THE DAYS OF ELIJAH

JOHN NOBLE

For my mom, who always believed in me, even when I didn't.

Contents

Chapter 1
Dances with Witches

Elijah watched as the Sons of Ba'al stalked in a slow circle around their altar, knives dripping red with their own blood as a haunting chant rose towards the sky. He stared for a moment at the blaze of opulent scarlet robes. There were so many... and not all were Sidonian. That fact stung worst of all.

Across the brown grass no more than twenty cubits away sat the crowd... no, not really a crowd, a multitude. People from all of Israel who'd come to Mount Carmel to ask a simple question.

Who was God?

The harsh wails of the priests reached a crescendo off to his left, and the crowd shrank back a step. A little boy in the front clutched his father's leg, a flicker of fear on his face. Elijah sighed and shook his head; he wanted to shout at them that there was nothing to fear, no more danger in the screams than the cawing of crows. But the truth was, outnumbered 450 to one – two if he counted God – there was still a part of him that was a little scared too.

What if this didn't work?

Four Years Earlier
Samaria

Jezebel strolled through the palace with smooth, measured steps, her skirts swishing in constant time like the beating of a timbrel. Outside she duplicated perfectly the dignified paces her mother had taught her back home. Inside though, she was a seething cauldron of anger.

The Israelite servants all slid to the side as she passed, their backs pressed against the walls and eyes towards the floor. Apparently news traveled fast. The only ones without fear in their eyes were members of her own retinue. Up ahead High Priest Baltazar rounded the corner.

"My Queen," he gave a curt bow, "we have him."

"Where?"

"This way." He led off through the maze of hallways that Jezebel had long since gotten to know like the back of her hand. They took two left turns and a long hallway to arrive at a small side room. This close to the servants quarters the door mantles weren't inlaid with ivory; instead they were just white plastered stone. Unlike the boundless wealth she'd grown accustomed to as a young girl, her husband's profligacy did have limits.

Two members of the royal guard stood at the door, spears held at a slight angle. They instantly stiffened when they saw her, their backs becoming just a little straighter, oval shields gripped a bit tighter.

Pushing through the door, she followed Baltazar into a cramped, torch-lit room. Several of his priests and an older woman all surrounded the beaten and bloodied figure of a man bound to a chair. Jezebel's eyes narrowed when she saw him, her lips twisting in anger. "Where did you find him?"

"The lower city, near the south gate." The older woman, Sisi, stepped forward. "Birkana was headed to Bethel with several of the priestesses when they found him spouting off his lies to a crowd there. She came back, and Baltazar led the guard down to take him."

Jezebel nodded and stared at the man a moment. Even before

he'd been attacked, he'd been dressed little better than a common peasant. Now his tunic was smudged with dirt and red streaks of his own blood. When she leaned close, her nose wrinkled at the sweaty, trash heap smell of someone who'd been on the road for far too long and didn't have the sense to use perfume.

She glanced at Sisi. "I assume he just arrived today, do you know where he…?"

"You…" the man's eyes finally cracked open, his voice weak.

Jezebel's gaze lanced in at him like daggers. "Yes, *me,*" she snapped, "and show a bit more respect when addressing your Queen."

The man took a halting breath before whispering, "Not… my… Queen."

Instantly Baltazar stepped close and slugged him hard across the cheek, knocking a tooth loose. Jezebel regarded it in disgust. "Right," she sneered, "I forgot, your 'God' still doesn't like my husband and me. Or is it a different song and dance this time? Has He changed his mind?"

Somehow the contempt brought a spark of defiance to the man's eyes. He spit blood at her feet. "You worship lies," he managed.

Baltazar pulled back his fist to teach the man a second lesson, but Jezebel raised a hand to stop him. "You really think that?" she taunted. "That Ba'al is a lie?"

The man's face hardened, "There is only one God and–"

His voice cut off as Baltazar stepped forward and pounded him again.

Jezebel shook her head. "And where is He?" she leaned in close. "I know where Ba'al and Asherah are, I sacrificed to them last week. What about this 'God' you love so much? If He's so glorious, where are his priests? Why are his altars forgotten while the altar to Ba'al is stained red with sacrifices?"

The man coughed and winced at the pain, his breaths heavy. He didn't reply though.

Jezebel's scowl darkened at his stubborn obstinacy. "Answer me," she hissed. "If your God is so powerful, where is He?"

"He doesn't need you..." the old man finally spoke, "or me... He *is*."

"Right," she rolled her eyes, "whatever that means." She was about to tell Baltazar to get rid of the old fool when the door creaked open behind him.

"Jezebel, I heard–" Her husband's voice abruptly cut off when he saw what waited inside. "I guess you already know."

The various priests in the room bowed as King Ahab stepped in and Jezebel dipped in a polite curtsey. "You're just in time, husband," she flashed him a smile. "My new friend here was explaining something about his *God*." She punctuated her statement with a sharp kick to the man's leg that elicited a low groan.

Ahab's mouth tightened in frustration. "And what was it this time?" he asked.

The old man managed a faint answer. "The Lord..." he coughed, and blood trickled from his mouth, "The Lord will judge Israel for her sins," he said. "Your sins, and..." he paused, an ember of fear in his eyes as they drifted to Jezebel, "and hers."

The queen's face twisted in rage. No one talked to her like that, least of all this ignorant peasant. She was Jezebel of Tyre, Daughter of Ithobaal, Queen of Israel, Priestess of Asherah, and High Matron of Samaria. Before Ahab could react, she whipped out the dagger she carried at her side and slammed it into his chest.

The man shuddered and gasped, a red stain spreading across his chest. She leaned close to his ear, her lips curling in a mocking taunt as she whispered, "If your 'God' is so great, then maybe He can save you... or not."

The old man was dying, but he summoned up one last sentence. "The Lord... is not... mocked."

His head slid forward, and the man slumped in the chair as he breathed his last, leaving her with nothing but a lifeless corpse to vent her fury on.

"Fool," she wrenched loose her ivory handled blade and handed it off to Sisi to be cleaned.

"Dearest," she felt Ahab's hand on her shoulder, "maybe that wasn't the wisest…"

"Don't tell me what's *wise*," she fumed, the anger still coursing like hot fire in her veins.

For a moment her husband said nothing, but finally she felt his fingers clasp at hers. "Let's go to the garden," the king offered. "Talk somewhere that isn't here."

She almost said no, but he knew her too well; she wouldn't refuse the offer. She let him guide her out of the cramped room that already seemed heavy with death, and stepping back into the hallway, she felt a renewed energy. Hand in hand they wandered the expansive palace until they came to the carved cedar door inlaid with a silver fig tree, each leaf graven in intricate detail.

Pushing it open, they stepped out into a verdant paradise of trees and chirping birds, with vegetation so dense she could almost forget she was in the center of a bustling city. This was the one part of the palace she enjoyed better than her home back in Tyre.

Her home city along the Great Sea was richer than Samaria, with merchants from the whole world bringing their goods to the market, but it was older too. Her father's palace had been an opulent, towering affair but with little greenery to recommend it. Samaria was still a young city though. Ahab loved to talk about how he'd helped his father design the palace at the pinnacle of a green hill in a lush valley. They'd had space to spare, and so a sprawling garden had found a place in the heart of the burgeoning city.

Strolling past a pomegranate tree heavy with ruby fruits, Ahab found a bench for them to sit.

"Dearest," his voice was consoling, "you know I don't like it when you handle these things yourself."

"Well what am I supposed to do?" Jezebel demanded, not meeting his eyes. "Ahab, your people hate me. These prophets keep pronouncing judgements against me… and *you*. Am I supposed to stand by and–"

"The people don't hate you, my doe," the king insisted, his hand laid on hers. "How many of them cheer when you greet them from the balcony? Ask your own priests, how many of my subjects implore them to make offerings to the gods on their behalf?"

His words softened her some. She leaned on his shoulder, the anger still simmering in her chest but no longer a bonfire. "And the others?"

They both knew who she was referring to – the followers of 'God,' who was still revered in Judah to the south. The ones who refused to worship Ba'al. The ones who'd been a thorn in both their sides since the time of Ahab's father Omri.

Her husband struggled a moment with the question. "They'll come around," he finally said.

Ahab's hands fell to his side and Jezebel caught the look on his face. He didn't really believe that, either. Nestling a bit closer, she let her hand caress him for a long, quiet moment. "We need to do something," she said, her voice pleading.

For what felt like forever he sat there, lost in thought, while she gently massaged at his shoulder. "Like what?" Ahab finally asked.

Jezebel didn't answer right away. She knew she had to be delicate. Instead, she stood and wandered over to the pomegranate tree, wasting a moment choosing a particularly ripe fruit that fell off the branch with barely a touch.

Wandering back to her seat, she passed him the fruit. Ahab kept a knife in his belt and busied himself for a moment slicing it in two.

It was only then she spoke. "If they won't sacrifice to Ba'al and insist on speaking out against you, then these God worshippers are a threat, not just to me, but to your whole kingdom. Just like Zimri before your father, when he tried to take power."

Ahab didn't disagree; instead he spent a minute scooping several rosy seeds out with his knife, offering them to her on the tip of the blade.

Taking the jeweled handle, Jezebel didn't hesitate to slip the little rubies into her mouth, the juice staining her lips blood red. "We can either wait for them to rile up the people against us or…"

She left the sentence unfinished and let her husband fill in the blank… *or* they could nip the problem in the bud.

She could sense his hesitation. He'd always shrunk back at the last when their talks inevitably came around to this topic. She slid her body close to his and was about to offer more encouragement when the garden door clattered open and two familiar voices echoed in the tranquil space.

"Mom, dad!" Joram's face appeared through the trees, red from running. "Ahaziah took my sword. The wooden one Obadiah got for me."

"Did not!" Ahaziah darted into view a second later. "Dad, he's making it up!"

"Well, in that case, one of you two is lying." Ahab's face took on a mock severity, but Jezebel caught a twinkle in his eyes at the sight of his boys. He passed her the sliced half of pomegranate and stood to go but she caught his arm. "Husband, we can't ignore this forever. If not for yourself, then for them," she nodded towards their two boys, "for their future."

Ahab's eyes drifted to his children and the argument finally seemed to sway the reluctant king. "What are you proposing?"

"Only that you let me handle it." Her eyes locked with his for a long seductive moment.

Finally he nodded, "Alright. Handle it, but… delicately."

Jezebel slid her body close to his like a luxuriant silken sheet, "Have I ever been anything but?" She stood on her tiptoes to kiss him on the mouth, and when she pulled back, his lips were stained just as red as hers.

Behind them she caught Joram rolling his eyes at their embrace, and she gently pushed him away with a glowing smile. "Your sons need you," she whispered.

Ahab turned back to his children, "Right boys," he grinned. "I believe the only way to settle this is to get a few more wooden swords from Obadiah and see if the two of you can take me. You up for a real fight?"

Joram hesitated at the challenge, but his older brother nodded eagerly and grabbed his father's hand. "Come on!"

Jezebel watched as they vanished from the garden and waited a moment, silently relishing her triumph. Finally, she'd show these stubborn 'God' worshippers the real power of her gods. Her thoughts drifted back to the old man earlier and the way he'd dared to insult her. Well, not anymore. She was queen here in Samaria, and soon the rest of Israel would know it too.

Chapter 2
The Last Prophet

Elijah," an urgent hand shook at his shoulder, "Elijah, get up, they're coming."

His eyes inched open to see Jesse standing over him, concern creasing the old man's wrinkled face.

"What… who?"

"The queen's men. Someone from the village saw them in the hills earlier today. They may be here soon."

"But…" The statement left him with more questions than answers. There'd been rumors, whispers of people disappearing for several months, but that had all been west of the Jordan, in Samaria and Jezreel. Not here.

He rolled off the rough straw mat that served as his bed and scrambled to his feet, "What do I need to do?"

Jesse tossed him a small bag, "Get your things and go. We're sending away all the students. Tonight."

"You're what?" The revelation took a moment to process. He'd been at the school for years, studying the Torah under the teachers, and now, out of nowhere, it was all ending in a single night.

"I'm not leaving," Elijah insisted. "Even if they are coming, I'll stay."

His master's eyes hardened, "You most certainly will not," he said firmly. "You'll leave this hour, and you won't look back. Understood?"

Elijah hesitated. At twenty-eight he was one of the senior students, but still not old enough to be considered a true prophet. Jesse must have glimpsed the ambivalence in his eyes, and for once his teacher's firm voice melded with despair, "Elijah, you have to go. If… if you don't who will be left to teach the children about The Lord?"

He swallowed hard, "What about you and the masters?"

For an instant Jesse didn't answer. He grabbed a rolled cloak off the floor and tossed it into Elijah's arms. "We… we've spoken and decided to stay, to buy what time we can for you and the rest of the students to escape."

The pronouncement left Elijah with a gathering lump in the pit of his stomach. A part of him had been hoping that maybe it was just a false report, but if the masters had already planned this far ahead… whatever hope he might have had evaporated like dew in the sun.

"You'll have to head into the hills. Try and go south; if you can make it to Judah, King Jehoshaphat may protect you." Jesse continued, "You'll have to cross the Jordan, though, and you may want to split into small groups to travel." He finished packing most of Elijah's few belongings into the travel bag. "Here," he handed him the pack.

For a terrible instant Elijah didn't take it. He couldn't. He couldn't just abandon his friends… his teachers to be murdered. Then a pained shout rent the cool night air.

"They're here." Jesse hurriedly shoved the bag into his arms and pulled a small pouch from his belt. "Take this."

He handed it over before the stunned Elijah could object. More shouts rose up like an awful chorus from every direction.

"Go!" Jesse pushed him towards the door, "You have to."

"You can come too," Elijah pleaded desperately, "please."

Jesse just shook his head, "You know I can't. I'll slow you down, then neither of us will make it." He paused one last second at the door. "You're the teacher now, Elijah. You're ready."

Seconds were precious now with the screams of the dying prophets marching relentlessly closer, but Jesse lifted a hand and almost instinctively the young prophet bowed his head as his teacher offered one last invocation.

May the Lord bless and keep you;
May He make his face to shine upon you,
And be gracious to you;
May the countenance of the Lord fall upon you,
And may He grant you peace.

He'd heard those same words hundreds of times before, but this time when Elijah looked up tears stung his eyes. "Goodbye," he whispered.

"The Lord go with you."

Jesse opened the door, and the two spilled out into the cold, dry night. Amid the flickers of dying fires, he heard the panicked screams of his friends being slaughtered and caught the dim flashes of firelight reflected off iron blades.

A part of him still wanted to stay and die here, but already Jesse was stumbling off into the night. "Over here!" he shouted to draw their attention.

His teacher was paying the price of his escape in blood, and Elijah couldn't bear to throw away such a precious last gift from the man he knew like a father. He turned and ran into the night, fear pounding through his veins.

Their school was little more than a loose collection of mud brick houses built around a central stone building where the scriptures were kept. Once there had been many more disciples, but now, with the worship of Ba'al rising like the moon across the countryside, there were fewer new students. The masters grew older, many without disciples to replace them when they died.

Up ahead he caught movement and the glint of metal in the night. He pressed himself into the shadow of the nearest hut as two soldiers dressed in brown tunics with light wooden shields and short spears charged by. Across the village green he saw a swarm of dark figures converging around another hut.

Aaron's house.

He silently prayed that his friend had escaped as the wraiths gathered and kicked in the door. A second later, that hope was torn away when he caught his friend's loud shouts in the night mingling with the chorus of others.

The soldiers were distracted though. Before they could return, Elijah broke cover and made a mad dash away from the cluster of houses, his heart beating out of his chest as he ran. His instinct was to make for the big hill south of their school, but a little voice in his head warned that they might expect that, it was too obvious. They might already be waiting there. Instead he diverted east towards a small grassy knoll a bit further off.

He didn't stop his pell-mell run through the pitch black night until somewhere near the top of the knoll. His foot twisted on a loose rock and he tumbled to a stop on the dark grass. For a second he lay there, his breath coming in hard pants, but with the looming fear of pursuit gathering in the back of his mind he pushed himself upright. The instant he tried to stand his ankle screamed in pain, and he collapsed back on all fours. Unable to run, he expected the sharp agonizing pain of a spear point between his shoulder blades any second now.

But it never came.

Hazarding a look back, he didn't see any shadows sprinting through the night towards him. They seemed confined mostly to the cluster of houses, smashing in doors and dragging the prophets out into the night. He couldn't tear his eyes away as he saw a small group of bloodied but alive prophets hauled into the light of the dying fire near the center of the buildings. Among them he caught the wispy grey beard of his teacher, Jesse.

Amid the pale orange glow he could make out the soldiers more clearly. There were at least ten close around the fire. As he watched, another man draped in the long black and red robes of Ba'al stepped into the flickering light. The soldiers kept a respectful distance as he strolled up to the kneeling prophets, contempt written on his face.

He briefly leaned down and spoke something to the prisoners. Elijah was too far to hear, but the priest must not have liked the answer because he scowled and turned away with a flick of his wrist.

Elijah tried to look away but couldn't. The soldiers stepped forwards and coldly slit his friend's throats, leaving them slumped like discarded dolls in the dirt. Before the horror of it all could even register, the priest gave an indistinct shout, and the soldiers busied about, dragging the fresh corpses into houses. He couldn't fathom what they were doing; that was, until several snatched burning hunks of wood out of the fire and began tossing them into the grass bundles that served as roofing.

Even just a smoldering log lit the already sunbaked straw into a bonfire in mere seconds. Soon every building in their little school was blazing away like so many funeral pyres. The granary on the north corner was next, and from there he knew it was a matter of minutes until the flames spread to the fig grove on the nearby slope and probably took their little vineyard too.

The fire illuminated the surrounding area, bathing the vale in a dull, orange glow. Realizing he was still on the near side of the hillock, Elijah scrambled up over the top. He did his best not to put pressure on his bad ankle, but even so, it wasn't long before he had to bite back a cry of pain when he stepped wrong.

He didn't look back until he was safely hidden on the reverse slope of the hill, with only his head peeking out. Looking down, he saw the soldiers assembling on the south edge of the village, while the buildings still blazed away, sending pillars of smoke spiraling into the moonless night.

Somewhere off amid the swirling flames he caught a creaking, wooden groan followed by a muffled *thwump* that sent sparks spouting into the sky as one roof collapsed. For a moment the terrible possibility came to mind that the soldiers might fan out to catch any stragglers. When the sun rose, his current spot on an open grassy hill would leave him as exposed as a dove with a broken wing. With his ankle lame, he couldn't imagine being able to move more than fifty cubits, let alone the half hour walk to the next large hill further east.

The fear gathered like lead weights in his chest, but peering over the hill-crest, he saw the assembled soldiers beginning to trudge off south amid the hellish gloom of the inferno, the priest near the front of the column.

He watched until they vanished into the night, then his eyes returned to the fires, watching as the place he'd called home for close to a decade burned to the ground. Slowly the terror of impending death faded, replaced by a gathering, hopeless despair. As the flames began to die low in the night, the exhausted Elijah slipped into a fretful sleep.

Chapter 3
Shattered Glass

When Elijah started back awake, the sun was already rising in the east. For a second he couldn't understand why he was face down in the grass, but his eyes rose to see the smoldering ruins in front of him and the memories surged back in a flood.

In the midnight gloom, the massacre had seemed more like a twisted nightmare, but now that he saw the wreckage in the day, reality began to sink in. They were dead. His friends, teachers…

The rush of images left him struggling to catch his breath, and he found himself on his knees, staring at the grass and trying to recover from the shock. Finally, he pushed himself up to sitting and tried to think what he was supposed to do.

His ankle still hurt, but an experimental push revealed it wasn't nearly as bad as the searing pain he remembered from the night before. A long look around the valley failed to reveal any signs of more soldiers lying in wait. Not that it would have mattered. He was already exposed, and if they hadn't found him by now he doubted they ever would.

His first instinct was to follow Jesse's last instructions, go south, try to get to Judah. But to do that he'd need to cross the Jordan, and with a sprained ankle he doubted he'd struggle more than a couple of hours before it gave out beneath him. With his options running dry, he reluctantly resolved himself to the inevitable. Elijah stood, taking delicate care not to put much weight on one foot, and slowly limped back towards the village.

It felt strange, eerie, wandering the wreckage that smelled of ash and death. At each step he found the burnt out shells of houses staring at him like blackened ghosts. Peering into one, his stomach churned when he saw two unrecognizable corpses crushed beneath a pile of charred roof timbers.

He felt that he ought to bury them, but he didn't have anything to dig a hole. Casting about, he noticed a discarded staff on the ground; it wasn't much, but he found the wooden rod could at least serve as a crutch. Forcing himself to move on, he finally stopped near the center of the village. The central building, a squat stone structure, hadn't burned, but the wooden door hung open blacked with scorch marks. Elijah hesitated to look at all, and when he did, the wanton destruction left him wishing he hadn't.

Ash. That was all that remained of their small library. Dozens of scrolls, several he'd helped to write himself, were reduced to nothing more than gray powder. The top shelf had held their most prized possessions, all five scrolls of Moses. Now though, the priceless copies, worth more than many people made in ten years, were scorched nearly beyond recognition.

For a long moment he stared at the ruin. All he could think was what Jesse would have said, and for an instant he was almost glad his teacher was gone. At least he didn't have to see his life's work end like this.

With that final discovery, the magnitude of the loss stabbed like a knife. His friends and teachers, gone. The one thing they'd devoted their lives to preserving, destroyed. With his back to the doorway, Elijah sank to the ground and wept.

He didn't know how long he sat there, tears of impotent frustration in his eyes, but when he finally looked up the sun was high in the sky.

It took a moment to pull himself together and stand. Elijah cast one last look at the charred rolls of bound animal hide. He almost left right there, but in a flash of curiosity he reached out and touched at the scrolls.

The first disintegrated into a pile of ashen flakes at the brush of his finger, but surprisingly the next didn't. He pulled it off the shelf, and while it shed off blackened bits of the outer husk, the core was somehow still intact. He tried the others, and none of them had survived, but... it was something.

He slid the fragmented scroll into his pack and glanced around. What now?

He couldn't stay. Not that there was anything to stay for. Maybe he should go to Judah, but would there be anyone to help him there either? They might not kill him, but...

His stomach complained with an audible growl, and Elijah finally made up his mind. He needed food and somewhere to rest for a few days before he could even consider getting over to the west bank of the Jordan River. There was one place he knew he would find both. He probably couldn't make it in a day, especially not limping as he was, and he wasn't sure what he was supposed to eat on the way?

His mind snapped back to the prior evening. The pouch, the one Jesse had given him. He hadn't looked inside, but he had a sudden suspicion what it was. Digging out the little drawstring pouch, he opened it to reveal several silver nuggets, maybe a shekel or two in total. Not a lot, but enough.

He pulled the small purse shut and uttered a quiet prayer of thanks for his departed teacher's forethought. When he opened his eyes there was a new spark of resolve in them.

That settled things. Elijah wasn't sure where to go afterwards, what to do when he got there, or how any of this carnage was supposed to be okay, but for right now... he was going home.

Tishbi seemed busier than Elijah remembered as he limped into town. Two older men trudged past carrying a heavy wicker basket brimming with grapes destined for the winepress. Across the dirt path that led into the village, Bilhah, an older woman with the first traces of gray in her hair, was busy sweeping out the first floor of her house. She couldn't veil her surprise and an ember of worry when she saw him. "Elijah? What are you doing here?"

For some reason the question caught him off guard. He came home often enough. His sister's mother-in-law had never cared before. Normally it was only a day's walk, although with his twisted ankle it had taken closer to two and a half. But still, his visit wouldn't have been odd except that he didn't normally come home at harvest time.

Typically everyone, students and teachers alike, were busy this time of year. Mostly they grew figs, as well as tending a few citron trees and a small vineyard. It wasn't much, but it helped pay for their modest needs, mostly barley for meals plus some parchment and ink.

"I…" He stumbled, trying to come up with an explanation.

Before he could, a tangle of raven curls and a young girl's face popped into the window overhead. "Uncle Elijah?" She burst into a grin when she saw him, "You're back!"

Her face disappeared, and Bilhah rolled her eyes at the sudden pounding from the stairs. A second later the excited eleven year old barreled out the front door and slammed into him like a little lioness, catching him in a big bear hug. "I didn't think you'd be back for a month!"

Despite everything, Elijah couldn't stop a grin tugging at his lips as he hugged her back. "Good to see you too, Lila."

He glanced up at Bilhah, "Is…?"

"Hannah and Nathaniel are both out in the vineyard," she answered, barely glancing up from her work. "They'll be back later."

"Thanks." Hannah was his older sister, which made Nathaniel his brother-in-law.

He glanced down at the little bundle of excitement that was his niece. "What are *you* doing here then, Lila?"

The question brought a pouting frown to her face, "Grinding flour," she muttered.

Her sarcasm was enough to bring Bilhah's sharp eyes back their direction.

"Well, that's an important job," Elijah said.

She scowled. "Doesn't feel like it. Dad let Tobin go pick grapes, and he's only ten."

He knelt down next to her. "You want to know a secret?"

She gave an eager nod.

"That's because Tobin couldn't grind flour if his life depended on it."

That finally brought the grin back to her face as she held in a giggle. "Are you going to see your parents?" she asked.

He nodded, and Lila looked back to her grandmother, still standing in the doorway and watching them with severe eyes. "Can I go with Elijah? I'm mostly finished with the flour."

For a second he was sure the old woman was about to say no, but she consented, "So long as you don't stay too long."

"Woohoo!" The young girl grabbed his hand to tug him on forwards. Elijah went a few feet then winced when he put too much weight on his sprained ankle. Lila paused with a concerned frown. "Are you okay?"

No, not really. He put on a brave face though. "I just took a wrong step earlier."

"Oh." She seemed to accept the answer and switched to wandering along beside him and occasionally skipping a few feet ahead despite her long skirt.

"Did you see there was a big fire up your direction?" Lila asked as they wandered through the small cluster of houses. "A few days ago? We could still see smoke the next morning."

Elijah swallowed hard at the question, "Yeah, I saw the smoke." He scrambled for a way to divert the conversation, "What's been going on here?"

"Not much," Lila sighed. "Orli had her baby, and Eli got in trouble for drinking too much a week ago. That's about all."

The main path through the village passed a wizened old oak tree. At its base stood a miniature prayer table set with several small brass bowls for incense, the local shrine to Asherah.

People had been burning little bits of incense at the tree longer than Elijah had been alive, but the table was a new addition. He nudged Lila as they walked by, "When did that get there?"

The girl glanced at the prayer table and her face dimmed a little. "A couple months ago. A priestess came and set it up." She paused and bit her lip nervously. "Mom's been going," she added in a small voice.

Elijah was sure he'd misheard. "What?"

"To the shrine," Lila explained, shamefaced, "in the mornings. She told me she wanted to have another baby and…"

Elijah wasn't listening though; he almost stumbled into the dirt, his breath coming short for an instant. When the news finally registered, he felt like he was about to be sick. Even his own sister was praying to Asherah too?

"I know you told me it was bad," Lila was saying, "but it doesn't seem like–"

"It *is* bad, Lila." He cut her off, angry for once. "There's only one God. It doesn't matter what your mom says."

"Well," her eyes fell towards the dirt path, uncertain, "Dad says it's okay. How do you know?"

Elijah's jaw tightened, of course Nathaniel did. He'd known her father since they were kids and even then his brother-in-law had never been a paragon of moral certitude.

"Look, Lila," he knelt down next to her so they were at eye level, "remember the stories I told you, about Moses and Deborah and Gideon and David?"

A hint of a smile pulled at her cheeks, and she gave an eager nod.

"All the stuff they did, that was because they believed in God. Asherah didn't split the Red Sea down the middle, Ba'al didn't send the plagues on Egypt, when David killed Goliath he prayed to God… the real God, not the fake ones they carve out of tree stumps."

That gave Lila something to think on for a minute, and her nose scrunched up a little. Finally, she glanced up at him, more confused than ever. "But that was all a long time ago."

Elijah's heart sank a little at the answer. He wasn't sure what he'd been hoping for, maybe a 'You're right, let's go chop down that stupid tree.'

He couldn't really fault her. It killed him inside but… he only came back a few times a year. Lila spent every day with her parents, and, even if he loved her like the child he'd never had, she wasn't his. Two weeks a year couldn't compete.

Truth be told, she wasn't wrong about it all being a long time ago, not exactly. David had lived – maybe a hundred years before – and for an eleven year old, that might very well be an eternity. He stood with a sigh, and they headed on past the Asherah tree in silence.

He'd never thought about it that way, but maybe, deep down, that was the problem. It wasn't just Lila, *everyone* had forgotten. The great miracles were just stories anymore. Meanwhile, the stupid tree was there every time you walked past until one day everyone forgot, and the tree became god.

He would have laughed except for the hollow feeling inside.

"I'm sorry," Lila said.

Elijah turned to see her, worried, like she was afraid she'd made him angry. His face softened, "It's not your fault, Lila." He put an arm around her shoulder. "It's not wrong to ask questions."

Even questions he didn't like to think about.

They took a right turn and followed a steep trail that switch-backed up the green hillside past a scattering of double-story, white plaster homes. His parents' was up near the top. He'd never really appreciated it until he'd left and discovered the crumbling shanty his school provided was a poor replacement. He'd always liked coming home, except this time… he still didn't know what to say.

Next to him, Lila must have thought he was still upset. "I can tell mom," she piped up, trying to be helpful. "What you said about Asherah not being real, I can tell her."

The tentative offer finally brought traces of a smile to his face. That was pretty darn brave of her. He knew his sister well enough. All that talk would earn Lila was a spanking and an early bedtime. He could see in her face that she knew it too.

"It's all right." He patted her on the shoulder and gave a conspiratorial wink, "Best not to bring it up. I'll mention it to Hannah sometime."

They were close to the top of the hill now and he could see his mom, a small woman with Lila's dark curls mingled with just a trace of grey. She was out along the side of the house, plucking figs off the huge bush of a tree that grew nearby and piling them into a wicker basket. She had her back to them and Lila took the chance to dart ahead with an impish grin.

"Grandma!" she shouted, "Look who's back!"

His mom looked back and, even from afar, he could see her eyes widen when she saw him. The basket slipped from her hands, spilling the tan fruits across the grass.

Elijah limped his way up to the house, and his mother hurried to meet him. He'd played out about a dozen different ways the conversation could go, but in the end all that came out was "*Shalom, ima.*"

'Hi, mom'

"Elijah," she threw her arms around him for a long second before stepping back to look at him, happy but confused, "the priests let you come back at harvest time?"

"Umm… sort of." His eyes flickered to Lila, and his mom's smile dimmed as she got the message.

His niece finished scooping all the palm sized figs back into the shallow basket and stood to proudly present it back. "Here you go, grandma."

"Thank you, darling." His mom walked over to the bucket by the door and poured about half the little fruits in before handing the basket with the rest back to Lila. "Since you came all the way up here, why don't you take these home."

Lila looked down at the basket with maybe twenty figs still inside, suddenly more excited than ever, "Really?"

Her family didn't have a fig tree, so Elijah knew the fruits would be a special treat. His mom nodded, "So long as you promise to bring back the basket tomorrow."

She nodded, with a quick thanks. "*Toh-dah*, grandma." A minute later she was jogging down the hill, the basket in her arms.

With Lila gone, his mother's eyes drifted across to him. "Elijah, what happened?"

Chapter 4
A Stranger in a Strange Land

They found his father along with his older brother, Michael, up in the family orchard. It wasn't quite harvest time for the olives, but close. A few early fruits showed the first traces of turning black.

"You're sure they were the queen's soldiers?" Elijah's father asked, his face surprisingly calm, as they wandered through the quiet rows of gnarled olive trees.

"They had a priest of Ba'al with them. I'm not sure who else would have sent them."

"Bandits?" Michael suggested.

"Bandits who burned everything?" Elijah shot him a skeptical look.

His mother's face turned ashen, "So, the smoke a few days ago…"

Elijah just nodded with an involuntary shiver at the memory. "They destroyed it all, the houses, the orchard, the vineyard; they just murdered everyone."

For a moment the words hung in the air between them. No one really knew what to say.

"You think they know you escaped?" Michael asked.

"I don't know. I'm—"

"Did you see which way they went when they left?" his father interrupted.

"South."

That elicited a chilly silence; south from his school was, more or less, towards them. He couldn't really fault them for being nervous. "Did they pass through here?" Elijah asked.

"Not yet." His older brother shook his head then followed it with a harder question, "Where are you going to go?"

"Michael," his mother's voice turned sharp, "your brother's been through a lot, you don't–"

"I was just asking."

"Look," his father stepped in, "we can talk about all this later. It'll probably make more sense after dinner."

That had a way of settling things, at least for the moment. They headed back to the house where Michael's wife Emma was busy laying out a meal and trying to keep up with his two little boys.

After two days on the run, fresh figs, mutton soup, and honey bread straight out of the oven was a welcome change. Even Michael, who was normally the big eater in the family, couldn't hide his surprise when Elijah went back for a fourth bowl of soup.

Afterwards, with a hot meal inside him, Elijah found someone had laid out a bed-mat for him in a small corner. He told himself he was just going to lie down for a little while, but in just a few minutes he'd drifted off to sleep.

When he woke it was dark outside. He felt better than he had in days, his back didn't hurt from laying on rocks, and for once he'd actually slept, not just spent hours tossing and turning. He might have dozed back off except for the hushed voices the next room over. In a house this small there weren't really any secrets. The only place anyone could truly talk in private was the olive grove out back.

"I'm not..." Michael's voice sounded frustrated, "I'm just saying it's not safe."

"You think he's safer out on his own?" his dad's voice didn't sound happy either. "There are bandits out there, people..."

"And what if the soldiers come here?" Michael asked, "Everyone knows who Elijah is and that he's back. You heard what he said, they're after priests of God. If they walk into town and ask, how long do you think until someone tells them?"

There was a pregnant pause, and Elijah bit his lip. He hadn't lived here in years, and even he knew the answer. Most people already regarded his family as the local weirdos, the ones who'd sent their youngest son off to learn about God instead of staying to help run the farm. His parents had never complained, but he knew it had been a sacrifice, one less pair of hands during harvest and spring pruning. They'd sent him money more than once, and he knew even getting Hannah married off had been more of a struggle, because who wanted crazies as their in-laws?

Now Michael had the farm and a family of his own to worry about. And here he was, back on their doorstep, a burden again with nothing besides a half burnt scroll to show for years of study. Plus, he had the royal guards out for his head too.

"We're not sending him away," his mom insisted.

"It's safer for him too," Michael fought back. "Everyone knows him here. At least if he leaves he'll just be another traveler."

The argument strung on for several more minutes before Elijah finally tired of listening. He stood, and a floorboard gave a loud creak beneath him. Instantly the voices hushed.

He rolled his eyes with a caustic humor and walked out into the common room. Bit late for that.

His mom looked up as he walked into the main space where a few candles cast their flickering light. "Elijah, we didn't wake you, did we?"

"Not really." His parents and older brother were seated in a tight knot, and Michael moved over to make space as he joined them. Elijah stared at the floorboards; the conversation stalled. "Michael may have a point," he finally said.

"Honey," his mother pleaded, "you don't have to leave. You can stay and help with the farm."

"It's alright," he tried to put on a positive face. "I was thinking it might be best to head south, to Judah. At least for a little while."

His parents clearly didn't like the idea. "And what would you do there?" his father asked.

Elijah had absolutely no idea. He wasn't much good as a day laborer, but at that moment he couldn't think of any other options. "I'll figure something out."

He tried to ignore the nervous lump in his chest. He'd said *a little while*, but, the way things were going, how long until it was really safe to worship God in Israel? With King Ahab and his wife in charge, it might be an awfully long time.

Elijah sighed. "I'll leave in the morning."

"Son," his dad said, "you don't have to–"

"It's better this way." He shook his head. "If anyone asks, I just passed through for the night. That way, no one will get in trouble."

For a moment none of them spoke, but finally his mom gave a reluctant nod. "You promise, you'll be back when this is all over?"

He nodded his assent, "When it's over."

***

The Next Morning

Elijah cast one last look back at the small village of Tishbi before turning his face west. Where to now? He still had to get across the Jordan, and even with his ankle mostly healed he figured it might still be half a day to the nearest crossing.

"Uncle Elijah!" a girl's voice shouted behind him. "Wait!"

He turned to see a young girl sprinting towards him. "Lila?"

She finally ground to a halt a few feet in front of him and spent a moment doubled over, panting to catch her breath. "I went to take back the basket, and Grandma said you were already gone."

"Sorry," he felt a sudden pang at his abrupt departure, "I… had to go."

"Without saying goodbye?" She looked up, and he saw hurt in her eyes.

Suddenly all his excuses didn't sound quite so noble as they had the night before. He knelt down next to her. "I'm sorry, Lila. I have to go. There are bad people after me, and I don't

26

want them coming here."

"Well," her lower lip quivered a little, "I'll help you."

He smiled. "I know you would, but this is the sort of thing I have to do alone. I'll be back, when it's all better."

From the look on her face Lila still didn't fully understand. "Well, why are they after you?" she asked, like maybe she could come up with a solution herself.

"Because I believe in God," he explained in the simplest way he could. "They don't."

She frowned, "That's not fair."

He shook his head, grinning a little, "No, no I don't suppose it is. That's the way things are, though."

She didn't look very happy, but Lila nodded. "I'll miss you." She put her arms around him in a big hug.

Elijah hugged her back, and when they finally broke apart, he was blinking away the mist in his own eyes. "I'll miss you too." He gave a long sigh. "Lila, before I go, would you promise me something? Don't worship Asherah, even if everyone else does. Promise me you won't."

The eleven year old thought about it for a second with a serious face; finally she gave a solemn nod. "I won't, I promise." Lila held up her pinkie finger, and she and Elijah shook on it.

Elijah stood and gave his niece one last, long hug. Lila looked up with tears pooling in her eyes. "Where will you go?"

Honestly, he wasn't quite sure. He had told his family he'd make for Judah, but the more he thought about it the less certain he was. "I… I guess I'll find out when I get there."

He paused, not sure what else to say and something else clicked in his mind. "Did you skip out on harvest to come say goodbye to me?"

The remark left her staring at the road with a guilty expression. "Maybe," she fidgeted with a loose strand of her curly hair.

"Well, don't get in too much trouble on my account. You better get back before Hannah starts to wonder if you got lost taking that basket back."

"Okay," she gave a sad nod. "Goodbye, Uncle Elijah."

"Goodbye, Lila."

He watched the little girl, the closest thing he had to a daughter, head back to town and brushed away the stubborn wetness in his own eyes.

It wasn't until Lila vanished back into the clustered homes that he finally turned with a deep sigh and began his trek west.

He made it to the Jordan River a little before noon, reaching a spot where the path cut along the river bank for about a hundred cubits before turning and disappearing into the shimmering blue-green water that marked a ford. It was still early fall at the tail end of a dry summer, and the river seemed shrunken compared to its banks.

It was busier here too, with travelers coming from both directions and wading across. There was even a thick rope strung across the river downstream with a square log ferry barge being pulled back and forth, hauling across wagons and travelers who didn't feel like wading through the waist deep water.

Elijah wasn't sure why anyone wouldn't want to wade the river. With the sun beating down overhead he was already sweating, and he finally paused for a break, finding a grassy spot with his back to an ancient willow tree along the riverbank. He probably would have just gone on across except his mom had packed him lunch that morning, and he didn't feel like eating soggy bread.

Breaking out his food, Elijah took a minute to relax and enjoy what might very well be his last home-packed meal for a long time. Up in the branches warblers chirped away in a chaotic melody that jarred with the gentle, hypnotic lapping of the river at its banks and the constant, pulsing hum of nearby locusts.

It was strange, but for the first time since that awful night, he didn't feel hunted. On the road and even at home, he'd been dogged by the constant fear of a troop of soldiers rounding the next bend in the road and making straight for him, the lone wanderer. Here though, he was safely anonymous amid the other travelers. Sitting cocooned beneath the willow branches that hung like a curtain of a thousand tiny vines, he felt a weight he'd almost forgotten about lift off his chest.

By the time he finished lunch, Elijah was so relieved he figured he might just hang around a while longer. It was noon anyway, and who really wanted to travel in the heat of the day? It wasn't like the Kingdom of Judah was going anywhere. He let his eyes slip closed for a nap, but he wasn't really tired. After about ten minutes trying to find a comfortable spot with his back to the rough bark, he finally gave up.

The sun was still beating down outside his patch of shade and, with nothing else to do, he spent a moment rummaging around in his pack for the pouch of dried jerky his parents had given him. Instead, his finger touched on the scroll still nestled in the bottom of his pack, and he froze. He'd been trying not to think about that. Technically, it was the only valuable thing he had, even charred as it was. He knew he couldn't sell it; it was all he had left. Besides, the scroll was God's word; selling it wouldn't feel right anyway.

He'd been avoiding looking at it, and even just thinking about it brought back a surge of memories, but he also knew he couldn't put it off forever. After a moment's hesitation, Elijah pulled it out. The fire had destroyed the bottom and left two unconnected but tightly wrapped rolls of hide. He wasn't even sure if there was anything still readable inside, but, taking a deep breath, he pulled it open.

At first there was nothing, just flakes of charred leather crumbling off the edges, but, amazingly enough, the hide skin parchment began to unroll, revealing writing still left behind.

Damaged as it was, the scroll wasn't exactly kosher or fit to use, but it was all he had, so he began reading. Elijah had been quietly hoping that he'd salvaged the scroll of Genesis. He'd always liked the stories about Abraham, Jacob and Joseph. Instead, he found himself staring at the front quarter of Deuteronomy. For a moment he skimmed through the words.

It was the part about cities of refuge. The sheet ended in a jagged black line but even so, he found himself reading through it. Back at his school they typically studied sections, little bits, he'd never been able to just… read. He had to pull out the other half of the scroll and rewind the loose end to go back more than a little bit.

Once he'd patched the scroll up, on the spur of the moment, he twisted all the way to the front, where it started. "These are the words Moses spoke…"

He started reading.

In a strange way it was cathartic. He didn't have to worry about memorizing or answering questions; he could just absorb the text at his own rate. Jesse would have thrown a fit, he thought with a hint of a grin. If he'd had his way, no student would have been allowed to even touch the precious scrolls, and yet here he was, camped out beneath a willow by the river, casually perusing his way through.

Reading the history of his people, he nearly lost track of time, until a voice behind him abruptly interrupted, "Can you actually read that?"

Elijah glanced back to see a large, slightly chubby man, dressed in plain clothes still wet from the ford standing at the edge of the willow tree and peering at him through the green curtain of hanging branches.

Startled, he fumbled for an answer. "Uh… yes?"

The man pushed aside the drooping branches and strolled over sitting down next to him, a curious gleam in his eyes. "If you don't mind, what is it?"

For a second Elijah hesitated. Did he tell him what it really was? With people out murdering priests of God, wandering around with the words of the Lord made him a pretty obvious target. Still, the man didn't look much like a soldier, and he wasn't wearing the red and black of a priest of Ba'al.

Elijah took a chance.

"It's the fourth Book of the Law of Moses."

"Really?" The man leaned forward, clearly he'd heard of Moses, "What does it say?"

"A lot of things, I suppose." Elijah paused, "Do you…?

"I've got time," the man nodded eagerly. "They still have to get my cart across." He nodded over towards the river where Elijah saw the ferry slowly hauling a bulky wagon over from the far bank, while a young boy tried to coax several skittish horses through the water.

"It's about God's promises to Israel and Judah," he explained. The man didn't object so he just picked up where he'd left off, reading aloud this time.

He read through the part about God's justice and faithfulness, the miracles He'd performed in Egypt, then the blessings God had promised and a warning about–

"Wait," the man interrupted, "could you read that last part again?"

"Sure," Elijah's eyes jumped back a few lines, "*Take heed to yourselves, lest your heart be deceived, and you turn aside and serve other gods and worship them, lest the Lord's anger be aroused against you, and He shut up the heavens so that there be no rain, and the land yield no produce, and you perish quickly from the good land which the Lord is giving you.*"

"Well, that's not good," the man frowned at the words. "Which god is this exactly?"

"It's *The* God," Elijah tried to explain, "the only one, the one King David followed."

That brought a glimmer of understanding to the man's face at the mention of King David, and Elijah could see things clicking into place, his face turning even more worried.

"Is that… true?"

Elijah paused; he'd never really thought about that passage. "I suppose it is, yes."

There was a clatter of wooden wheels and clopping horse hooves behind them. "Master, we're ready to go," a youth interrupted from the dirt path.

"Right," the merchant stood to leave, "I have to get moving." He hesitated, his gaze drifting back to the scroll. "You should probably tell someone about that," he added. "It would be really bad if there was no rain."

Elijah just nodded, and with a parting wave the man and his wagon were off, slowly diminishing into the distance. He found himself staring at that line of scroll over and over again, the words almost jumping out at him.

It wasn't that it was unclear – worship other gods, and there won't be rain. Pretty straightforward actually. But why hadn't it already happened?

'Maybe because nobody asked?' a little voice nagged in the back of his mind. He considered it for a moment before shaking his head; no, that didn't make any sense. It wasn't like he was the first person to read Deuteronomy.

He shoved the confusion to the back of his mind and started rolling up the scroll. As he did, he glanced back at the still diminishing figure of the merchant, and a second thought struck him. *Should* he tell someone?

The man had seemed pretty insistent, but the image of the soldiers butchering his friends flashed to mind. If he stayed, sooner or later that was his fate too.

Elijah sat there thinking, unsure what to do. In a flash he could see both paths, go south to Judah and scratch out a living as a scribe, or stay in Israel and tell… someone.

His thoughts drifted back to Lila that morning, with a sudden resolve. Because of him there was at least one person in Israel who wouldn't worship Asherah. Maybe he could make it a few more.

He toyed with the possibility for several minutes. He'd have to keep a low profile, perhaps work as a scribe on the side, but it might be doable. He'd read the stories where God provided for his people, God might provide for him too. Besides, it was what Jesse would have done.

In an instant, Elijah's plans changed. He slid the scroll back into his pack. It was past the heat of the day now, and so he headed down to the river, holding his pack overhead as he crossed and enjoying the cool water.

When he waded out, still dripping wet, he cast one quick look south, towards Judah. Then he headed west, into the heart of Israel.

Chapter 5
By Faith

6 Months Later

Elijah stared at the scroll on the desk in front of him, reading the same words over and over again, *"lest the Lord's anger be aroused against you, and He shut up the heavens so that there be no rain"*

He must have read that line a thousand times over the last half year. It was getting to where he could unroll the scroll straight to the spot. He still didn't understand it though. Specifically, why hadn't the judgement already happened?

Right on cue the little nagging suggestion popped right back into his head, 'Because nobody bothered to ask.'

In a way, the more he thought about it, the more it almost made sense. If it just stopped raining for a year, it would be a catastrophe, but there had to be someone to explain why. Otherwise it was *just* a catastrophe. So instead the promise lurked there, waiting for someone brave enough to use it.

If he was being honest though, Elijah didn't really want it to be him. Calling down divine disaster was okay when it was the next country over, not so much when it was your own. He looked around the small guest room he'd been offered for the night. What about these people? They'd been kind enough to open their house to him for a few days. He'd been helping them write up a few contracts they needed for their barley harvest in exchange for their hospitality, and they seemed like nice people. What would happen to them if the rain stopped?

What about his parents? What about Michael? The thought struggled to the surface, not for the first time. What would they do with no rain? He bit at his lip: what about Lila, his sister, and her family?

The chorus of horrible possibilities had been enough for him to just put the scroll away the prior night, but now he fought back the urge.

He shook his head. Maybe nothing would change. In that case he wasn't sure if he'd be relieved, or devastated. He'd spent the last several months wandering the countryside, keeping a few steps ahead of the royal guards and trying his best to denounce Ba'al. But what if he prayed to God and… and nothing happened?

Would that mean he was wrong? That God wasn't God, and he was just a lunatic? The possibility churned his stomach, and it took a moment to calm his breathing

It was easier to just let it alone. Nobody got hurt, and he didn't have to put everything on the line for some obscure part of the Law of Moses.

The problem was, no matter how much he tried, the verse wouldn't let him alone. The words hovered in the back of his mind like a thorn that wouldn't go away. And they were wearing him down.

In desperate confusion, he glanced at the ceiling, his voice a whisper. "What do you want me to do, God?"

In a way, he already knew, but it felt better to ask. He couldn't avoid the way the answer loomed over him like a long shadow. Israel had sinned, so decree the curse.

His hands clenched a little and he shook his head. Why him? Why couldn't someone else have gotten stuck with this job? Even so, he looked back down at the scroll and took a deep, terrified breath.

If God was God, and this really was His Word, then Israel had sinned, and the promise to seal up the skies was real. If not… well, he was about to find out.

Elijah closed his eyes, hesitated a long agonizing moment,

then prayed for the rain to stop so that all Israel would know who the true God was… himself included.

He finished and looked up, more than a little on edge. Peeking out his window at the flickers of light that marked the town in the gathering dusk, the cynical part of him frankly expected it to start raining right then and there, the world's way of mocking him.

It didn't, though.

Granted, it was almost summer, and it hardly rained at all in summer, so that wasn't a huge shock, but it was a bit of an encouragement. For a minute, he wasn't sure what else to do, right until a pounding knock on his door nearly scared him out of his seat.

The mood shattered, he hastily rolled up the scroll. "What is it?"

A young boy's head cautiously poked inside. "Sir, we uh… there's dinner downstairs."

Elijah slid the damaged scroll back into his bag. "Thank you, Noam. I'll be there in a second."

He wandered downstairs to catch the wafting yeast and honey scent of fresh bread, mingled with the rich, meaty smell of cooked lamb. The whole family was waiting for him at a long low table with cushions for seats. There were a lot of them – three young sons and two daughters, a matronly grandmother, a cordial lady of the house, and of course Saul, the man of the house, a jovial, middle aged fellow who sometimes got a little too deep in his wine.

Elijah found a spot and bowed as the blessing was said. He'd almost forgotten how hungry he was and was quick to start on the delicious food. Saul was eager to hear about his progress getting the delivery terms for his crops finished up, and Elijah was explaining that he'd likely finish tomorrow, when there came a heavy pounding on the front door and a gruff voice. "Open up! In the name of his Majesty the King!"

Elijah's heart froze in his chest at the words, and Saul muttered a curse. He hadn't exactly been subtle during his time here in Tanaach, and part of the reason Saul had offered to let him stay and work was because his family followed God, too.

"Go," he sharply gestured Elijah toward the stairs, "out the window. I'll stall them." He stood and headed for the door as the fist pounded yet again. Elijah bolted for his room while, behind him, Saul's wife quickly cleared his spot at the table so no one would suspect a guest.

Darting into his room, Elijah jammed the few things he still had into his bag and peered out the window into the night. It was a four or five pace drop down to the packed dirt along the side of the house. There wasn't much room in the narrow side alley, only a few cubits gap separating it from the next house over, but from there he could probably vanish into the rest of the town until morning.

He crawled out the window sill until he was hanging down along the outer wall with just his hands holding on.

Flickering torchlight suddenly spilled down the narrow alley and a loud shout, "Captain, around here!"

In a swell of panic his hands slipped loose and he tumbled to the ground below. The impact jarred his legs and left a sharp sting in one foot. The light was closing in behind him, but Elijah ran anyway.

He got all of three steps before someone tackled him like a bull from behind, sending the young prophet crashing to the ground. He desperately tried to kick off his attacker, but in a moment the soldier had his arms pinned behind him like a vise, shoving his face into the dirt.

"Got him!"

Elijah's breaths came in short frantic pants as more footsteps thudded behind him. He twisted his head until he could see the whole squad of King's Guards gathering around him, their spear-points glinting like razors in the torchlight.

"Get him up," the leader commanded. Several pairs of hands hauled him upright, face to face with the guard commander, a stocky man in a studded leather jerkin, and the only one to carry an expensive sword at his side.

"Are you the one called Elijah?" he demanded, his eyes narrowing and his hand sliding towards his blade.

Elijah swallowed hard. He'd always known they might catch him, but he'd imagined putting up a slightly more glorious struggle than almost breaking his legs and getting tackled in a back alley. "The people inside, they didn't know–"

"I don't care about them," the commander cut him off, his voice acrid. "Are. You. Elijah the Prophet?"

His eyes darted back to the man's sword. This was so unfair; he'd just taken a huge step of faith praying for no rain, and this was the response he got? It didn't make any sense. He'd run over this scenario a hundred times in his head though, and despite the cold fear strangling his chest he forced out the words, "Yes, I am."

He pressed his eyes shut and winced, expecting the agonizing bite of sharpened iron in his gut.

After a long moment, though, nothing happened. He inched his eyes open to see the guard commander staring at him like he was a moron. "Take him back to the post," he ordered with a flick of his hand. "We'll move out at first light."

It took Elijah a second to process that they weren't about to murder him right on the spot, but when it did he let out a breath he hadn't even realized he was holding. "What… where are we going?"

The commander's voice was sharp, like even deigning to answer was a trial. "Jezreel."

Jezreel, the fortress city of King Ahab. Whatever relief he'd felt at retaining his life evaporated as he realized what that meant. His execution was still on the horizon; he'd just have a bit longer to dread it.

***

King Ahab of Israel lounged back in his chair and sipped at a silver goblet, savoring the red wine, a product of his own vineyard right here at Jezreel. He'd come to the city to oversee the ongoing construction of several new towers, and had gotten a pleasant surprise as his news this morning. It was shaping up to be an excellent day.

"So where did they find him, Obadiah?"

"Tanaach, sir," his steward replied. "They found him yesterday evening and brought him first thing this morning."

"Tanaach," he mused. "What is that? Three hours walk? They made good time." Before Obadiah could answer, he nodded towards the door, "Go get him."

"In here, sir?" Obadiah asked, surprised.

"Just bring him in."

Obadiah nodded, and Ahab settled back on his throne. Normally, he would have passed sentence from his throne at the city gate, but he could always do that later. Right now he wanted to meet this odd prophet who'd been popping up all over his kingdom for the last several months. He could save the judgement until after inspecting the royal stables this afternoon.

Meeting this Elijah in public would just cause more problems. Plus, Jezebel would show up. As it was, she was busy with her hand-maidens, doing... something.

Frankly, it was better that way. She'd probably be all *'off with his head'* and really he just wanted to talk for a minute. Besides, this Elijah hadn't made any particularly grim pronouncements against him yet. Maybe there was an easier way to solve all this.

The carved cedar doors to his chamber swung open, and Obadiah strode in at the head of two guards, escorting a man who hardly looked a day over thirty.

"The Prophet Elijah, sir." The steward bowed and gestured Elijah forward.

"So," Ahab regarded him, "you're the Elijah I've heard so much about? I don't suppose you know who I am?"

Elijah hesitated, his answer cautious. "You are King Ahab of Israel?"

"Indeed." Ahab noticed with a twinge of annoyance that Elijah didn't bother to bow. A lot of the prophets seemed to be sticklers about that, yet another reason he hadn't done all this down at the city gate. Here he could ignore protocol if he wanted. "I want to talk," Ahab said, "about this God of yours."

The bewildered confusion on the young prophet's face almost made the king chuckle.

"What... what do you mean?"

"I mean I'm tired of his followers constantly harassing me. I was hoping we could come to some sort of understanding. If you want to worship Him, that's fine. I prefer Ba'al, but I can definitely offer a few sacrifices to your God if that would appease Him. I can even offer you a position as a palace priest if the sacrifices need to be done in some particular fashion."

He had been hoping the prophet would accept his olive branch. Normally, that sort of thing did wonders to deal with discontent. It was amazing how many people just wanted an easy job, a room at the palace, and an important sounding title.

Elijah froze at the offer. Ahab suspected he'd been marched in expecting a summary hearing followed by an execution. Clearly the prophet hadn't anticipated anything like this and for a long moment his mouth hung open a half inch, considering the offer.

"I…" Elijah took a deep breath, "I don't think that is something that would appease The Lord."

Ahab felt a flash of frustrated anger. "Well, what would?" he demanded. "What do I have to do to get your God to leave me alone?"

Elijah visibly swallowed, a nervous look on his face. Ahab guessed he wouldn't like the answer. "If you cut down the Asherah poles, tear down the altars to Ba'al and destroy the golden calves at Bethel and Dan–"

"That's not going to happen," Ahab snapped, his fists unconsciously tightening at the trumped up prophet's obstinacy. "Why does it even matter?" he threw up his hands. "Why does your God care if I worship Ba'al? Does He need a certain number of prayers? I can arrange that."

"He doesn't *need* prayers," Elijah tried to explain. "He–"

"Then why does He seem to be so insistent that everyone worship Him?" Ahab cut him off.

For a second the question hung in the air between them. Finally, Elijah spoke, his voice quiet, "Because He is the one true God, and truth matters, at least to Him. I'm sorry," he sounded genuinely apologetic, "but you cannot worship both The Lord and your statues of Ba'al and Asherah… He demands a choice."

Ahab could barely believe what he was hearing. Here he was making every effort to come to an understanding and yet, at *every single* turn, this Elijah was basically begging for death. Could he *not* make an impossible demand?

Stranger still, he seemed to understand exactly what he was doing. For someone pronouncing the judgement of God he looked pretty scared, but for some obtuse reason he just wouldn't let things go. Ahab had half a mind to write him off, just another deranged prophet that wouldn't work with him. He was still measuring what to do when the door at the end of the hall swung open, admitting a graceful feminine figure draped in satin robes of crimson and beige.

For a moment Elijah faded from Ahab's attention, and he couldn't help but stare at his wife. Whatever she'd done with her hair, it looked exquisite, braided and curled like a crown around her head with little threads of gold sparkling within. The rest of her didn't look too bad either.

One hand adjusting her golden armlet, Jezebel's eyes honed in on Elijah.

"Dearest," Ahab gestured her over to a seat next to him, "I'd like to introduce you to Elijah."

Instantly Jezebel's eyes narrowed at the young prophet. "You found him?" She strode across the room and slid into the seat beside Ahab.

"Last night."

"And he's still alive because?"

Ahab sighed. She didn't have to be so extreme. "Because I was talking with him," he said, "seeing if we couldn't resolve things amicably."

"And can you?" There was a snide smugness to Jezebel's voice that almost made him wish he had.

Unfortunately, he couldn't shake Elijah's words about being forced to choose. "I don't believe so."

Jezebel rolled her eyes and shook her head like she could have told him that without all the hassle.

"So, little prophet," she leaned forward off the chair with a fierce gleam in her eyes, "since you're here, did you have anything from your 'God' to tell us before it's off to the executioner?"

Ahab saw a flicker of horrified despair in the prophet's eyes.

Probably wishing he'd taken the deal earlier. As it was though, Elijah took a nervous, halting breath. "I do," he said. "Because Israel continues to worship false idols, the Word of the Lord is clear. As the Lord God of Israel lives, before whom I stand, there shall not be dew nor rain these years, but according to my word."

Ahab's jaw dropped. Had this man lost his mind? He was being threatened with death, and this was what he came up with? It didn't even make any sense. "You realize it rained three days ago, right?"

Elijah's face reddened some in embarrassment. "I didn't pray until last night."

"Oh, right." Ahab had an inkling Elijah was flat out mocking him now. Yes, technically it hadn't rained since last night, but if one overnight weather prediction was all it took to be a prophet, he suspected every five year old in his kingdom qualified. Besides, of all the predictions he could have made, this one was… stupid. They were nearly to summer, and it rarely rained in summer; *he* could have predicted that and been right four times out of five.

"Obadiah, get rid of this…"

"Wait." He turned to see Jezebel with a fiendish smirk and a glimmer in her eyes like a fox. She wet her lips, "So, if I understand this, you're saying there will be no rain, *anywhere* in Israel, until…?"

"Until I pray for the rain to return," Elijah said. "And that will only happen when Israel rejects Ba'al as a god and turns to The Lord."

Jezebel glanced at him and lowered her voice, an almost insane joy on her face. "Let him live," she whispered.

Seriously? Ahab was sure he must have heard wrong. Had the whole world turned upside down today? First he had a prophet who wanted to die, and now, for some reason, Jezebel *didn't* want to kill him.

"Obadiah, take him outside," Ahab ordered.

He waited until everyone disappeared into the hallway before turning towards his wife.

"This is perfect." Jezebel grinned like a cat toying with a

mouse.

"Perfect? How is this perfect? Did you not just hear any of what he said about the rain?"

Her voice fairly bled sarcasm. "Oh, don't tell me you actually *believe* him?"

"You don't?"

"No, he's obviously out of his mind. That's why we need to let him go."

Try as he could, Ahab couldn't put that together at all. "You suddenly have a soft spot for crazies?"

Jezebel gritted her teeth, like he was trying her patience. "Look," she said, exasperated, "I don't care what he says, *it is going to rain.* But he obviously believes his own lunatic fantasies, so let's use that."

That made slightly more sense, even if it still wasn't a cogent plan. "How so?"

"Let him tell the world," she made a sweeping gesture. "Let him go out and tell the whole nation that until they stop worshiping Ba'al there won't be any rain. It's summer, so it won't rain for a while anyway. Everyone knows that so no one will get too nervous until fall. Early fall I'll have my priests go around the kingdom making offerings for rain. You know what will happen? Ba'al will send rain. It doesn't even have to be that much, but it will prove him wrong, and *no one* will believe in his God after seeing that."

Ahab tapped at his thigh for a moment; that was… pretty clever. It would fix a lot of problems. In an instant he latched onto the idea. "Bring him back in!" He had to shout to be heard through the door, and a moment later the prophet Elijah was back in front of him.

"I've made my decision," Ahab said.

Elijah tensed for the worst as the judgement came, "You're to be set free."

For a second, everyone, even Elijah, stared at him like he'd lost his mind. "Sir," Obadiah stepped forward cautiously, "You realize you just said–"

"I know what I said," Ahab snapped. "Let him go. He's to be allowed to travel the kingdom and preach unmolested."

Jezebel threw in a smirk and an alluring wave from her own seat. "It's your lucky day, little prophet. Go tell the world what you just told us."

Obadiah looked dumbfounded, but he didn't object; if anything he just looked relieved. "Yes, sir," he nodded and gestured for the guards to bring a stunned Elijah.

***

No one said anything until they were well away from the room with Ahab. Elijah couldn't quite believe it. He'd heard of miracles happening, but he'd never expected to see one, let alone have it happen to him.

Next to him the man the king had called Obadiah, a tall fellow with a short, smartly trimmed beard and stubby hair to match, gestured for the guards to leave.

"So you're the one they call Elijah?" Obadiah regarded him with a sort of awe. "Was what just happened in there..."

Elijah shook his head an emphatic no. "That wasn't me."

"Huh..." Obadiah mused, "well I've never seen *that* before." He paused and bit his lip for a second like he was deliberating saying more. "You should probably leave," he cautioned, "before the king and queen change their minds."

"But they just said..."

"I know, but Jezebel was plotting something. I doubt it's anything good, and if her mood changes, your head will be right back on the block."

Elijah was more than a little surprised one of the king's own men would be warning him, but he nodded anyway. "I'll be careful."

Obadiah nodded. "What you said, about it not raining, was that the truth?"

Was it the truth? Elijah wasn't exactly sure himself. He hadn't meant to bring it up at all. It was less humiliating if he was wrong. When the queen had asked if he had anything to tell them though... he'd just known that was what he was supposed to say.

Maybe that was the point, he realized. Either he believed

enough to tell someone, or he didn't and if he didn't, did he really have much faith at all?

"It is," he nodded to Obadiah. "I've asked the Lord not to send rain until Israel repents."

Surprisingly, Obadiah didn't get angry or even hostile; he just gave a grateful nod. "I'll plan ahead then." He followed it up with about the last words Elijah expected from a ranking member of the king's household staff. "The Lord go with you, Elijah."

He was so surprised it took him a moment to muster up the reply. "The Lord be with you as well."

Obadiah walked him the short distance to the exit, and in a few moments Elijah found himself standing outside the palace gates in the compact, fortress city of Jezreel.

For a moment Elijah wasn't exactly sure what to do, but he kept coming back to the queen's words, 'Go tell the world.' He took a deep breath and fought down the butterflies in his stomach at the prospect. Finally, he found a spot to stand above the ocean of people, and cleared his throat. "People of Jezreel! The Lord your God has decreed his judgement upon Israel!"

Chapter 6
The Word of the Lord

Elijah cast a glance back on his way out of Beth-shan, an extra bounce in his steps. Being a traveling prophet wasn't nearly so bad when the queen wasn't out to murder you. It was kind of fun, actually.

Half out of habit his eyes scanned the cloudless sky, and a spike of nervous excitement roiled in his stomach. Still no rain.

He'd be lying to say he hadn't had his moments of terrified doubt, the creeping feeling that summer would end, the rains would come and all of Israel would see him for a fraud and mock the Lord. The ridicule he'd gotten over the summer when he'd proclaimed the drought hadn't helped.

Now though, the mood was starting to shift. He'd seen it in Beth-shan, a few uneasy farmers shuffling at the back of the crowd, thinking back over the bone dry summer. It was happening, slowly, but it was happening.

About a mile outside town he halted at a fork in the road. Where to now? He stroked at his stub of a beard, south to Jericho or maybe east, back across the Jordan?

He was still making up his mind when a gust of wind swept down on him, kicking up a churning cloud of dust. Elijah shielded his eyes just as another, stronger blast of air slapped at him from behind. There hadn't been so much as a cool breath of air all day, but suddenly the wind swirled around him like a cyclone, sweeping up a spiraling pillar of soil. He caught a mouthful of sandy grit as the storm intensified, the wind howling like a banshee in his ears while the thickening dust veiled the whole world in a brown shadow.

His face stung from a thousand tiny pinpricks of dirt, and a confused Elijah hunkered down into a little ball as the sudden storm raged around him. Even curled up on the ground he could feel the sharp winds whipping at him, like a living force trying to drag him away.

For a second the winds strengthened faster than he'd ever imagined, then it just… stopped.

Nestled close to the ground, Elijah peeked out, thinking it was over. What he saw was a twisting vortex of dirt barely an arm's length away that towered up far overhead, higher than any building. In the eye it was dead quiet though, almost oppressively so, despite the windstorm raging so close he could touch it.

Confused and more than a little scared, he was about to get up when a deep voice rolled out of the storm, shattering his island of stillness with a physical force that washed across his body. "Elijah!"

Elijah froze and swallowed back the lump in his throat. For an instant he thought he was losing his mind but even so he stammered back an answer, "Who… who are you?"

The storm itself seemed to pulse and thrum at the reply, "I AM!"

Elijah's heart dropped into his gut at the words, and he pressed his face to the ground. He'd read the scroll of Exodus. He knew it was death to look upon God. "My Lord," he whispered.

"Leave here," the voice boomed, "turn eastward and hide in the Kerith Ravine, east of the Jordan. You will drink from the brook, and I have directed the ravens to supply you with food there."

Elijah didn't dare lift his head, and a second later the wind swept back over him so powerful he was sure it would lift him up like a child's doll and fling him across the landscape. At the last second the storm weakened, the pelting dust lessened, and the shrieking howl diminished to a murmur then vanished entirely.

For a long moment he lay there, face down, not daring to move. Gradually he was aware of the beating sun on his back and finally chanced a glance up. His whole figure was draped in a fine layer of dirt, and further out he could see dissipating billows of dust hurled outwards like a titanic shockwave had punched into the ground right on top of him.

He struggled to even breathe, his mind spinning like a loose wheel. Had God just talked to him?'

Just the idea sounded borderline insane. He'd read all the stories about how 'The Word of the Lord' came to Moses or Samuel or Joshua, but they were ancient heroes and he was… the local lunatic.

He felt a twinge of irritation. They could have mentioned the giant windstorm, too, that would have been polite. Regardless, he finally controlled his breathing enough to stand and glance around. He could still see the white plaster houses of Beth-Shan in the distance, but no one appeared to be coming to investigate.

The words forced themselves to the front of his mind, almost like he couldn't forget them if he'd wanted to. The Kerith Ravine on the east bank of the Jordan, he knew the spot, maybe a day from Tishbi. He and his brother had snuck off there on little adventures when they'd been younger.

He brushed off the layer of grime that coated his cloak. Well, at least he didn't have to wonder where to go anymore.

Elijah took the road towards the Jordan.

It was only a half day's walk to the Kerith Ravine, a steep-sided winding canyon that cut through the hills east of the Jordan River. From the top it looked like just another scrub patch in eastern Israel, but half sliding his way down the rocky hillside he found a verdant, grassy paradise in the narrow valley below.

The brook gurgling through the center was clear and cool, a cubit and a half wide, with a bottom of smooth rocks and a padding of emerald grass running right up to a little lip at the edge. He'd come down near where the steep canyon took another sharp curve, and as far as he could see, the place was deserted. Sipping some water from the brook, he found a rock and sat for a moment.

Well, he'd made it. It wasn't exactly a step up from his prior accommodations, but he figured it could work. A little ways down he noticed a cluster of fig trees and several scattered olive trees heavy with nearly ripe fruit. Elijah stood to take a closer look when the harsh screech of a bird rent the air. He glanced up to see a low altitude black streak overhead and a rounded golden lump tumbled out of the sky.

His eyes widened in surprise, but before he could move the golden brown rock thing pounded him straight over the head. He winced, expecting a whack like a brick, but instead all he got was a soft *thunk* and a crunch like dry leaves.

He looked around to discover a round loaf of bread laying at his feet, split roughly in two and a little smushed in the center from the impact with his head.

Another honking *cronk* sounded nearby, and a few feet away a black raven beat its wings to a dead stop and dropped the last few inches onto a log. Elijah was so surprised he just stared at the bird for a moment. The black-eyed raven tilted its head, gazing right back from his perch, first to Elijah, then to the bread, then back to Elijah.

It wasn't hard to guess what the raven wanted, but Elijah hesitated. Normally he wouldn't have anything to do with the scavengers. Not only were they unclean, he didn't relish the thought of all the disgusting carcasses the bird's talons had sunk into before bringing him his dinner.

The hook-beaked bird kept staring at him, though, and after a long moment Elijah slowly reached out and tepidly grabbed at the bread. It was still warm, almost fresh out of the oven. Pinching off a small bit he tossed it to the raven. The bird caught it midair and wolfed the snack down in just a few bites.

He turned over the bread to see small puncture holes in the blackened bottom where the bird had gripped it. His stomach grumbled as the yeasty scent hit him full force. He hadn't eaten since breakfast.

He bit at his lip. Maybe he could just eat around that part? Give it to the bird? Besides, he mused, God wouldn't have sent him all this way and ordered the raven to bring him snacks if God just meant to kill him with some tainted bread. Elijah took a tentative bite.

He was busy savoring the honey-sweet taste when a second raven's distinctive *craw* echoed in the valley. This time Elijah was quick enough to dodge when a limp puffball of brown feathers tumbled out of the sky and *thwumped* to a halt on the grass at his feet.

He looked down to see a dead chicken, and a second later another raven alighted next to the first, cocking him that same, 'I'm hungry' stare.

Okay, this was weird, and that was coming from the guy who'd just taken moving advice from a talking cyclone.

Either way, there weren't many options. Touching the dead chicken broke a whole bunch of rules about unclean carcasses and that sort of thing. But he was pretty hungry. He wasn't technically a temple priest, and he was pretty sure God was running the whole deal anyway. He had a small knife in his bag, so he set to cutting a spit to roast his newfound bounty.

The pair of ravens watched him for a few minutes before flapping off to their aerie in the canyon above. It took a while but soon he'd plucked and gutted the chicken and had it slow cooking over a small fire. It was near evening by the time he made much real progress, and in the canyon the shadows grew long so quickly he could nearly see them creeping like colossal veils up the opposite wall.

As Elijah slowly rotated his dinner, he couldn't help but wonder what was going on. What was he even doing here? When he'd prayed for God to stop the rain he certainly hadn't been asking for something like this, stuck in a ravine with scavenger birds for friends. How long was he even supposed to stay here?

The beating of wings sounded in the evening air, and he looked up from his culinary adventures to see the two ravens flapping their way onto a nearby log, eying his very tasty looking dinner. Of course, he sighed, they wanted their share. A wild hunch came to mind.

"So," he asked aloud, "you two birds married or

something?"

The pair of ravens didn't answer. They just cocked their heads at him like he was acting particularly crazy. Okay, so they didn't talk. He picked off a few of the less appetizing scraps of chicken and tossed them on over to the hungry birds. Maybe expecting talking ravens had been a bit foolish, but he'd been having a fairly strange day. It was worth a shot. If they had been talking birds it sure would have helped the tedium.

The question pushed back to the front of his mind, how long *was* he supposed to stay here? He nibbled on a bite of chicken as he mulled it over and threw a few more bits to the ravens. Well, he figured, God had gotten his attention when He wanted him to come, so maybe He'd let him know when to leave. He pulled his cloak tight to shield against a breath of cool night air. Hopefully, God didn't leave him waiting here too long.

Chapter 7
Raven Man

Elijah scanned the sky, watching and waiting. It wasn't like there was much else to do here. The ravens would be coming soon and today–

A black streak dipped into view far overhead, and as it coasted lower he could see the wings beating hard to carry a white object almost as large as the bird. For an instant he couldn't help but be impressed. The bird must have sighted him because it lined up its attack run and a moment later released its catch, the white object falling in a lazy arc aiming straight for his head.

This time Elijah was ready, and he neatly sidestepped the raven's rude hello package so it tumbled onto the grass near his feet. "Haha, take that, Aaron."

It felt weird, but he'd taken to naming the ravens, helped with the tedium and all. They seemed to be a pair so he'd called the bigger male Aaron and the smaller female Abbey.

With the danger of aerial bombardment passed, Elijah knelt down to take a look at today's meal and was more than a little shocked to see the mangled remains of a baby lamb. Aaron was big, but even so, the carcass looked to be at least as heavy as he was. Aaron coasted to a stop and dropped onto the grass a few feet away, strutting around as if to show off his prize. Overhead Elijah heard a low distinctive *craw*.

Instantly he tensed. That sounded like Abbey, which

meant…

Too late he looked up to see a flying loaf of bread lancing straight for his head. He tried to move, but it smacked into his shoulder before tumbling to a stop on the grass.

He growled and fought back the sudden desire to kick a rock. "Stupid birds," he muttered. Was this his life now, dodging airborne presents from two ravens? He felt like they were mocking him.

Abbey swished to the ground near her partner and let out a demanding *croak*.

"Oh shut it," Elijah fumed, gathering up the bread and hauling the lamb over to where he'd been building a small pile of wood for the fire. He'd have some work cleaning the lamb, but as far as meals went, this was definitely a step above his normal fare. He glanced back to see both ravens cheerfully trotting over towards his bag on the ground.

"Oh no you don't." He darted over and swatted them back before they could tear into his things. Darn birds were too curious for their own good.

Eventually he had to tear off a few bits of bread to keep the razor beaked terrors occupied while he went about cooking. A part of him wondered where Aaron had found a baby lamb to cart off, but in the last few months he'd stopped worrying about where his food came from so long as it showed up. He figured somewhere out there was a village with a bunch of very angry wives suffering a plague of stolen bread. He laughed at the thought and went about gutting the young lamb, tossing the insides over to the waiting birds.

"Hey, you!" A sharp voice rent the afternoon air, and Elijah looked up to see an older boy with a staff weaving his way down the side of the ravine towards him. "Where'd you get that lamb!"

The boy, maybe fourteen, with scruffy black hair and the first shadow of a beard on his chin, slid the last bit down to the valley floor. He leveled his staff at Elijah, his eyes jumping between him and the two birds. "Those birds yours?" He glowered at the ravens who apparently sensed trouble and spread their wings just an inch, ready to soar away.

Elijah shrugged, "I'm not really sure they belong to anyone, but they hang around. What does it matter?"

"One of them stole my lamb!" the boy scowled. "That lamb," he pointed to the carcass Elijah was slow cooking over the fire.

Ohhh. He shot the raven Aaron a dirty glare and sighed. "I'm sorry about your animal. I didn't realize–"

"Well, are you going to do something about it?" the boy demanded, visibly angry.

Elijah dug in his pouch for a second. "I've got a few silver bits left," he offered.

That didn't really cover the loss of a lamb, and from the boy's frown he clearly knew it.

"Look," Elijah scrambled for a way to patch things up with the young shepherd, "I'm really sorry about all this. Why don't you have dinner here and we can talk."

That was poor form, offering the boy his own lamb for dinner, but he eventually nodded.

Elijah gestured at the ravens. "You two, scram. I'll feed you later."

He was afraid the birds might insist, but on command they turned and flapped off, sweeping out of sight down the valley to their nest up in the cliff wall.

The boy waited until they had vanished around the bend before taking a seat on the grass. "You know," he muttered, "for not being your ravens, they sure do whatever you want."

Elijah shook his head. "Not really."

He caught a whiff of the boy and wrinkled his nose. Well, he was a shepherd all right. Smelled like it too, a rank mix of sheep's wool, sweat and dirt. Didn't look great, either. Tattered clothes hung off his scrawny frame and a fading black eye had left a purple splotch on his face.

"So," the boy probed, "you live around here or something, raven-man?"

"Or something," Elijah nodded, slowly rotating the hunk of lamb meat over the fire. "What about you? Got a name?"

"Jaron," he said without elaboration.

"And you're…?"

The boy didn't answer for a long moment. "I help with a flock," he explained in a voice like he'd rather not talk about it. "They're up there," he gestured towards the top lip of the ravine with a dark look in his eyes, "a little ways north, looking for grass. When your bird grabbed the lamb, I saw it dipping down in the canyon, so Gili sent me over this way to get rid of it." He slouched over and rested his chin on his palm. "Probably shouldn't have said anything. Not like it matters anyway."

Elijah wasn't a master shepherd; his specialty ran more to trees and plants. But even so that was a bit hard to square. "What do you mean it doesn't matter?"

Jaron shot him a quizzical look like he'd been living under a rock, which was... not necessarily untrue, given that his current bed was situated beneath a stone ledge. "Where have you been?"

"Here, mostly. Something going on?"

"There's been no rain... anywhere." The boy swung his hands around like it was obvious, "Not a drop all winter, the grass was already dry from summer, and in a lot of places it's barely growing. What are the sheep supposed to eat?"

Strange as it was, Elijah had more or less forgotten about the no rain thing. Sure, he was aware and still caught himself glancing warily at the sky whenever he noticed a stray cloud. But, amid the daily visits of his raven friends and all the little chores of subsistence living, it didn't occupy his thoughts like it had. Besides, he was camped out in his own little patch of green gully where the world seemed oddly unchanged.

Jaron, though, he'd been living it. The young visitor bit his lip. "It should have rained by now, at least a little." He stared at the ground with a sour face. "It's all that prophet Elijah's fault."

Elijah froze; should he pretend like he didn't know who that was? The boy caught the confusion on his face. "Oh, don't tell me you don't know him either?"

"The guy that said there wasn't going to be rain, right?"

"Yeah," Jaron fumed, "that guy." He paused for a second before perking up a little. "You know there's a reward out for him?"

A feeling like iron settled in Elijah's gut. "There is?" he

stammered.

"Yep," the boy nodded eagerly, "two hundred silver shekels for the person who brings him to King Ahab alive."

Elijah didn't say it, but… that was a *lot* of money just for the king to chat with him. He hadn't realized he'd made that sort of impact. Suddenly, he was glad he hadn't gone home. The temptation had been getting to him the last few weeks. Tishbi was little more than a half day's walk from the ravine. He could have gone there, said hi to his parents, and still been back in time to enjoy his supper with the ravens. At least they'd know he was still alive.

With that sort of price on his head though, he couldn't go home, not anymore. The people in his village were nice and all, but for a payday like that, somebody would turn him in in a heartbeat. For money like that *he* might have turned himself in.

"I wish I'd seen him," Jaron added. "He was near my village a while back. Mom said he was crazy but…" The shepherd boy's voice trailed off in dejection.

Elijah couldn't stop himself from asking. "Which village was that?"

"Ramoth."

Elijah couldn't hide a momentary smirk. He remembered Ramoth and not in a good way. They were close to the Jordan, and everyone there had more or less laughed at him when he'd told them there wouldn't be any rain. A few of the bolder ones had pointed to the river and told him to try and stop it if he could, then they'd be worried. But from the look on Jaron's face, nobody was laughing now.

The lamb was close to done now. Elijah sliced off an outer piece and offered it to the shepherd boy, who gobbled it down like he hadn't eaten properly in weeks.

Elijah's mind flickered back to the other refrain he'd heard so often across Israel. "Has anyone prayed to Ba'al for rain?"

He feared the boy would get defensive at the question or maybe angry with him for asking. What he got was a fed-up scowl and a sarcastic eye-roll. "You didn't hear?" Jaron shot him a skeptical look. "How long have you been down here?"

Elijah almost didn't say. It was awkward enough being here

without admitting he'd been camped in a crevice for three months now. He sighed, the kid was barely fourteen or fifteen; if Jaron thought he was a bit crazy, it probably didn't matter. "Since the end of summer," his face heated a little in embarrassment.

The boy eyes widened, but he was apparently discrete enough not to point out how ludicrous that was. "Well, I guess you missed it then," Jaron said. "A few months back the King and Queen made this big proclamation about how they were going to sacrifice to Ba'al to ensure good harvest and rain. They had messengers going around summoning elders from villages all over the kingdom to come witness. My friend's dad went, said they had a big festival with drums and flutes, and the Queen herself got up and sacrificed a bunch of bulls to Ba'al, so we'd have rain and good harvest weather."

Elijah had been starving for news the last few months and the queen making public sacrifices to Ba'al was about as interesting as it came. It meant the game was on. For real. It was The Lord God vs Ba'al, and after his preaching and the Queen's flamboyant display, all of Israel knew exactly what was happening.

Elijah sliced off two more cuts of lamb and offered another to the boy, who was eyeing the juicy meat with ravenous eyes. "They don't feed you shepherds very well I take it?"

He meant it as a joke, but the boy's face darkened, his eyes falling towards the ground. "Not really," he muttered.

"Is there… not much to eat?" Elijah had the sense he was walking on a thin ledge.

Jaron folded his arms, more upset than angry. "The way the grass is looking, they'll probably have to slaughter half the flock by next summer if we don't get rain. In that case, there'll be plenty to eat," he said bitterly, "just…"

His voice trailed off leaving Elijah to fill in the last bit, 'Just not for him.'

All the pieces fell into place, and suddenly the boy's black eye made a lot more sense. Shepherds didn't have a reputation for being the nicest folk, and it wasn't hard to imagine Jaron having a rough time as the runt of the group. The sort that got sent off on foot to track down ravens, while everyone else bedded down for the evening. That was about as pointless as tasks got.

Elijah offered him another thick slice of lamb. "I'm sorry."

Jaron just shrugged. "It's fine," he said, emotionless.

"Is there anything I could do to help?"

"I don't suppose you could get your ravens to go bring a live lamb?"

"I don't think they work that way."

Jaron frowned a little in disappointment. "Well, can I at least take the ear?" he asked, with a flicker of optimism. "Prove that I found it."

"Sure." Elijah had removed the head before putting the rest of the body on a spit. In a minute Jaron had deftly sliced off a milky white ear and set it aside, his mood visibly improving. They spent the next half hour sitting around the fire enjoying the meat while the sky darkened overhead. With the boy's appetite he wasn't sure there'd be enough to go around, but somehow there was plenty for all. Elijah even set aside a pile of tasty bits for the ravens when they came by later. He did miss the lack of wine, but stream water served well enough, and as the first stars began peeking out, Jaron laid back on the grass, a contented smile on his face for the first time in what Elijah suspected was a long while.

For several minutes he stared up at the cloudless twilight. "Do you think it's going to rain?" Jaron wondered aloud.

Elijah sighed, "I don't think so."

The answer caught Jaron off guard, "You don't?"

"Well, you said Elijah told everyone it wouldn't rain, and so far it hasn't rained. So…"

Jaron gave a slow reluctant nod, "I guess that's true." He fidgeted with his lower lip for a moment. "I don't understand why Ba'al won't just send rain though? Some of the other shepherds said it was because he's angry with the King and Queen for letting Elijah go around speaking against him, but… we've been sacrificing to him."

Elijah didn't answer right away. The only things he could think to say sounded condescending at best. That was an interesting way to rationalize things, Ba'al was angry at Israel because of *his* preaching. He wasn't really sure what to say to that.

Glancing at the confusion in the boy's eyes the possibility occurred to him, maybe he didn't *need* to say anything. Maybe Israel needed to see and come to their own conclusions.

Chapter 8
Tremors

E lijah couldn't suppress a twinge of worry as he scraped out a little hole in the streambed maybe a hand-length deep and another hand across. "There we go," he mumbled to himself. It wasn't much but he lined the base with a scattering of water smoothed pebbles to keep the muddy sides from sliding in and waited a minute as the trickle of water slowly filled the hollowed out depression.

He stuck a single finger into the water until he touched a rock on the streambed, then pulled it out, staring at the line of wetness that hadn't even made it up to the top of his fingernail. "Getting kind of low today."

He'd been digging out just enough water to get by for days now, but with the heat of summer starting to creep back it didn't take a genius to see his water source was failing. A part of him wondered if somebody upstream wasn't drinking it all. The shepherd boy Jaron dropped by every now and then, so Elijah knew his much diminished flock wasn't that far off. Supposedly the ravine was too steep for them to get their sheep down the side, but from what he could tell they were getting desperate. They might have found a better way down somewhere upstream.

Leaving his hole to slowly fill with precious water, Elijah paced off to avoid the urge to mess with it and stir up anymore silt. That just left him with a creeping anxiety though. Alone, wanted by the king, and his only water supply going dry… he had some problems. Near the brook the grass was still an emerald green, but towards the edges of the canyon an inexorable brown wave had been slowly inching inwards for the last several weeks, leaving dead, wilted flowers and yellow stalks of grass barely clinging to life. He couldn't suppress a shudder; it felt like the drought was steadily coming for him too.

Overhead he heard a now familiar *crawk*, but this time mingled with an echoing chorus of harsh screeches, the *caw caw* of several crows. Glancing up he saw Abbey the raven swing low over the valley, pursued by a squadron of crows, a little limp figure like a field mouse tight in her talons.

Clearly she'd managed to anger the smaller crows, and one flapped his wings to gain altitude, right before diving down on her from above.

She dodged, flipping her whole body on the side and sweeping right, but the rest of the aerial platoon chased after her. She circled once with the crows beating hard to catch her and finally dropped to the ground near the canyon edge, flaring her wings wide and screeching to scare off the smaller birds.

Elijah rolled his eyes. "Hold on, Abbey!" he shouted to her and jogged for the nearest path up the steep ravine wall.

A part of him couldn't help but wonder if he was going a bit crazy as he grabbed his way up the rocky hillside; he figured talking to birds put him pretty close. Might as well add that to his list of issues.

Reaching up, his palm scraped on the coarse brown stone and, getting a firm grip, he worked his way up the steep slope. By the time he reached the valley rim his hands were coated with powdery dust. Twenty feet away Abbey was still screeching, hopping little jumps forward and frantically beating her wings as she tried to fend off five crows all going for her prize.

"Hey!" Elijah darted towards the crows throwing his arms out wide, "Get away! Scram!"

In a few steps he was in among them and the crows panicked. They scattered in a storm of wings and feathers and flapped off into the sky.

Turning back to his bird friend, Elijah found Abbey still there, watching him. She didn't panic; after spending the whole winter together, she wasn't very afraid of him anymore. Instead she looked almost proud, so much as a raven could. Abbey pecked at her treat, a small dead mouse, and strutted a little like she'd just come back lugging a buried treasure in tow.

With nothing else on his schedule he watched his raven friend for a few minutes. Food must be getting scarce if a little mouse was enough to fight over.

He paused, 'raven friend?' Yeah, he was losing it. Apparently, living alone for half a year with only two birds and an occasional shepherd boy to talk to wasn't great for your sanity.

While Abbey munched on her mid-morning snack, Elijah situated himself near the edge of the ravine, enjoying the view. Down below snaked a thin, vibrant strip of green grass while the hills above were carpeted with the ubiquitous sand brown of dry brush and dirt. He was about to head back down and see if the mud had settled out of the water so he could scoop up a drink when the ground shuddered.

The rumble came faint at first, far away like a whisper from below, but in a second it swelled like a fast approaching drum. Before he realized what was happening something like an underground shockwave jerked the ground sideways beneath him.

Elijah had been in earthquakes before, but perched close to the edge of a dizzying drop he panicked and scrambled away as another wave of raw force washed through the earth. Nearby, a growing roar echoed into a cacophony as countless stones from pebbles to boulders as thick as his arm were ripped loose from the ravine wall and tumbled to the valley floor below.

Elijah threw himself flat, the crescendo of banging rocks assaulting his ears as the shockwaves kept coming. His whole body lurched back and forth like the ground was thrumming to the heartbeat of the earth itself. He grabbed for a hold in the hard dirt, but with the whole world shaking there was little to hold on to. In the corner of his eye he caught a black flash as

Abbey took to the skies, the one safe place.

He was just thinking he might be able to ride out the quake when another titanic ripple pulsed through the ground, kicking his whole body a hand-width into the air.

A second later he thudded back into the churning dust, arms flailing and still dangerously close to the edge.

Then everything froze.

Around him Elijah could see the ground still shuddering, but the spot where he lay was somehow still as a mountain. The smashing roar of falling rocks had vanished, replaced by an impossible quiet where he could almost hear the terrified pounding in his chest. Amid the island of calm, Elijah heard a voice calling his name. "Elijah."

He didn't have to guess who it was. Fortunately, he was already facedown. "Yes, Lord?" he whispered.

"Get up," the voice tolled like the hammering of a bell. "Go to Zarephath that belongs to Sidon and stay there. Look, I have commanded a woman who is a widow to provide for you there."

Before Elijah could even process the words, let alone scrape up an answer, the thunder of the earthquake swept back over him. Another shudder ripped through the earth beneath him amid the echoes of a hundred tumbling boulders.

The earthquake seemed to go on forever, and even when it ended, the sharp clatter of rocks still rang in the ravine before gradually dying away to a stunned quiet. Only when he was sure the tremors had stopped did he finally push himself to his feet and turn towards the canyon.

The valley floor was a wreck, with rocks strewn everywhere. Back to the east a whole part of the wall had slid down, and a tumble of sand hid where the stream had run. What had been his camp now had several rocks bigger than his head strewn about, and several trees had been completely crushed, splintered beneath tumbling rocks.

For a few minutes he sat there, forcing his hands to stop shaking. He certainly didn't trust his grip enough to climb back down, and instead found himself dwelling on the big question.

What was going on?

Of all the places God could have sent him, the land of Sidon was quite possibly the *worst* option outside Ahab's capitol in Samaria. Not only did the people in Sidon worship Ba'al and Asherah, but Tyre and Sidon were ruled by a profoundly unfriendly man, namely, Queen Jezebel's father, King Ithobaal. The priests of Ba'al who'd murdered his friends, they'd been from Tyre.

It certainly wasn't where he would have picked. Jerusalem would have been a much better choice. At least they actually worshiped God there. For a moment he felt a spark of hope at the possibility that it had just been a slight mistake.

He figured it couldn't hurt to ask. "Umm, God… are you sure about that? Go to Sidon?"

A faint shudder raced through the ground beneath him, not enough to knock down any more rocks, but enough to give Elijah a jolt. He sighed, knowing exactly what that meant. No mistake, just orders.

Elijah exhaled. This was *not* what he'd had in mind when he'd started learning about God under Jesse. Frustrated, he flung a loose pebble down into the gulley, waiting for the crack of stone on stone as it hit the bottom. Well, he tried to see the bright side; at least he'd have someone to talk to now… even if they did want to murder him.

After a while he felt confident enough to weave his way back down into the gorge. Sliding down banks of loose gravel, he finally reached the bottom.

The stream was gone. It had been on its last legs even before the earthquake. Now, with a dam upstream, nothing flowed. The only water left was in the little hole he'd dug out, and Elijah scooped up what he could for one last drink as that, too, gradually drained into the mud.

Then he turned back to survey the ruins of his camp. His two pots had been crushed by a rogue rock, and the stone overhang he'd been using as a tent had collapsed. Pretty much the only things that had survived were his cloak, pack and a tinderbox with several flint pieces to start a fire.

Good thing he hadn't been down in the ravine during the quake, he realized, swallowing back a hint of dread. He spent a moment picking through what little he had left. Apparently God didn't want him dead, at least not today.

Behind him came the sound of beating wings, and Elijah turned to see the ravens alighting on a fallen branch.

"*Crawk*"

A hint of a smile came to his face at seeing them. "Good to see you two made it through." He spent a moment shoving what little he still had into his travel bag. He hesitated, "I'm leaving."

Aaron cocked his head a little to the side in a jerky, avian way. Elijah figured it for a question. "It's going to be a long ways away. Much as I've enjoyed the company and all, I can't stay here with the creek dried up. At least you two won't have to worry about dropping dinner on my head anymore."

Abbey turned her head to the side, one eye lingering on him. "*Craw.*"

"Yeah, I'll miss you too, Abbey," he nodded. "Both of you."

In truth he doubted the ravens knew what he was talking about. They were clever but obviously not quite conversant. Even so, Aaron dipped his head in something reminiscent of a nod.

Elijah grinned as he donned his traveling cloak. "You two stay out of trouble, alright?"

In answer he got a chorus of screeches from the two ravens, and they took to the sky one last time. Flapping up high overhead, the pair tucked their wings and gave a parting dive before catching a thermal and soaring upwards and out of sight beyond the canyon rim.

Elijah watched them for a few final moments before shouldering his pack and starting the long trudge out of the ravine and towards Phoenicia.

Chapter 9
Dema

Dema stared for a long while at the entrance to the Temple of Ba'al-Sur. She almost went in. Almost. But she'd kind of stopped caring, and it was clear Ba'al didn't care about her either.

A little ways down stood the city shrine to Asherah, a carved, slender legged statue of the goddess set on an ornate pedestal outside a small round temple building.

The priestesses were inside, but a cluster of young girls, the oldest barely over ten, were gathered around the shrine, giggling as they burned pinches of incense. One of them sighed and draped a scarf across her shoulders, like an older girl would after she was married. Dema watched for a moment before tearing her eyes away as the sight dredged up a slew of memories. She could still remember being that age, all starry-eyed and hopeful, dreaming of her life and burning little prayers to the goddess. At the time it had been fun to imagine her future husband and having children of her own… being a mother.

Now though it just seemed like a cruel joke.

"Dema," a feminine voice intruded from behind, "Dema, wait!"

She spun and caught a hooded woman in a modest, well-worn dress hurrying across the street.

"Istarah?" Dema couldn't hide her surprise at seeing her childhood friend.

Istarah grinned and caught her in a hug. "Dema, how are you doing?"

"I..." For some reason the question caught her off guard. The truth was, she was doing horribly. She was broke, her life was in shambles, and her last fragmented hopes were rapidly evaporating. "It's been tough." She swallowed back her urge to cry and managed to put on a brave face. "The last few months, I um..."

She couldn't bring herself to finish the sentence, and Istarah put a comforting arm around her, "I know." She tried to smile for the both of them, "It'll be okay."

Dema had heard that line so many times it was hard not to be jaded. She knew her friend meant it well though, more than most. Istarah was one of the few who'd actually spared some to help her these last several months. Istarah and her husband didn't have much, but they'd offered what they could.

Unfortunately, it hadn't been enough.

"We were going to the temple," Istarah offered, "to pray to Ba'al for rain. Do you... want to come?"

Dema had to fight to hide the defeated shame that threatened to spill onto her face. No, not really.

It wasn't like she could afford a sacrifice. Even if she could, she didn't know what good it would do. Everyone inside was praying for rain, an end to the drought. Many of them were farmers like Istarah's husband. But as far as Dema was concerned, it didn't matter. She didn't need rain, she needed food. *Right now.* Not in a few weeks or when the harvest came around. She didn't have that long.

Besides, Ba'al had cursed her, everyone in town knew it. Why else would he have taken away Simmias and left her... like this? She felt it every time she went outside the house without the shawl she'd worn as a token of being married. All going into the temple would do was set off another wave of vicious whispers, everyone wondering what she'd *done* to deserve her fate. From what she'd gathered the current theory was that she'd cheated on her husband, and Ba'al had punished her by taking him away.

She tried to bottle it all up in the face of Istarah's smiling optimism. "So, you want to come?"

"I… not right now," Dema tried to be polite, even with frustrated tears brimming at her eyes. "I… I have to go." She turned before Istarah could ask any more questions.

"Well," Istarah's tone lost some of its cheer, like she didn't know what else to say, "let me know if you need anything. Alright, Dema?"

Dema gave a sad nod and watched just long enough to see her friend turn away, then she fled.

She finally stopped in a back alley not far from the city gate. Slumping down against the wall, she buried her face in her hands and wept. She didn't know what to do, and little Hammon was back home, expecting her to have answers. All she could see was her ten year old's eyes staring at her, not understanding why his dad was gone, why all this was happening.

For a long while she cried and didn't care who passed by. It wasn't like she'd have to deal with them much longer anyway. After what seemed like forever she looked up and saw the shadows growing long as the sun dipped low in the sky. A part of her just wanted to stay here, but she couldn't, not with her little boy waiting.

Pulling herself upright, she thought about things for a second, the same terrible circle she'd been going in for days now. A part of her had been hoping something would change. Anything. Nothing had though, and as reality set in she felt a cold lump in her stomach despite the summer heat.

She was out of options. A grim horror tightened around her chest so she almost couldn't breathe. She'd tried everything, and now she only had one awful option left. Wandering out of the alley she took a deep breath, tried to be brave, and headed towards the city gate.

There was… well, it was basically a glorified trash pile a little ways beyond the entrance. Most of the actual garbage went in another dump a bit further away so the wind wouldn't waft the stench of refuse straight back into town. The one near the gate was just wood, discarded sticks, boughs from trees, pruned vine stems, that sort of thing. It wasn't ideal firewood, but it was dry.

Leaning down she picked up a few sticks and began snapping them into usable lengths. The work helped distract her for a moment, enough that she could brush away the last of her tears. In a few minutes she'd fallen into a routine and had a decent pile going.

Dema was still busy when a voice interrupted from behind her. "Excuse me, ma'am?"

She turned to see a man she didn't recognize with a poorly kept beard and worn clothes. From the way he shuffled one foot to the other she got the sense he was nervous, although she couldn't see a reason why.

Her tone was short and sharp, "What?"

"I uh…" he looked lost. "Is this Zarapheth?"

She forced herself to take a deep breath before answering. Even if she was upset, politeness didn't cost anything. It was about the only thing she had left to give. "It is," she replied more subdued. "Are you looking for someone?"

"Kind of. I'm not sure who exactly."

Okay? She really wasn't sure what she was supposed to do with that. His beard might not be well trimmed, but from the style and his accent, she figured him for an Israelite.

Most of the Israelites who came to Zarapheth were from the hills to the west, in Naphtali. Mainly they came to buy fish, especially now with the famine growing more severe. He should have gotten here in the morning though; last night's catch was all gone.

"Well, why are you here?"

He hesitated. "Would you believe me if I said God told me to come here?"

Okay. So he was crazy. Dema stared at him, completely lost. "Ba'al told you to come *here*?"

"Not Ba'al, the Lord." He must have caught her bewilderment because he clarified, "The Israelite God."

Right, Dema sighed, she'd heard some of the Israelites worshiped a God who was different than Ba'al, although she wasn't sure how exactly. The conversation was going nowhere. "If you don't mind, sir, what's your name?" she tried to get a straight answer.

He seemed to have to think really hard about that one, "You can call me... Elias," he said. "Would you please bring me a little water in a cup? It's been a long trip, and I drank the last of mine an hour ago."

Dema was sorely tempted to point him toward the literal oceans' worth of the stuff, three minutes walk east. Who knew, this Elias seemed clueless enough, he might just drink it too. She couldn't though; her mother's words echoed in her head like a mantra, 'it never hurts to be hospitable.' He probably didn't mean to be rude either. She was just upset.

Glancing down, she discovered the bundle of sticks at her feet was fairly large, more than enough for what she was doing. If she was heading back to the house anyway...

"I suppose I can." She knelt down to gather up her wood, "I'll be back in a minute if you can wait."

"Thanks," Elias nodded.

He followed her inside the gate and found a spot to sit there. This late the streets were mostly empty while the sun dipped behind the western hills. The sticks were more bulky than they were heavy, and Dema had to fight to hold them close to her chest as she walked.

She hadn't gone more than ten steps when Elias spoke up behind her. "Bring me a bite of bread, too."

Dema stopped cold, the request like a stake through her chest. Something so trifling, she couldn't say no but...

Her hands loosened for just a second. Dema panicked and scrambled to adjust her grip, but in an instant the bundle of sticks slipped loose, bouncing and scattering across the packed dirt road until they were just a jumbled mess at her feet.

Kneeling down, she desperately tried to gather everything, her cheeks turning hot in shamed frustration. Nothing seemed to work though.

"You okay?" Elias hurried over.

No, she was not *okay*. Nothing about any of this was *okay*. The wave of emotion hit her like a storm off the sea, and she couldn't fight back the tears any longer. Kneeling on the street she broke down in sobs as the impossibility of it all crushed whatever strength she'd had left.

"I don't have any," she said.

"Any what?" Elias knelt down beside her. "Are you alright?"

"Any bread," she whispered, humiliated to have to admit it to a stranger. "Sir, I swear by the Lord your God that I don't have a single piece of bread in the house. And I have only a handful of flour left in the jar and a little cooking oil in the bottom of the jug. I was just gathering a few sticks to cook this last meal, and then my son and I will die." Her voice broke. "I'm sorry, just... please find someone else."

The tears came freely now that she'd admitted it, and she shuddered with quiet sobs. Normally she would have pulled herself together, but it wasn't like it really mattered.

When she finally wiped away her tears and looked over she expected Elias to be gone, but for some reason he was still there, his eyes distant.

"I'm sorry, sir," she drew in a halting breath. "I don't have anything."

He nodded but still didn't leave. Instead he asked the last question she could have imagined, "What if I could help?"

Dema was sure she'd misheard. "What do you mean?"

"Look," Elias said, "don't be afraid. Go ahead and do just what you've said, but make a little bread for me first. Then use what's left to prepare a meal for yourself and your son. For this is what the Lord, the God of Israel, says: There will always be flour and olive oil left in your containers until the time when the Lord sends rain and the crops grow again."

Dema stared at him, open mouthed. That was... impossible. Elias seemed to believe it though, and she desperately wanted to believe it too. "How do you know?"

"Because The Lord sent me here," Elias said, an excited gleam in his eyes as he helped gather the scattered sticks. "He told me to come here and find a widow who'd have food."

A widow who had food? That was like a farmer who had a ship or a beggar with buried treasure. Even when times were good it was hard enough to scrape by with no husband when the only work you could do was patching clothes and you had a child to feed.

Elias apparently saw her hesitance and shot her a wry grin. "I thought it was a strange plan too."

Dema didn't answer, she hadn't a clue how. Instead she spent a moment staring at the dirt, stacking her scattered firewood. Was this some sort of weird trick? Some cruel way to rob her of the last thing she had? She honestly had no idea, and she was too hungry to think straight anyway. Elias seemed earnest enough, and if it was a trick… well then she'd die a day sooner. In a way, maybe it didn't matter.

As they finished with the wood, her eyes drifted towards the strange traveler. "You promise?" she whispered.

He smiled and nodded. "I promise."

Dema's breath drew sharp at the reality of what she was contemplating, but finally she pressed her eyes shut, fought back the terror stinging like a poison in her chest, and nodded. "Okay," she stood. "My house is this way."

Chapter 10
The Magic Jar

Dema dipped the measuring cup down into her flour pot, feeling it scrape against the clay bottom. It came up full though, and two scoops later she had enough for a small loaf. In the other room she overhead her son Hammon eagerly asking Elias where he was from and silently prayed that she was doing the right thing. She wasn't sure who she was praying to exactly, but she did it anyway.

The recipe wasn't difficult, just flour, oil, and water. Lately she'd been adding mostly water, but if this really was the last batch of bread she was ever going to make, it might as well taste good. She went back to her old recipe – half water half oil, poured together then mixed.

Soon she was kneading the small loaf and added in the last ingredient, the seor or leaven, a lump of dough from a previous batch that she'd set aside and allowed to rise. Now she mixed it in with her current batch to spread the leaven through the whole loaf.

She wasn't sure how long she kept at kneading the dough, but when her fingers were finally sore, and her stomach had churned more than a few times at the smell, she set it aside. Poking her head out into the main room, she found her son and Elias were apparently getting along well enough. Elias was telling a story about visiting Samaria in Israel, and Hammon had a smile on his face for the first time in a long while.

They both looked up as she entered. "Do you care if it rises?"

Confusion flashed across Elias's face. "Care if what rises?"

"The bread. I can leave it, but it will take a while to rise. If you're hungry I can just put it in now. It'll be a bit heavier."

Elias shrugged, "That's fine, doesn't matter to me."

Dema nodded and vanished back into her small kitchen to light the cooking fire. It didn't take long to bake and a short while later, she walked back out with a small but dense loaf, sliced into quarters. She set it in front of the hungry Elias who'd found a cushion on the floor. "Here you go."

He gave her a polite thank you and took a bite, "Mmmm… this is good." He glanced up with an encouraging smile, his tone optimistic. "You should make more."

More, right. Dema felt a lump in her stomach at the prospect of walking back in and finding just scraps in the bottom of her jar, but she sighed and dutifully found her way back into the kitchen. Reaching inside the jar she scooped out a cup of flour and froze. The cup hadn't scraped the bottom. A quick look inside the flour pot showed it was about as empty as ever, and pressing the cup down a ways she could still tap at the bottom, but…

Confused, she took five – six more scoops, then peeked back inside with suspicious eyes. Somehow it looked the same. There still wasn't a lot, but somehow there was about enough.

She picked up the pot for a second and glared at the bottom, like there was some sort of secret hole, but it looked perfectly normal. For an instant she was sure she was losing her mind, until, in a rush, reality crashed down on her.

It was happening.

Her breath caught in her throat. It was happening, just like Elias had said. In a sudden frenzy she grabbed at the jug of olive oil and swished it around to feel how much was inside. There wasn't much – but there was enough.

She delicately put the jug back on the counter, slumped back against the wall in a swirl of shock and relief, and slid to the floor, her hand covering her mouth.

They weren't going to starve. She wasn't going to have to

watch her son die.

For the third time that day she cried.

But this time, tears of joyous relief.

"Mom? Are you okay?" She looked up to find Elias and Hammon poking their heads in the door, where she was weeping on the floor.

She wiped away the tears. "I'm fine, I just… everything's going to be fine."

Her son seemed to accept the answer and disappeared back into the main room, but Elias waited for a minute, a grin playing across his face. Dema's eyes wandered across the room to the flour pot and the heaping pile of ground wheat next to it.

"What did you do?" she asked, breathless. "What did you do to my pot?"

"What do you mean?" He nodded towards the main room. "I've been in there the whole time. Did something happen?"

Dema stared at him, speechless. "How did you know?"

"I told you." Elias's smile widened till he was beaming, "God takes care of things. Trust me, this is *not* the strangest thing I've seen this week." He paused, "Your bread was great, by the way."

Dema just gave a stunned nod and forced herself back to her feet, with a sudden heady realization: she had people to feed, and for once she had the food to do it.

That night, all three of them went to bed with full stomachs, and Dema had a smile she just couldn't wipe off her face. The memory of her son wolfing down bread in gigantic, hungry bites was fixed in her mind. She'd been a little concerned Elias would ask to share her bed, but he didn't refuse when she offered the spare straw mat upstairs. It wasn't the softest, but she'd pulled out whatever blankets she could find to give him extra padding. With her son already in bed she lingered for a moment.

"Thank you," she said for what felt like the hundredth time.

"I appreciate it," Elias said, "but really, it wasn't me. If you want to thank someone, thank God."

Dema thought about it for a second. The thing was, she

didn't know his God. "Would you… thank your God for me?"

"I can, yes," Elias agreed. "If you did want to thank him yourself though," he added, "I'm pretty sure God sees everything, so just say thank you. He hears."

Dema bit her lip and didn't utter a word; she just nodded and went to bed, leaving him to his own sleep.

For a long time she lay there awake on the straw pallet, staring at the ceiling and enjoying the wonderful feeling of a full stomach. Finally, her hands nervously clasped together, she took a deep breath and whispered, "Thank you… God of Elias."

She drifted off to a deep, blissful sleep.

***

Elijah knew he ought to hate these people. Very likely some of Jezebel's priests, the same ones who had murdered his friends, had come from this very village. The temples to Ba'al and Asherah in the center of town were constant reminders of just how woefully deep in enemy territory he was.

Still though, he couldn't, not with excited little Hammon bouncing along at his side as they wandered down the shoreline back towards town. "You said your mom will know what to do with this thing?" he asked, trying not to look at the hulking fish they'd spent the morning reeling in. Just glancing at those big glistening eyes sent a shudder down his back, like the fish was staring back, silent, accusing.

"Oh, yes." Hammon nodded eagerly, wading through the ankle deep waves that lapped at the sand. "Normally she grills it. We used to catch seabass all the time back when…" his voice abruptly trailed off, the excited light dimming in his eyes.

It wasn't hard for Elijah to guess, 'back when Hammon's father was alive.' No one really talked much about it, and he hadn't felt right asking. It always managed to come up at the oddest moments though, and he hated seeing the way it crushed the boy's mood whenever he seemed the happiest.

They walked in an awkward silence a long moment before Elijah came up with something to distract him. Besides the small fishing boats, there were several big ships farther out to sea, among them a sleek cruiser beating its way north. With the square sail lowered, the rippling double banks of oars made it look like some sort of monstrous centipede snaking through the ocean.

"What is that?" Elijah pointed.

"That?" Hammon only had to glance, "A bireme, from Tyre. They come by every now and then."

"You ever been on one?"

The boy shook his head and gave a little snort of laughter. "They're warships." He glanced up at Elijah, "You've really never seen one?"

Elijah shook his head. "Where I come from, the biggest stream wouldn't even wet the hull on a ship that size."

For some reason Hammon seemed to think that was particularly funny, and the last traces of gloom faded from his face. "The only way to get on a bireme is to be in the fleet, either as a soldier or a rower." He shrugged, "I don't think it sounds that great. I always wanted to go on one of those," he pointed towards a huge, rounded ship like a barrel cut in half with a single square white sail beating its way south along the coast. "It's a Gauloi, a trading ship. They go everywhere."

"You want to be a trader?"

The boy nodded. "Nicias used to be a trader. He saw all sorts of amazing things."

Elijah wasted a second trying to remember who exactly Nicias was. He wanted to say it was old wizened fellow with the pronounced scar on his neck who lived several doors down. By the time he sorted that out Hammon was already talking three thoughts ahead of him again.

"Nicias told me if you sail all the way west, as far as you can, even past Tarshish, the Great Sea gets narrower and narrower until you could almost throw a stone from one side to the other. Then you find these two huge mountains on either side, and if you sail through them there's another sea that goes on forever with huge waves and storms and monsters. I want to go see that."

"Really?" Elijah couldn't keep a trace of sarcasm out of his voice. Sounded like *great* fun.

"Yeah." The boy didn't seem to notice Elijah's half frown and kept right on talking. "He also told me about the 'Sea of Islands' to the north. There are other traders there, the Hellenes. They live in these little cities and fight each other all the time. Nicias even showed me one of their helmets."

Elijah half tuned the boy out on their walk back. He wasn't quite sure it was the best idea for the neighbors to be filling his head with fantastical tales, but he didn't see any reason to crush his hopes. Hammon had had plenty enough of that lately.

Wandering back into town, they passed several workmen and a few other small-time fishermen back with the morning's catch. Most just ignored them, although a few greeted Hammon, and one even offered a polite nod and a, 'Morning, Elias.'

Elijah tried not to take it too personally. Despite the wild stories a few of the odd ones would spin, most of these people had lived in Zarapheth since they'd been born. He'd been here three weeks, so, as far as being accepted, he had a bit of catching up to do.

Granted, this was the same community that had been fine with letting Dema and Hammon starve, so he wasn't sure he cared that much what they thought, nor did he care to get too involved.

Finding their way back to the white plaster house in town, he saw Dema sitting up on the upper floor, a patch of the roof arranged with seating cushions and a curtain awning for shade. She looked busy sewing, but Hammon was quick to draw her attention and point to the fish. "Look what we caught!"

Dema's face lit up to match her son's smile, and a moment later she was down to greet them in the main room, staring at the hefty bass, "You caught this, Hammon?"

"Elias did. But I helped fight it."

She shot Elijah an amused half grin. "I thought you said you didn't fish?"

Elijah shrugged and tried not to look too embarrassed. "I guess I can now."

Dema pulled the fish off the line they'd been carrying it on and took their bounty into the small kitchen. "Well, no matter who caught it, I'm sure you'll both agree to eat it. Hammon, could you run and find some wood for a fire?"

The kid was off like a bolt of lightning, leaving just the two adults. Dema didn't start preparing the fish right away though. Instead, she hesitated with an apprehensive grin. "I have something for you."

"You do?" Elijah honestly didn't have a clue what that could be. Before he could ask, the woman gave an excited nod and vanished upstairs.

There was the creak of floorboards overhead, and a moment later she reappeared, holding his worn cloak. "I patched it," Dema said, excited. "When you left this morning I noticed all the holes and tears, so I went through and tried to fix it up as best as I could."

She held the cloak up and spread it wide for him to see. After using the thing every day for the last two years it wasn't exactly in the best condition, but she'd managed to fix it up where the only trace of many of the worst tears was a line of layered stitching across the grey-brown fabric. The color of the thread was similar, so from a distance the stitching melted into the rest of the cloth

Dema nibbled at her lip. "I hope I wasn't intruding, I just…"

"Are you kidding? It looks great." Elijah strode over to have a closer look. "This is good work. Really good."

"Thanks," a modest grin crept onto her face. "I could do the rest of your clothes if you want. Really, if the fabric wasn't so expensive I could do a whole new outfit."

"New clothes?"

"It's not hard," she shrugged. "Normally I do patches and stitching for a lot of people around town. With the bad harvest, business has been slow, but I could definitely come up with something."

Elijah thought about it for a second. A new outfit. He hadn't had one of those in… years. His mom had never been the handiest with a needle and thread, and he'd never had the money to buy anything particularly nice. The more he mulled it over, the more the idea stuck with him. He'd need to earn some money to buy cloth, which might necessitate a job, but… a new outfit.

"Did you want me to work on the rest of your clothes when I have a chance?" Dema asked, jolting Elijah out of his daydream.

"That'd be great. Thank you."

She nodded and headed back to the kitchen to work on their lunch, leaving Elijah to admire his newly repaired cloak. He cast a quick glance toward where she was humming to herself peering at a loaf of bread crisping in the oven. This was… kind of nice, he realized. It shouldn't have been. He was on the run from King Ahab, living in a foreign country in a house with a strange woman and her son, and yet, he was happy here. It was almost like having a family of his own.

The novelty of it all nudged him like a wave lapping at his ankles. This wasn't what he'd expected. When he had first come, he'd been certain he was in for more misery, but, looking around the house, it didn't feel miserable at all.

Chapter 11
The Jewel of Cities

Sitting on the shaded upper porch, Elijah stared at the tan papyrus for a few seconds before finally dipping his quill in the inkwell and scratching out the next line. The people here might not speak Hebrew, but the Sidonians were nothing if not dedicated to business. Fortunately, they traded enough with Israel for his services as a scribe to still be valuable.

Letting his mind drift for a moment, his eyes wandered towards the sea, where several trade ships had their sails raised as they made for the harbor in Tyre on the edge of the horizon. He always found it so strange how they seemed not to be moving, but if he looked away for a few moments they'd jump across the water.

Farther out to sea, he could just make out a dark shadow clouding the horizon, a storm, a big one by the looks of it. The first time he'd seen one he'd panicked, thinking the rain was returning. Anymore though it didn't worry him much; it wouldn't reach land. He'd seen several in his months here, and they all sputtered out some distance off the coast, like they'd run up against a giant, invisible wall.

He blinked and focused back on the contract in front of him. He'd already spent half an hour too long on this thing. With the soft shadow of sunlight leaking through the cloth awning it was hard to focus, and instead he constantly had to fight back the desire to enjoy a nap.

Dema's piercing shriek jolted him awake, followed by the smash of pottery on the stone floor.

Bolting upright, he leapt down the stairs three at a time and burst into the kitchen. "What's wrong?"

He expected to find something horrid, but instead he discovered Dema staring at the shattered fragments of a pot and brownish white flour sprayed across the floor, half burying some shards. The woman's eyes fixated on the spilled flour and the little puke brown insect worms writhing around in it. "There's maggots in the flour," she said, her voice reeking of revulsion. "How did they get in there? I only put it in the pot yesterday."

Well that wasn't as bad as he'd imagined. Elijah stooped down, staring at the little insect larvae wiggling in the fine powder. There sure were a lot of them.

It didn't take long to realize the one odd thing about the whole situation. "Where did you get all this flour?"

The woman's face reddened. "From the jar," she pointed over to the other clay pot, the one that had been feeding them for the last six months or so. "I took some out and used it to fill up this jar."

It took Elijah a moment to grasp what was going on, but when he did he couldn't hide an amused smile that danced across his face. "Why?" he asked, more curious than accusing.

Dema frowned, "It doesn't bug you that the jar is always *almost* empty?"

"Honestly, I don't really spend much time looking at it so…"

"Well it bugs *me*." Dema put her hands on her hips, frustrated.

Elijah stood and walked over to the other jar, the 'almost empty' one. He peeked inside and checked, no bugs and there was still flour at the bottom. "Dema, I know you were trying to save some extra, but that's not how these things work."

"What do you mean?"

Elijah tried to think of a way to explain it that would make sense. "Have you ever heard of a thing called manna?"

Dema shook her head.

"Hundreds of years ago, before my people lived in Israel, they spent years in the desert. We would've starved, but God fed us with this bread called manna. Every morning the people would go out and collect it off the ground. There was always enough, not too much, not too little, but enough. Some people worried though and tried to collect more than they needed. The next morning, their manna had maggots in it, and there was fresh manna on the ground outside."

Dema frowned and glanced from him to the flour, then back, her eyes echoing confusion. "Why would your God ruin perfectly good food?"

"It wasn't about food."

"You just said they ate it."

"Well... they did. That wasn't the point though."

Elijah sighed. This wasn't the first conversation they'd had about God. Dema had been more than a little curious about who exactly was behind her infinite flour jar. When he did try to explain God though, she had a way of grasping some things perfectly and completely misunderstanding others. When he'd tried to explain that God was the only god and sovereign over everything, she'd seemed to get it, right until the end when she'd asked who God was married to.

Elijah trumped most of it up to a cultural divide. "Look," he said, "the manna was about trust. God wanted us to trust him and *keep* trusting him. Saving it all up is the opposite of that, it's telling him you're not sure there will be enough tomorrow."

That seemed to finally get through. "I guess..." Dema fidgeted with a loose strand of hair. "Why does your God care?"

Elijah paused; that was a good question. "I suppose because people forget otherwise. I mean, look at my people, they spent forty years with God and now they don't even recognize Him when he turns their land into a desert." Elijah shrugged and tried to ignore the sting of realizing just how badly Israel had fallen. He'd always imagined that somehow Israel was better than the pagans that surrounded them, but suddenly he wasn't so sure. Were they really better, or had they just started higher and fallen so much further?

He pushed the thought to the back of his mind. There was

something else he'd been meaning to ask. "Dema, you said you could make new clothes, right?"

Her face brightened, "So long as you have the fabric."

"And I could get that?"

"If you know what you want, you could always order it with Erubeth; he makes runs down to Tyre every now and again. The only problem is he tends to get creative with his billing. Really, if you're not too busy the best way is to just take a day and head down to the city. It's not that far." She paused, "I could go with you if you wanted, help you pick out something, and I know Hammon would love the chance to see the city. It's been years since we were there."

Elijah mulled it over for a moment. Tyre didn't exactly top his list of favorite places, but it wasn't like he was going to bump into Jezebel in the market. He could definitely use some new clothes, and for the first time in his life he actually had extra money to spend on something nice. Plus, all his pants itched whenever he got sweaty.

Finally, he nodded. "I suppose we could do that."

Dema's face lit up in a wide grin. "It'll be fun."

Yeah, Elijah mused, it might be fun… or someone would figure out who he was, and he'd end up dead. Hopefully *not* the latter.

***

Two Weeks Later

Elijah felt the sharp jolt as the wagon trundled along through the early morning gloom. Up front, the hanging lantern swung and twisted at the bumps, casting wild shifting shadows in the predawn.

Sliding off the back of the wagon, Elijah left Dema to what couldn't be a very comfortable nap and walked alongside the squeaking cart for a while. Off to the east the first golden tendrils of sunlight peeked across the horizon, and ahead he caught his first real look at the mainland city of Tyre, a towering curtain wall behind which a jumble of glittering spires and arched buildings stabbed skywards.

Out towards the Great Sea, ships were thick on the water. Smaller rowed skiffs and ferries deftly wove their way around lumbering potbellied traders, all while sleek triremes painted with fierce warrior eyes on their prows patrolled the vast blue. In the center of the tangled armada, like a stalwart giant among starlings, rose the real pride of Tyre. A thousand cubits out in the ocean sat the island city, a jewel to dwarf the imposing mainland portion of Tyre.

At the very outer edge of the island, so close the ocean waves lapped at their foundations, stood a battlemented wall studded with soaring towers that ringed the fortress. Behind the stout defenses he caught glimpses of a grand city. At the north end of the island, golden roofed palaces soared far over the ramparts, and across the rest a dense forest of stone buildings poked out. Some were a blaze of decorative color with painted archways and curtained balconies, while others were flecked with strips of green from roof gardens. In the center, among them all, rose a man-made mountain, a raised building surrounded by a colonnade of pillars so enormous it was hard to imagine anyone lifting them into place. They supported a peaked triangular roof carved with reliefs that were indistinguishable from so far away.

At the corners, facing towards the mainland, sat two unmistakable markers of the building's purpose. A pair of statues, each the body of a man seated on a simple stone chair but with the head of a bull and two wavy, spiked horns. Statues of Ba'al-Sur. Staring across the wide strait they almost seemed to challenge visitors, even from so far.

Mainland Tyre was set a little south of the island city, and as the sun finally burst over the horizon their little cart drew alongside the opulent island.

Sitting up in the front of the bouncing cart, Hammon was, of course, wide awake. Next to him rode Erubeth, Zarapeth's local trader, who'd been friendly enough to offer the three of them a ride and act as a guide for their trip.

"That's the Sidonian Harbor," Erubeth pointed to the thick seawall shielding an inlet on the north end of the island where, already, ships were filing in and out. "There's another one, the Egyptian Harbor in the south."

While Hammon bombarded the merchant with questions, Elijah watched as their donkey drawn cart lumbered closer to the city. Even this early, tendrils of smoke from cooking fires threaded their way into the sky, and as they drew closer, a long throbbing blast rung from the city, slowly rising to a powerful, solemn crescendo before fading.

"The horn to open the gates," Erubeth explained.

As the sun drew higher, the long morning shadows fell away, replaced by a verdant seaside paradise. He'd expected a walled city surrounded by wheat fields and sheep pens, like Samaria. Instead, the plain around mainland Tyre was carpeted with, well, more city. Close to the main road sat several inns, and peddlers selling fruit and fish camped their carts in little clusters. Further away, giant mansions and sprawling stables dotted the rolling landscape, each one like a sentinel guarding its own private hilltop and somehow surrounded by thriving greenery. Despite the drought he saw palms and fruit trees bursting with growth, even bushes and emerald grass, the sort he'd almost forgot existed. At first, he couldn't fathom how they kept it like that. Then he started noticing troupes of slaves in worn work clothes trudging steadily north in groups of four, hauling large urns mounted on poles between them. For a moment he puzzled over what they were doing, then it clicked: the river.

They'd crossed the small Litani River that morning, shrunken and struggling from a lack of rain, with a bridge that seemed huge compared to the stream beneath. It boggled his mind, but the Tyrians were actually sending slaves to cart in water for an entire city and, from the looks of things, they weren't short a drop either.

He didn't have long to gawk, though. As they neared the city and the walls loomed ever higher a loud shout went up behind them, "Make way! Make way!"

For a second Elijah wasn't sure what to do. Erubeth nudged the cart to the side of the wide, packed dirt road and Elijah glanced back to see what looked like a whole army of gleaming charioteers, their horses tromping straight towards him and not slowing. He managed to scramble out of the way as the squad of lavish chariots rode through, a blaze of color and spears escorting a stern faced young man and a gorgeous but somber young lady decked in a glittering dress with several liveried servants close behind.

Those were the first but definitely not the last. By the time they reached the soaring mainland walls, other members of the nobility were pouring into the city, each with their own retinue of guards and servants.

At the city gate they found a press of people, petty merchants, slaves, and commoners all crowding to get inside. Amid the chaos it wasn't really possible to stop. Erubeth was saying something about meeting later if they got separated, but Elijah could barely hear it over the din of so many voices. He'd thought it was more comfortable walking, but a quick glance at Dema still perched in the back confirmed she'd made the better choice staying put. Crowded against the cart, with room barely to step, the tide of humanity swept them into the great city of Tyre.

Chapter 12
The Most Savory Offering

The crowd thinned a little once they were inside, but Elijah still couldn't hide the borderline claustrophobia that gripped him. There were so many people.

He'd always imagined Samaria as a big city, but at least there you could breathe. The buildings loomed up all around him. Everything at least two or three stories high, with heaps of rubbish strewn along the street where people had dumped it, leaving the stench to ooze through the streets like a dank fog. He was shocked to find the roads were paved too, and not just the main ones. Nearly every street was blanketed with a smooth carpet of stones so the cart hardly even bumped as it trundled over them.

"We'll head to the bazaar!" Erubeth had to shout over the din and, flicking his reins, he urged the donkey onward, battling through a tight press of people at the nearest intersection. Taking a break from walking, Elijah slipped onto a seat next to Dema in the back of the cart.

"What do you think?" she asked, an amused grin tugging at her lips.

"It's... big," Elijah managed, his eyes wandering across the crowds, so overwhelmed he almost couldn't process it. "I... how did they build all this?"

She gave a little shrug. "The wealth of the world flows to Tyre. At least that's what they say. All those ships have to bring in something."

"Still it's…"

"Chaotic?"

Elijah nodded and watched for a second, his gaze lingering on several old women sitting along the side of the street, clothed in hoods and rags with pewter cups held in front of them. Normally in Israel beggars would sit at the city gates, but here he figured they'd get trampled if they tried.

"Don't stare," Dema interrupted.

"Huh?"

"At the beggars, they'll assume you have something for them."

Elijah hesitated. Normally he was borderline broke so he'd never had much to offer, but now he actually did have some money and a bit of his heart went out to them. He wasn't sure how Dema could be so callous when she'd been close to the edge herself. He jumped off the back of the cart, but she caught his arm. "Elias, they're not real beggars," she said, with a hint of exasperation.

"What?" he frowned.

"It's a job," she explained, like she was talking to a child. "They dress up to look pitiable and sit there to make a living begging. Some of the ones with their heads down aren't even women, they're men who dress the part. They make their money off people coming in from the countryside who don't know any better."

For a moment Elijah stared in disbelief. In Israel people begged but they didn't do *that*. Maybe they had in Samaria and he'd been too naive to notice, but still…

Dema must have glimpsed the confusion on his face. "Simmias and I used to live here," she said, "before Hammon was born. If you watch long enough you'll see some of the beggars leave and others replace them later today. They work in shifts. It's a scam."

Staring at the pitiable wretches, Elijah couldn't believe how cold hearted Dema sounded, but he let her drag him away regardless and a moment later they'd disappeared into the swirl of people. Elijah was torn though, and glanced at Dema. "How do you know who the real beggars are then?"

She shrugged, apparently inured to the whole thing. "You don't."

Elijah didn't like that answer, but staring as they passed a lone beggar on the side of the road, he realized he didn't have a better one. Stepping down to walk for a ways, he had to avoid a pile of dung right in the street, and up ahead he saw another churning intersection they'd have to plough through.

They'd just entered the blob of people when a loud wooden crunch and a horse's panicked whinny sounded nearby. Looking left he saw two carts had gotten tangled up, their wheels locking together. With people surging everywhere, one driver whipped at his beast to pull free until the wheel snapped with a sharp crack, sending the cart sideways. Curses rung in the air as bundles of wool broke loose and tumbled to the street, and over the noise a loud voice shouted, "Make Way!"

Before Elijah realized what was happening, he was separated from the cart. The crowd shoved him back as it desperately parted for a richly decorated palanquin escorted by several guards strong-arming people out of the way. In the chaos he lost sight of Dema, and by the time the palanquin passed through, traffic was so congested he could barely move let alone see the cart in the impossible crowd. He glanced around, swallowing. He didn't recognize anyone and cold reality set in.

He was lost.

Before Elijah could get his bearings, the river of people had shoved him on, like a current pulling him further from his friends. This was apparently a main thoroughfare too. Unlike the smaller streets where there was space to breathe, he found himself trapped, his only options being to go with the flow or get trampled.

By the time he could slip onto a side road, Dema and Hammon were long vanished. He wasn't even sure which way they'd gone, except they'd headed towards the bazaar... wherever that was.

Three Hours Later

"Move it!" A blow from a spear-haft stung at Elijah's arm, as the guards shoved him and a dozen other people up the enormous steps of the temple.

"Wait," Elijah insisted, "there's been a misunderstanding, I'm not supposed to…"

The guard abruptly punched him straight in the gut, and Elijah doubled over on the steps, gasping for breath. A second later the pain hit him, and his eyes involuntarily filled with tears at the throbbing agony in his stomach.

Pulling in deep, frantic breaths and clutching at his abdomen, he was only half aware of the guard bodily grabbing his arm and forcing him up the steps. Elijah stumbled his way forwards, but it wasn't until near the top the guard finally loosened his iron grip.

He paused a half second. They were so high up. Looking back, he could see over the steep walls that ringed the island all the way to mainland Tyre and into the foothills beyond.

He shook his head. Okay, maybe taking the island ferry on a stranger's advice had been a mistake.

The guards had fallen back but only to herd up another group of civilians. What was going on?

Someone tugged at his arm. "Hey, come on."

He looked back to see a man about his own age, gesturing him inside. "You want to get beat again?" the man insisted. "Come on, before they get back."

Elijah hesitated at the massive entry doors flanked by two mammoth statues of Ba'al. He really *didn't* want to go in there, but the man was right. It was either walk in or be dragged in. He sighed and followed the man into the colonnade. Two enormous bronze doors greeted them, flanked by temple guards with long spears and round shields polished to a mirror finish, their lavish armor plated with silver and accented with threads of gold. Their helmets were a style Elijah didn't recognize, sleek and terrifying to hide most of the guards' faces, each plumed with a black and white crest that fanned out around their head like a lion's mane.

He couldn't help but stare. He'd seen warriors in Israel

before but no one like this. "Are you stupid?" the man hissed at him. "Don't mess with the Hellenes, come on."

They hurried inside, but Elijah glanced back. "Who are they?"

The man shot him a skeptical look, but Elijah couldn't tell if it was his Israeli accent being too pronounced or just that he'd asked a dumb question. "Kings-guards," the man answered curtly, "mercenaries from Hellas. Somewhere called Lacedaemon, I think." He paused, "You're not from around here?"

Elijah shook his head. "What's going on?"

The man grimaced, "Sacrifices." He didn't elaborate as they wandered into the Temple of Ba'al-Sur.

Despite his time railing against the false god, Elijah couldn't help but be impressed. A vivid tapestry hung from the left wall stretching dozens of cubits long. The intricate threadwork depicted the exploits of Ba'al, a larger than life figure, as he battled an impossible lizard bodied serpent with three heads while eagles circled overhead. It was so detailed it almost felt real.

The only true tapestries he'd seen were in King Ahab's Palace. At the time he'd thought them excellent, but this one made them look like pale forgeries. The needlework was so fine and the details so precise he could swear he was looking through a window into the frozen image of another world. The way it shimmered in the light like it was laced with glittering gold and silver left a part of Elijah wondering if there wasn't really some strange magic in the tapestry.

The rest was equally daunting. Huge red banners draped down like curtains from the ceiling that soared impossibly far overhead, and from behind the banners came the low *thwumping* beat of a drum.

A churning crowd filled the space, all sorts from beggars to middling merchants mingled together. At the edges, priests of Ba'al hurried about the room clothed in their distinctive red and black robes, carrying braziers filled with glowing coals. From within the sanctuary, the rhythmic beat seemed to intensify until it was almost a force pressing at him.

The crowd was loud enough no one would have overheard him, but even so, Elijah lowered his voice and leaned close to the man. "What is this?"

"Like I said, sacrifices," the man answered, his voice cautiously quiet. "The king always has them bring in commoners so everyone will know they didn't get substitutes."

"Substitutes?" Elijah asked. He couldn't figure why these people would make such a huge fuss about sacrificing a few bulls.

The man didn't seem to want to answer but, before Elijah could press, a chorus of trumpets sounded, a deafening cacophony that echoed in the temple until Elijah almost couldn't think. Off to either side he saw groups of several priests tugging on huge silken ropes to haul aside the massive curtains that veiled the inner sanctuary. Slowly the behemoth veil was pulled aside, revealing a hellscape of fire and bronze.

The inner sanctuary was dominated by a raised platform upon which sat the towering bronze statue of a seated man with a bull's head and curved, spiked horns. Unlike the ones out front, this one was bigger and gleamed of burnished golden metal. Instead of a simple stone carved seat, the statue's throne was an opulent affair of white limestone, inlaid with ivory and crusted with freshly polished, sparkling jewels.

Strangely, Elijah's first thought was that it must have been a horror to clean. Within the statue of Ba'al burned a terrible furnace, with flames licking out of a square hole in the torso, lighting up the thing's face with a hellish, flickering glow. A second pyre of orange flame blazed in the statue's lap, and its thick arms stretched out above the fire, palms up and cupped together.

Elijah steeled himself. It wasn't real, just a statue cast by smiths and filled with fires tended by priests. But with its hands held out, he couldn't escape the eerie thought of the statue pleading for a sacrifice to be dropped into the inferno rising from its lap.

He wasn't the only one taken aback by the vision. Several shrill screams went up from the crowd, genuine fear in people's eyes, as the rise and fall of the dancing flames in the statue's chest made it look uncannily like the enormous graven image was breathing. Amid the swirling smoke its stern features twisted into a horrible nightmare visage.

As he watched though, something clicked. It *was* scary, but it was also just a statue. His heartbeat slowed to a more measured pace, and amid the aura of fear that swept through the room, he realized something else. These people were genuinely frightened.

He'd never given much thought to *why* people worshipped Ba'al. He'd always just assumed they hated God, or maybe they didn't know any better. Suddenly, though, it made perfect sense, and he understood just how wrong he'd been. It wasn't any of that.

They were afraid.

They were afraid of what awful fate would happen if they didn't appease their angry demon of a god, and, looking at the grotesque statue, Elijah couldn't blame them.

As he watched, more instruments joined in the dark melody: piping flutes and gentle harps, underlined by the ominous booming of drums and the smash of cymbals.

His interest piqued, Elijah shouldered his way to a better spot as the priest strode to the base of the statue. He stopped at a simple flight of steps situated between the statue's legs that led up to the outstretched hands. Raising his arms, he brought the grim music to a halt.

Amid the sudden quiet, the whole temple could hear the robed man's chanting as he bowed, facedown, before the statue. Around the room the other priests took up the chant, until it echoed in a hundred voices, all beseeching Ba'al for his favor. Elijah listened, more curious than scared. The first part was about the protection of the city and its trade ships, strength for its walls. The next part caught his attention. The priest begged Ba'al to hear their pleas and send rain for their crops. There was a long bit about Ba'al wakening to their struggles and turning his eyes to their city, and so on. He ended his cries with the promise of a *most savory offering* to waken the god from his slumber.

Elijah looked around at that bit, expecting to see someone

leading in a bull to be sacrificed, or maybe another animal even more exotic. He didn't though.

The people around him seemed to turn even more grim at the pronouncement. Men's eyes fell to the floor, and he saw one woman with a hand over her mouth and a look like she might be sick. Far in the front of the crowd of commoners stood a different sort, at least based on their clothes. He guessed them to be wealthy merchants, officers and members of the aristocracy, but even some of them shrank back at the decree. It was as though everyone knew what was going on except him.

He watched for a moment as the priest finished his speech and gestured for someone to come up. A young couple wearing exquisite robes slowly ascended the stairs to where the priest was waiting, the woman cradling something in her arms. It wasn't until they reached the top and faced out over the crowd that Elijah could see it was a… baby?

He stared, and it dimly registered that they looked exactly like the young couple whose guards had nearly run him down that morning. Most of his focus was on the squirming bundle in her arms though; were they dedicating their baby or something? If so, they didn't seem very happy about it.

The priest leaned over and whispered a few quiet words in the woman's ear, and she dutifully held up the child overhead so the whole crowd could see the infant wrapped in a beautiful quilt. No one cheered though, not even a clap echoed in the space. Instead there was a solemn silence, broken only by the young child's wails.

The drum sounded again, a dark forceful beat, and the chorus of trumpets joined in as she handed the baby over to the priest. Elijah couldn't stop from looking, it didn't make any sense. The woman didn't look happy; if anything she had tears in her eyes, what were…

It clicked, a truth so horrible he almost didn't believe it, until he saw the priest carrying the child up the steps to the altar. It *was* the sacrifice.

He looked around, expecting someone to object, but no one said a word. Some looked away, most just looked grim, even the couple didn't move to rescue their child. The music rose to an oppressive, triumphant crescendo, and a sickness caught in his throat as he finally understood why it was so loud. So they wouldn't have to hear the child screaming.

The priest slowly held out the infant over the outstretched hands of their nightmare god.

He let go, and Elijah looked away, a taste of bile in his mouth.

Chapter 13
Land of Nightmares

Elijah fought his way through the crowd, pushing people aside and not daring to look back. Behind him the horrible music halted, and the priest spoke again, ritually calling for another sacrifice. Elijah made it back to the door as the drums beat again but found it barred by more ornately armored Hellenic guards. "Let me out!" He tried to push his way through the hulking men, but one of them caught his arm in vise grip. "Please, you have to let me…"

A spear haft slammed his head and he collapsed, dazed on the floor. The pain spiked through his skull and for a second he struggled to get up. The drums hammered in the background, pounding at his ears, as the single thought surged through his head, 'Get out!'

He tried to stand, but one of the guards lashed out at him, landing a kick right in his chest. More agony surged through him and Elijah curled up, barely able to breathe. Vaguely, in the background, he felt the guards grab at his arms, and he was too weak to stop them.

They pulled him away across the floor, and it was only when the bright midday sunlight splashed across his face that Elijah realized he was back outside. The guards unceremoniously dumped him at the top of the stairs outside the temple with a mocking snicker before turning and striding back in.

Elijah lay there a minute, sprawled out on the gleaming

marble, trying to catch his breath. Finally, he forced himself to his feet despite the throbbing in his head, and stumbled down the steps, desperate to get as far from the awful place as he could.

He made it down to the street, his stomach roiling and stinging with pain where he'd been kicked. He still didn't have a clue where to go but, staggering to the side of the road, he couldn't force himself any further. Slumping down against a building, he stared at the ground dizzy with the foul tang of vomit in his throat. He took a long breath, then retched.

When he was done, he didn't feel any better, but his stomach was empty enough that it finally stopped revolting and quieted. Leaning up against the wall he spat to clear the acid taste from his mouth, his mind replaying what he'd just seen over and over again. He could still hear the faint thundering of drums in the temple, and now that he understood what it meant, he almost couldn't breathe.

How could they just… stand there?

Strangely, it wasn't the priest murdering children that shocked him the most. After seeing Priests of Ba'al murder his own friends he was ready to believe the worst about them, but how could everyone just watch? He'd seen their faces; no one had looked happy about it, but they hadn't done anything, either.

A horrible image stabbed at his mind, a vision of his sister Hannah back in Tishbi, clutching little Lila in her arms before a robed man in black and red pulled her away to feed the screaming girl to the fire in exchange for a good harvest. All while everyone just… watched.

He tried to force away the awful scene, erase the imagined screams of his niece, but it wouldn't go away no matter how much he tried to tell himself that couldn't happen.

Because one day it would.

Maybe not today, or tomorrow, but it would. He'd always imagined the Phoenicians were different somehow. Worse. But in a flash he saw that they'd just been wandering down the path much longer. Israel wasn't better, they'd just fallen from a lot higher.

He'd be lying to say he'd fully understood what he was fighting against. Before today, people had asked him why it mattered whether they worshipped Ba'al or God, and he'd talked about truth and why it was important. But now he saw a different reason; there were no prophets left, and without him, what he'd just witnessed would happen in Israel too. Children burned for the pleasure of a demon.

He leaned back against the wall. The throbbing in his head had faded some, but he still didn't trust himself to walk, and his breath still came in sharp gulps.

"Elias!" a familiar woman's voice cut into his thoughts, "Elias, are you okay?" He looked over to see Dema hurrying across the street to him. "Elias, what happened?" She knelt down at his side, her eyes pausing at the pool of vomit nearby and the dirt that stained his clothes.

What *had* happened? Elijah wasn't quite sure where to start, "How did you...?"

"When you didn't find us at the market, I thought you might have gone to the bazaar on the island instead, so I came over. I heard they were dragging people into the temple for the Ideal Sacrifices, I was afraid you might have gotten caught up in everything and..."

Her voice trailed off in the face of Elijah's burning stare, and she looked away, as the drums inside pounded again. "Do you know what they're doing in there?" he demanded, angry.

Dema glanced up at the temple, her expression shadowing from joy to somber restraint as she realized what he meant. After a moment she swallowed and nodded, "Yes. But you have to understand..."

"Understand what?" Elijah demanded. "That they're murdering their children to get a better barley harvest?"

"Elias, you..." She struggled to explain even as he could see the disquiet in her own stomach at the thought, "It's always been this way, and it's not just for Tyre. It's for the whole land."

"And that makes it okay?"

"No but..." Her expression hardened at his attack. "It makes it what it is," she finally snapped.

For a minute neither said anything. Finally Elijah let out a breath he hadn't realized he was holding, "How many?" he asked quietly.

Dema looked away. "I don't know," she said. "Things are bad and we really do need rain, so maybe twenty, thirty." She swallowed, "Maybe more."

The number made Elijah want to vomit again, but with nothing left in his stomach all that came out was another question. "Why do they haul in so many people?"

"So no one can say they didn't do it," Dema explained, her voice little more than a whisper. "People will say they stole a baby from a maidservant, or didn't really–" she skipped the last words. "If everyone sees no one can dispute what happened."

Dema stood and took his hand, "Please, let's just go."

A morbid curiosity kept prodding Elijah to ask more, but finally he nodded and let her help him up, wincing as he stood.

"Are you alright, Elias?"

He massaged at his forehead a moment. "Not really, but… I'll manage. They threw me out."

"You're lucky they didn't kill you." Dema said.

Yeah, Elijah mused grimly, he probably was. All the *stuff* he'd seen today was expensive, but apparently life was cheap in Tyre.

The Grand Tyrian Bazaar would have been a lot more impressive if Elijah had been feeling better. Unlike many parts of the city that stank of garbage and manure, or the docks that mingled the salty tang of the sea with the reek of putrefied fish, the bazaar was a strange blur of wonderful scents. Women clothed in a blaze of alluring gowns offered exotic perfumes and powders. Merchants handed out tiny samples of rare wines from Gaul and cooks offered savory slices of fresh grilled meat stabbed on a skewer. A tall man and woman with dark brown skin were hawking gold jewelry studded with precious stones, claiming it was from Cush, while children skirted about peddling water and warm rounds of bread.

Elijah had never seen anything like it. They had Egyptian glass, silver from Tarshish, strange black hardwood carvings, fabrics from the far east, swords and spears of hammered steel, and rolls of luxuriant fabric.

Dema seemed eager to ignore what had just happened and made straight for a stall selling a rainbow of strange cloth. "What do you like?" She offered him a few samples to rub between his fingers, everything from plain coarse linens to a bizarre *serikos* so smooth it slid like water between his fingers and shimmered like dyed oil in the sun.

The *serikos* was expensive enough to have come from the far ends of the earth, which, according to the merchant, it had. The fine linens were more reasonably priced though, and as he and Dema fell into the familiar habit of haggling with the shockingly greedy trader, the horrors of earlier that day slipped to the back of his mind, at least for a few moments. They finally settled on a price that wouldn't bankrupt Elijah and, despite the merchant's pleading that it *would* bankrupt him, he seemed eager enough to make the deal.

Their next stop was a dye shop where an older woman sold little clay pots filled with various hues. Elijah couldn't stop glancing at her dress. He'd never seen anything quite like it, a mind-bending swirl of blue, green, and red splotches in strangely symmetric spirals covered her chest. It wasn't the sort of thing he could wear outside and be taken seriously, but a part of him wanted it anyway.

He'd never done anything with dyes before, but apparently Dema knew quite a lot. "What about this color?" She dabbed a pinprick drop of scarlet red on his finger. "It'll come out a bit lighter when we actually dye the fabric."

Elijah stared at the dye. It looked pretty but also uncomfortably close to the scarlet robes of the priests of Ba'al.

"How about a different color. What else is there?"

Dema was quick to wipe down her sample pin and dip it into several other shades, "We could do green maybe?" She paused, then shook her head, "No, you'd look like a tree. How about yellow?" She deposited another drop on his finger.

Elijah let out a long breath, imagining himself walking around looking like a giant yellow citron fruit. "Does it have to be the whole outfit?"

That set Dema off to thinking again. "No, if you pick the

right color you could do a dyed tunic and keep the rest white. You'd have to be careful about washing them separately though. You'd need something subdued like–"

"Blue?" Elijah peeked inside a little pot containing a fine royal blue powder.

The older woman nodded eagerly. "You have a good eye, sir, that's Egyptian Blue. They ship it up the Nile to here. Very special."

From the skeptical eyebrow Dema raised, it probably wasn't *that* rare. It did look good though, the color reminded him of the ocean, and if he ever did have a real run in with the Priests of Ba'al at least everyone would know exactly what side he stood on.

He stared at it for a moment longer and shot a quick glance at Dema to make sure this would work. She nodded and he turned back to the merchant woman, "How much?"

For being as *special* as the woman said the dye was, she sure sold it on the cheap; at least she did after Dema spent ten minutes hammering her down on the price. He'd never really enjoyed bartering. It always felt unnecessary. Dema was in her element, though, fighting hard for every *gerah* and even threatening to walk away at the end to grab a last fraction of a discount.

When they left toting a bolt of fine cloth and a small squat clay dye jar, Dema seemed positively ecstatic. "Did you want to get anything else?" she asked as they wandered past a stall selling 'magic potions' in colored glass vials.

"Not in particular. You?"

From the look on Dema's face she would have loved nothing more than to spend the next three days perusing every cart in the labyrinth of a market. He knew she didn't have the money for that though. Finally, she sighed and shook her head regretfully, "I guess not."

Elijah glanced up at the sky to see the sun was already well past noon, and a sudden thought jolted him. "Where are Hammon and Erubeth? Shouldn't we get back to them?"

"Oh, they're over on the mainland." Dema started walking at a leisurely pace. "We can catch the ferry back."

"The mainland? I thought they were going to the bazaar?"

"There are two markets in Tyre," Dema explained. "The one on the island is technically called the Great Bazaar, and the mainland one is usually called the Morning Square. It's... not as fancy."

"Oh," that explained a lot, like why everyone had kept pointing him towards the ferry docks when he'd asked after the bazaar.

Dema nodded, "When you didn't show up I figured you might have come here instead."

She left it at that and very studiously didn't mention the temple. She even guided them far around it, like she'd rather keep the memory out of sight and mind. Caught in the narrow streets of island Tyre lined with tall multistory shops and houses, Elijah couldn't even see the temple until they got to the ferry and slowly pulled out of the Egyptian Harbor at the south of the city. As the imposing walls and bastion towers slowly shrank, the peak of the temple crept into view like a disguised dragon, thin trails of smoke still belching from within.

He watched briefly from the gently rocking boat, then glanced over to see Dema studying at him with anxious eyes. "You alright, Elias?"

He glanced down at the bolt of cloth laid across his lap and deflected the question. "Well, I guess we got a good deal so..."

"That's not what I meant. Are *you* alright?"

He hesitated a half second before answering, impassive. "No. I'm not."

Dema tugged at a loose strand of hair. 'I'm sorry you had to see that."

Elijah couldn't keep the accusation out of his voice. "Are you sorry about what happened, or just that I found out?"

Dema didn't answer.

In a way that was all the answer Elijah needed.

He looked back towards the Temple of Ba'al-Sur as it rose like a miniature mountain. The drums were silent now, but things were very definitely *not* okay.

Chapter 14
Echoes

Dema stared at the bolt of cloth strung out in front of her, trying to figure out where to start. She'd measured it three times already, so she knew she had enough. But for some reason she couldn't bring herself to make that first cut.

She was still puzzling over the outfit when the front door swung open and Elias trudged inside with a fresh fish in one hand. Normally he'd have said hi, but today he simply nodded in recognition and wandered into the kitchen without so much as a word.

It stung, his ignoring her. It was stupid, childish even, but ever since Tyre, it felt like there was a widening river between them. Like he'd discovered the city's dirty little secret, and now he wanted nothing to do with it. That wouldn't have been so bad except the classification apparently extended to her too. She was 'one of *them*.'

She sighed, idly twisting a loose lock of hair between her fingers. Maybe she shouldn't have said she used to live there; maybe then he wouldn't blame her.

Dema glanced back at the door. She'd expected her son to be out with him fishing. "Elias," she called into the kitchen, "Where's Hammon?"

"Last I saw he was upstairs," Elias answered curtly. "Said he was tired this morning."

Dema frowned, he wasn't still in bed was he? They'd gotten

back late from Tyre, but that was two days ago and it was already mid-morning. He ought to be up by now. Setting aside her sewing, she walked upstairs and peeked in his room. Inside she found the lump that was her son still dozing in bed with his blanket cocooned tight around him, "Hammon? It's time to get up."

His eyes drifted open, just long enough for him to roll over and mutter, "I'm tired."

Well, he shouldn't be. She crossed her arms, "You weren't up late, were you?

"No," he muttered. "It's just cold."

That finally popped a warning flag, and in a few steps she was across the room, a hand on her son's forehead. "Hammon, you're burning up. Do you need a drink?"

All she got in response was an indecipherable mumble.

Worried, she hurried back downstairs and found Elias still in the kitchen cleaning his catch. "Hammon's sick." She grabbed a cup and half full pitcher.

That finally got Elias' attention, and a real question, "Sick? What happened?"

"I don't know, he has a fever. Probably picked something up in the city."

He hesitated, "Is there anything I can do?"

"Yes, but I don't know what right now." She headed back upstairs. "If you could just… be around."

He nodded, and she hurried back upstairs.

Unfortunately, Hammon's fever ran high the rest of the day and into the next. Even with Elias' help, between tending to Hammon and holding the rest of the house together, Dema was dead tired by the time she finished late the second evening. Nothing was getting any better either; her son was shivering beneath a heavy blanket, and they couldn't seem to help. Slumping down on the bed she didn't go to sleep so much as she passed out cold.

It was still pitch black outside when she jolted awake to a loud, hacking cough upstairs. It went on for a few seconds then thankfully paused.

The cough returned with a vengeance though, an awful

sound like he was fighting just to suck in air. Struggling out of bed she couldn't find a candle and had to half feel her way upstairs, trying not to stumble in the dark. Hammon's door was on the right, and Dema groped her way along the wall till it finally pushed open. Inside, the pale moon cast just enough light to see her boy's figure shuddering at each cough.

"Hammon?" She knelt beside his bed and took his hand, "Sweetheart, are you alright?"

He sniffed and swallowed to clear his throat. "I can't sleep."

"I know, sweetie." She laid a palm on his forehead and her gut twisted. His fever was still running brutally hot. She'd left a little water basin by the bed, and dipping a cloth in, she laid it across his forehead. "Try and sleep, sweetheart."

He coughed again to clear his throat but nodded and settled back on his bed. For a long while she sat there at the side of his bed, silently counting every wheezing breath, until they gradually slowed to a regular sleeping pace. She knew she needed to get back down to her own room but was afraid of the loose creak of a floorboard jolting him back awake. Leaning her head on the side of his bed, she figured she could wait a little while longer, just a few more minutes... till he was fast asleep...

"Dema?"

Someone shook her shoulder. She tried to move but instead felt a stab of pain from an awful crick in her neck, "Dema, it's almost noon."

"Huh?" Her eyes inched open to see Elias standing over her.

"Have you been here all night?"

"Where...?" She mumbled and massaged her neck. Next to her, Hammon was still asleep, except now, instead of pale moonlight, the midmorning sun poured in through the window. She squinted and rubbed her forehead. It couldn't be noon already? She felt like she'd taken a nap on a bed of spiked rocks, and somehow she was every bit as exhausted as when she'd gone to bed.

"Is it really noon?"

"Getting close," Elias nodded. "I tried to leave you alone

this morning but…"

"It's fine. I need to be up." She winced and forced herself to stand despite the ache in her back. Her gaze lingered on her son for a long moment. Even asleep, his breaths were still coming in pained rasps. She didn't know what else to do.

Elias must have been thinking the same thing, "He's still hot." He led her out into the hall and downstairs, his voice turning hushed. "Is there someone around here who might be able to help Hammon? Some sort of physician?"

Dema's first instinct was to say *absolutely not*. She wasn't dealing with that man again, not after last time. She paused, though, at the thought of her son struggling through another horrible night, barely able to breathe.

"There… sort of is," her eyebrows knit in frustration. "He's across town, Hyclaeus, he's a Hellene but he's lived here longer than I have. He *claims* to know something about medicine."

Elias shrugged, "Well, that's better than nothing."

Dema wasn't so sure it was. More often than not, it seemed a little bit of knowledge just made things worse. She didn't try and stop Elias from going to get him though. It wasn't like she had a better plan.

The door tapped shut behind Elias, and it was just her. Dema slumped down on a small square cushion in the living room, not really sure what to do. Finally, she realized she probably needed to make food before they starved.

By the time she got some flour set to rising, Elias was back, dragging the portly old doctor and his leather medicine satchel in tow. Hyclaeus looked even worse for wear since she'd last seen him, a bit more wrinkled, a bit balder and definitely a bit heftier. Not precisely the image to inspire confidence in a physician. Still, he was polite as ever, giving a slight bow when she walked out of the kitchen to meet him. "Dema, a pleasure, as always."

Just seeing the man in her house again conjured up a surge of memories, most the sort she'd rather forget. "I wish I could say the same."

"Of course." Hyclaeus didn't seem to take it as an insult, "Elias here said Hammon wasn't feeling well?"

"No, he isn't," she shook her head. "He's upstairs."

She might not have liked Hyclaeus, but at least he wasn't an insufferable know-it-all. Hammon was only vaguely awake, but the old man set to examining him, checking his arms, neck, and chest but apparently not finding much of interest. "Elias said he's been like this for two days?"

She nodded, "This'll be the third."

"Hmmm," the doctor rubbed at his beard, just as a slight knock sounded below.

Elias had been watching from the hall, and he disappeared downstairs to get the front door.

"Has the window been open?" Hyclaeus finally asked.

"Partly."

"Leave it closed," Hammon muttered from beneath his sheets. "I'm cold."

"I think that's more from the sickness than the temperature," the physician waved him off. "I'd suggest you leave the window full open to get some ventilation. That should help wash away some of the bad air. You've been giving him water?" She nodded.

"Good," he said, digging through his satchel. "Normally I'd suggest bleeding him." Dema's face went absolutely pale at the suggestion, but he continued, "Unfortunately, I've spoken with several others physicians in Sidon and they've all noticed it doesn't seem particularly effective with young children. In my personal opinion, it's because they aren't old enough to have truly stale blood, but I digress. I believe this should help." He pulled out a small jar fill with dried, crushed leaves. "This is oregano leaf. Mix it with some sort of food or water, and it should help tone back his sanguine humor." He pulled out another jar. "And this," he declared proudly, "is something I picked up from a truly odd fellow down in Egypt, said he used to give it to the Pharaoh himself. It's a willow bark extract; I've noticed it has a particularly potent effect on fevers. Give him two pinches with water and wait an hour to see how it reduces his temperature before giving him more."

Hyclaeus handed her the medicine and Dema let out a relieved breath. Well, that was certainly better than she'd been expecting. At least he wasn't going to insist on bleeding her son white, and she actually had something to give him that might help.

"How much do I owe you for…?"

"Don't worry about it," Hyclaeus raised a hand to wave her off. "It's a small thing, and I'd hate to see anything happen to Hammon."

The generosity was more than she'd expected, and for the first time that day, Dema felt a little ember of optimism kindling in her chest. A few minutes later Hyclaeus had helped her mix the tonics. From the look on Hammon's face they didn't taste very appetizing, but he'd pressed his eyes shut and swallowed down the medicine anyway.

"If you have any honey, a spoonful would be good, especially right before bed," Hyclaeus was saying as they headed downstairs. "Most patients say it helps them breathe easier."

Dema nodded, and thanked him one last time. At the base of the stairs her eyes flicked across the room to where Elias was seated, talking with…

"Istarah?"

"Dema," her friend glanced up, concern written on her face, "Is everything alright? Elias said Hammon isn't feeling well." Her eyes widened as she noticed Hyclaeus. The old doctor tipped his head to her too and headed outside.

Istarah waited until the door was safely closed behind Hyclaeus, her face growing even more concerned. "You called *him*?"

"I… well," Dema wasn't really in the mood to explain, "Hammon's not good." She paused, "You're here for the fabric, aren't you?"

"You're busy," Istarah shook her head, "you don't have to…"

"It's fine." Dema hurried into her bedroom where the bolt of cloth and thread ball she'd picked up for her friend back in Tyre were still on a little stool at the foot of her bed.

By the time she walked back out, Istarah was already up off her seat. "How about I stay for the day?" she offered. "Help out.

Akbar isn't expecting me back until late."

Dema hesitated, Istarah wasn't exactly who she would have… well, whatever, she needed the help. "Sure."

"Great," her friend led her over to a seating cushion, "how about you rest for a minute and I'll go make some food."

"Okay, I just… I need to go make sure Hammon's doing okay." Dema forced herself upstairs to where her son was still buried in his blankets. For a moment she just watched, wondering if maybe she ought to give him a bit more of the willow bark. Eventually she settled against it and held herself back from going over to check his fever yet again.

It wasn't until she came back downstairs that her exhaustion finally hit like a torrent washing over her, draining whatever strength she had left. Dropping onto the nearest floor cushion, she took a deep breath and closed her eyes, trying to gather herself for whatever came next.

Istarah wandered out of the kitchen, her hands powdered with flour, "I'm working on a second batch of dough, did you need anything else?"

"I… probably not, thanks."

Istarah paused a half second. "Uh, your flour pot was getting kind of empty. Did you need me to go get some more?"

Dema shook her head, "It's always like that. Hasn't run out yet."

She caught a flicker of confusion on Istarah's face, but her friend didn't press. Instead she found a seat nearby. "How is he?"

"Hyclaeus said to wait an hour, so I guess we'll see." She glanced around. "Where did Elias go?"

"He said he was getting kindling for the fire." A sly grin danced across Istarah's face. "I think he's hungry."

Her smile was infectious. Even given the dour circumstances, Dema felt a grin tugging at her lips. "He's always hungry."

"If you don't mind my asking," Istarah probed, "is there… something going on with you two?"

"What's everyone saying?" Dema asked, expressionless. Apparently it wasn't good, because Istarah's cheeks shaded a deep scarlet at the question.

"That bad?"

"Well, it's just rumors," her friend tried to cushion the blow. "You know how people are."

"If it matters, there's nothing going on between us."

"Really?" Istarah tried not to let it show, but Dema caught more than a little surprise in her voice.

"Yes, *really*. He just lives here."

Istarah seemed to accept that, but even so she nibbled at her lip and lowered her voice. "Why is he here? Where did he come from?"

Dema shrugged, Elias had never gone into much detail about his past, even when she'd probed. "I guess things were pretty bad in Israel, so he left."

"And came *here*?"

"Well, don't spread it around, but according to him, his God told him to come here."

"So… he's crazy?"

Dema couldn't fault the sentiment, but her mind drifted back to the impossible pot of flour sitting in her kitchen, the one that hadn't run out in the last half year. "Not exactly, no."

From the look on Istarah's face, Dema got the sense her best friend was starting to wonder if *she* was crazy.

"I try not to worry about it too much," she added. "It's that whole 'Don't pawn gifts too close to home' thing. He's here, and… I'm glad."

Istarah seemed to get her point but even so, she couldn't veil her skepticism. "Dema, I um…. I ran into Ameleah at the Temple of Asherah. She said you haven't been there in a long time?"

Dema froze at the question. This was really *not* what she wanted to talk about. "Elias doesn't like Ba'al or Asherah. That's the one thing he's really particular about," she gave the easy answer. "It's just simpler if I don't go."

Istarah bit at her tongue, like she wasn't sure about what was coming next. "Have you considered," she glanced toward the stairs, "maybe, because you've been ignoring the gods, Hammon getting sick is their way of getting your attention?"

The words cut, and for a moment Dema wasn't sure what to say. She knew her friend meant well, but she wasn't sure that 'your son is sick because of you' came across politely, no matter how you put it. Really, it felt more like a dagger in the chest.

"That…" she almost said that wasn't what was happening.

But was it? Could this be Ba'al's way of getting revenge because she hadn't honored him? Hammon wouldn't be the first child he'd taken. A sudden, torn panic gripped at her chest. She didn't know what to do, and the uncertainty gathered like a lead lump in her stomach.

"I'm not trying to say it's your fault," Istarah added quickly. "Just, if Hammon doesn't get better, maybe you should consider making a sacrifice to Ba'al."

Dema swallowed hard. Istarah had a point, but the possibility that her son was upstairs in pain all because she'd invited Elias into her home felt like a boulder strapped around her neck.

"It's just a thought." Istarah stood, "I need to check the bread."

She headed back into the kitchen, and for a long while Dema didn't move, her mind grappling with a horrible choice: who *did* she trust to save her son's life?

Chapter 15
Narrow Paths in A Strange Wood

Dema slipped outside the door to her son's room and slumped back against the wall. She held there for only a few seconds before burying her face in her hands and sobbing.

Hammon wasn't getting better.

The willow bark helped a little. She'd watched him rally, his fever dimming and the life flooding back into his cheeks, but it hadn't lasted. Like a moment of calm amid a storm it had faded, and now he was even worse than before.

She'd spent the last two days fighting it, but now she didn't know what to do. She was losing her son, and her best efforts had bought maybe two days… maybe.

Inside she cringed at the painful sound of Hammon retching again, as the last of what he'd been able to keep down at lunch came back up. She knew she ought to go back inside, but she couldn't.

A moment later Istarah walked out carrying a bucket, her face grim. She hesitated and cast a pleading glance at her friend before heading downstairs to empty the bucket around back. Dema slowly followed, the same question spinning through her head that had been there for the last two days. What was she supposed to do?

With Elias gone to gather wood, it was quiet downstairs. A still desperation pervaded the house. Dema glanced at the door, half wishing he'd come back and half dreading it like the plague.

"Dema," Istarah returned from the back, "we need to go. Please."

Dema drew a sharp breath, "I told you I'm not going back there."

"You're not going to try and save your son?" Istarah demanded, a spark of anger in her voice.

"I…" Dema bit at her lip and looked away, "what do you think I'm doing?"

A long pause hung between them. "Dema," Istarah's voice softened, "it's not working."

She took a long shuddering breath, "Look, I'll get Hyclaeus back here and he can…"

"Hyclaeus can't save anyone," Istarah's lips drew tight.

"You don't know that, maybe if…"

"He couldn't save Simmias," Istarah said bluntly. "Dema, he couldn't save your husband, why do you think he'll be able to save Hammon?"

The words sliced like a cutting knife. Always trust Istarah to bring that back up. She swallowed back the choking sensation in her throat. "I don't want to talk about it."

"Well, someone has to," Istarah said, "before Hammon runs out of time, too."

"Shut up!" Dema snapped, tears in her eyes, "Just… shut up."

She fled the room, retreating out the back. The narrow alley behind her house was shrouded in lengthening shadows amid the afternoon sun. Leaning up against the cool plaster wall, Dema pressed a terrified hand over her lips. Her eyes pressed tightly shut as shivering sobs rippled through her body. She didn't know what to do, and Istarah wasn't wrong; she was running out of options. Hyclaeus probably couldn't fix things, and Elias didn't seem to know what to do either. He said he had prayed to his God, but apparently that wasn't helping.

Upstairs she heard more of her son's choking coughs carry from the window above, each like a punch to the gut.

She knew exactly what Istarah wanted, and she'd been

putting off the decision as long as she could, but now Dema felt the creeping sense that it was time to decide. But she still didn't know what to choose.

Next to her, the back door squeaked as it inched open. Istarah stepped, wordless, into the muggy alley. For a time neither woman spoke, and Istarah slumped against the outside wall nearby, her feet scuffing at the packed dirt. "I'm sorry. I shouldn't have said that."

Shivering despite the heat, Dema pulled her arms close, brushing away the tears that stained her cheeks. She drew in a long halting breath, whatever resistance she might have had left beginning to crumble. "You still think I should…" Dema's voice trailed off midsentence.

Istarah understood, "Yes." She paused before continuing, "Dema, I don't think you have a choice. Go to the Temple of Ba'al, make a sacrifice."

"You think it will matter?" her voice came out flat, dead.

Istarah stared at the ground like she wasn't quite sure herself. "Two years ago, you remember when Elora's daughter Athaba was sick?" she said. "Elora was telling me how she went and made an offering. The next morning, Athaba went from having a fever to feeling good enough that she tried to sneak out of bed."

Istarah didn't come right out and say what they both knew; that wasn't an answer, it was an anecdote. Still, it was enough to conjure up the possibility, an image in her head of Hammon back to his old self, walking in the front door carrying a fresh caught fish and bursting with excitement. The image left Dema strangely gasping for breath.

A part of her wanted to shove it away, but right now it was the only flicker of hope she had, her only chance to get her son back. Dema swallowed back the rest of her hesitation, her voice small. "What do you want to do?"

Istarah gave a relieved sigh, a sudden optimism brightening her face. "Come on," she took her friend's hand and led Dema back inside. Istarah's bag was resting on a chair in the front room and, reaching in, she pulled out a small Ba'al statuette, a sleek little bronze figure of a man. She found an incense tray too, a flat board with a curved groove cut down the middle.

"We'll go to the temple, make a quick offering, then come back and hopefully Hammon will start to get better tomorrow." She offered Dema the figurine. "When he came by again this morning Hyclaeus explained how sometimes sickness is a warning from the gods. Maybe this will help fix whatever's wrong."

Dema took the little statue and stared for a moment, praying to herself that it really could help her child. Her eyes jolted away at the sound of the front door banging open, and she froze. Elias was standing in the doorway, his arms full of sticks, eyes fixated on the little god in the palm of her hand.

"What's going on?" he set his bundle aside, wary confusion on his face.

"Elias," Dema stammered, "You're back."

"Yes." His eyes drifted between the two ladies then back to the Ba'al statue. "I thought we agreed not to have those in the house."

Istarah's expression twisted in a frown. "It won't be here for long." She took the statue back and shoved it, along with the incense burner, back in her satchel. "We were just leaving. Weren't we, Dema?"

Dema gave a small nod and moved to follow her friend. She tried to ignore the piercing look Elias gave her and ended up staring at the floor.

"Leaving where?"

Dema couldn't bring herself to make the words come out, but Istarah didn't have a problem. "We're going to get help for Hammon," she said curtly. "We'll be back in a while."

"You mean you're going to Ba'al?"

"Yes," Istarah snapped, "we are. Come on, Dema."

From the shocked look on his face, Dema half expected Elias to try and stop them. He didn't move to block the door though. "Dema, wait," he said. "Don't do this."

"Elias, I know you don't... I'm sorry okay, but..."

"Ba'al won't save Hammon."

Standing in the doorway, Istarah narrowed her eyes. "What makes you so sure?"

"Because he's not a god," Elijah shot back. "He's a lump of cold metal, made by a craftsman who could have made him into a bracelet, or a cup or a decoration on someone's wall, but chose to make a little bronze man instead. He's as much of a god as your washbasin."

That earned him a dark scowl from Istarah. "You shouldn't talk that way. Besides, is *your* God going to save Hammon? Or haven't you tried that already?"

The jab seemed to take Elias back a pace, and Dema caught the truth in his eyes. He *had* tried, hadn't he, and it wasn't working.

"Elias, please," she said, "I'll be back in a little while, just watch Hammon and…"

"And what? You'll go worship that… *thing*. The thing that eats little children, and somehow it's supposed to save Hammon?"

Her gut clenched at the words. "What else am I supposed to do?"

"Dema, Ba'al hasn't been the one providing for you all these months. The Lord has and He can save your son. Ba'al can't."

For an instant the decision had felt simple, but suddenly Dema felt the tangle of impossible choices surging back. Istarah was still standing in the door waiting for her to come, but she couldn't make herself move.

Images cycloned through her mind, all those little offerings to Asherah for a good future she'd made as a girl. Her husband Simmias, the man she'd thought a gift from the gods, dying of a fever. Standing in the Temple of Ba'al after he'd died, a pariah, people whispering as she passed. The day she'd met Elias and his strange God that had saved her with a flour pot that always had enough for one more loaf.

She didn't have to go far to find a miracle. She had the odd feeling she could walk into the kitchen, turn her oil jug upside down, and flood the world with what came out. The God of Elias had been good to her. He'd saved her and her son – when Ba'al hadn't.

But then why was Hammon sick? The doubt gnawed at her. What had she done wrong? What had she done to deserve to lose her son?

"Dema," Elias must had seen her indecision, "I don't know why this is happening to Hammon, but Ba'al can't save him, only God can. You know that. You've seen that."

She had, and as hard as it was, she knew he wasn't wrong. Dema's voice came out as a desperate whisper, "Okay."

She stepped away from the door.

Istarah stared at her, eyes wide in incredulity. "Are you serious? Dema, you don't actually believe?"

Dema swallowed hard, her eyes on the floor. "I do."

Istarah's glare honed in on Elias like a lance, bitter hurt in her voice. "What have you done to my friend?"

She turned away, and Dema glimpsed tears of frustration in her friend's eyes. "Well, if none of you care about Hammon, *I* still do." She stalked outside, "If you come to your senses, Dema, I'll be down at the temple, trying to keep your son alive." Istarah slammed the door shut, and it was just the two of them.

"Dema," Elias said, "I–"

"Don't… just don't." Dema held up a hand for him to stop, still half in shock. What had she just done?

It took a moment to catch her breath, and when she did it finally sunk in that she didn't really know what else to do. She glanced toward Elias, "Just save Hammon, okay?" She headed upstairs, "I'm going to go be with my son."

Chapter 16
The Lost Boy

Elijah jolted awake to a piercing wail that cut like a blade through the pre-dawn dark. From the sound, he didn't have to ask what had happened, and his heart sunk in his chest at the thought.

Upstairs, Dema's horrified screams split the warm night, and when they faded it was only to be replaced by haunting, torn sobs.

He'd fallen asleep sitting on a cushion downstairs, up late into the night, praying.

Apparently, it hadn't helped.

For a long time the awful sound of Dema weeping upstairs permeated the house. Elijah would have gone up to say something, but he honestly didn't know what. What was he supposed to tell a woman who'd just lost everything?

And a second question hovered like a black shadow in his mind, sending tendrils of confused fear into his chest. How had this happened?

It didn't make any sense. He'd prayed, he'd asked God to save Hammon, he'd believed, he… he'd done everything he could.

He'd cared for Hammon too, but from the distraught weeping upstairs, Hammon was dead, and God hadn't showed up.

For a long while he sat there, chasing the question like a

rabbit in his head, yet not finding any answers. Finally though, as the first embers of dawn glowed on the horizon, Dema's quiet sobs faded and in the gloom he heard the wooden creak of floorboards followed by the soft scrape of bare feet on the stone steps.

The darkness hung like a shroud over the stairs, but in it he perceived motion, like a shifting shadow. Out of the murk came Dema, her hair a scattered bird's nest, her cheeks streaked with tears, and the limp figure of a little boy nestled in her arms.

She didn't look at him, she didn't look at anything. Her eyes were fixated on the floor, and in the dead quiet, each pat of a foot sounded like the hammer of a bell. She carried the lifeless boy into her room and a moment later emerged without him, her steps slow and tired, like she was sleepwalking.

Plodding across the room, she sunk, cross legged, down onto a seating cushion nearby where she didn't have to see him, her eyes staring dead ahead, like it might just break her to look anywhere else. For a long while, she said nothing.

Outside the embers of dawn spread, glowing like wildfire across the horizon, until a faint orange light pushed at the windows.

Only then did she speak, her voice a choked whisper. "You promised," she said. "You promised me."

"Dema, I…"

"YOU PROMISED!" She screamed, the words like an inferno between them. "You promised me your God would save him!"

Elijah didn't know what to say, "I'm sorry."

Dema drew in a halting breath, "I am too. I'm sorry I believed that your God cared."

"Dema, don't say that."

"Don't say *what*?" the poison dripped in her voice. "That your God stole the one good thing I have left? That… that Hammon is dead… because you lied to me?"

Elijah stared at his lap for a time biting at his lip so hard it hurt, "Dema, God does care about you," he finally said. "You can go open your pot in the kitchen if you don't believe me."

That just made the hurt in her voice worse. "I don't want

flour," she said in bitter disbelief, "I want my son back." She pointed to the kitchen door, her hand shaking. "I would smash every pot in this house, if it would bring Hammon back." She looked over and their eyes locked. "Tell me it will," she half pleaded.

Elijah looked away and shook his head. "I'm sorry."

She shook her head in disgust. "I should have gone to the Temple of Ba'al. Istarah was right. I've ignored the gods and… and they've taken…" Her voice broke, and she couldn't finish as tears flooded her eyes, drowning in grief.

"Ba'al wouldn't have saved Hammon," Elijah said in a small voice. It didn't feel like the right thing to say, but he wasn't sure there *was* a right thing to say.

Something snapped deep inside Dema, and her eyes stabbed at him like twin spears. "How do you know?" she demanded, her voice rising in a cold fury. "How do you know! Your God couldn't save him, how do you know Ba'al couldn't?"

For some reason the question caught Elijah by surprise. How did he know? His first thought was that her god was a glorified lump of bronze, but his God was invisible most of the time too. So how did he…

The words sprung to his mind, "Because I saw," he said. "I saw how they worshiped Ba'al in Tyre, and the god that you worship, he didn't care about children, except to devour them."

It was enough to give Dema pause. She stared at him, a sudden wildness in her eyes. "Is that what this is about?" Her hand covered her mouth, her voice turning desperate. "This is about Tyre, isn't it? About what the high priest does, the children they kill? This is your God's vengeance on me?" She drew in a sharp, panicked breath, and looked at him with a horror on her face, like the pieces were finally falling into place. "What do you have against me, man of God? Did you come to remind me of my sin and kill my son?"

The accusation stung like a hornet, "I cared about him too," he said, the anger rising in his own voice, "If I could have saved him, I would have."

For an instant she glared at him, rage in her eyes, but soon even that dimmed and Dema's shoulders slumped, all the fight drained from her, like there was nothing left now but terrible, relentless loss. As the sun peeked over the horizon, Elijah sat there, silent, with Dema's words ringing in his head.

Why *had* he come here? Why had God sent him to Dema? He'd saved her from starving, but now Hammon was dead, and he could see in her dim eyes that a part of her had died with him.

How was this better?

"God," he whispered, "why?"

He waited for a moment, wishing for an answer, but none came. His face creased in a defeated frown. Maybe she was right, maybe this was some sort of judgement. He shook his head. Maybe he should just leave. Dema didn't want him, and he couldn't bear the thought of spending another week trapped in a house with the memories of what had happened. All he'd done was bring trouble.

He was seriously considering offering to pack his things when a second thought popped into his head. Why *had* God sent him *here*, to Dema? To a woman who'd lived in Tyre? There were widows in Israel, so why go to another country, to somewhere like Zarapheth? Ahab hadn't found him here, but there were places to hide in Israel too.

His eyes drifted across to the shell of a woman sitting nearby, what had God seen in her? In response, a strange question came to the forefront of his mind; it didn't make much sense, but it pestered him for an answer.

"Dema," he asked quietly, "why did you leave Tyre?"

The question caught her off guard. For an instant she looked like she'd rather not answer, but finally she spoke, "Because the city is poison." Her voice was subdued, "Slow poison, the sort that takes a lifetime to kill you. I suppose most people don't really care but living there, surrounded by so much pain and knowing you have to ignore it… it eats away at your soul a little bit every day. Behind all the money and clothes and ships and walls and sacrifices, there are a lot of dead people wandering that city. I didn't want Hammon to grow up dead and cruel like that."

"I convinced Simmias to move out here when he was born.

Less work, but you live better." She pressed her eyes tight shut, as they misted over. "At least, that was what I thought." She pressed a hand to her mouth, the tears flooding back. "I guess I was wrong."

Something hardened deep inside him, anger and frustration at the unfairness of it all. "You weren't wrong," he said, a sudden firmness in his voice, "about Tyre, about it being evil. You were right."

Dema shook her head, "Then why is everyone I love dead?"

A sudden thought flared in the back of Elijah's mind, something impossible, or at least, he would have said it was impossible a few years ago. But that was back before he'd stood before the king and survived, before ravens had brought him food for a year, before he'd met God in the whirlwind and the earthquake... before he'd prayed and believed and turned the sky to bronze. Maybe it *wasn't* supposed to be this way.

"Give me your son," he whispered.

"What?" Dema glanced at him with a look like he'd lost his mind.

"Give me your son." He saw the hurt bewilderment written in her eyes. "Please, just this once."

For a moment, he was afraid she was about to say no, to scream at him again, shout for him to leave and at least grant her the dignity of suffering in peace. She didn't though. Instead she offered a tiny nod and stood.

She disappeared into her room and a moment later returned with Hammon's lifeless figure. Elijah stood and took the child's body from her arms, stunned at how light he felt, like holding a ghost.

Elijah carried him up the stairs to the room where he was staying and laid the body on his bed. For a long time he stared at the cold, frail figure, still struggling to understand. The question '*why*' circled through his head over and over again.

Finally, he knelt down next to the bed and looked up towards heaven. "O Lord my God, why have you brought tragedy to this widow who has opened her home to me, causing her son to die?"

If he was expecting a voice from the sky, he didn't get an

answer. A faint breeze whisked its way through the window, carrying the chirping of birds and the sharp tang of salt as the rapidly growing light of dawn crept its way into the home. No booming voice though, no answer, just the sounds of the morning and the smell of the sea.

For what seemed like forever he knelt there, contemplating his thought from earlier. What if it wasn't meant to be like this? He couldn't get the possibility out of his head, and it left another one hovering there too; if it *wasn't* supposed to be like this, how could he change it?

His fingers shook, but Elijah stretched out his body over Hammon, and prayed for something impossible.

"O Lord my God, please let this child's life return to him."

He prayed once… then again.

Nothing happened, and Elijah's heart began to sink like lead in his chest.

Finally, holding on to his last shard of hope, Elijah prayed one last time…

Hammon breathed.

Laying on the bed, the child gasped down a deep breath. Elijah jolted back at the shock, his eyes wide and his hands frozen like the coldest winter. For a half second his mind struggled to believe what he was seeing. Then Hammon took another breath, more regular this time, and his eyes flickered open, tired, drained, but alive. His face burst into a faint smile, "Elias? What's going on?"

Elijah had a hard time even speaking, let alone coming up with an answer. What *was* going on? He took Hammon's hand, "How do you feel?"

"Tired." The boy's stomach gave an audible gurgle, "And hungry."

Elijah felt the boy's forehead. The warmth had flooded back into Hammon, but he wasn't hot anymore either. He seemed… fine.

Hammon glanced around, "Why am I in here?"

"We were worried about you." Elijah scooped the boy up in his arms, "Come on, let's go see your mom."

Downstairs, he found Dema still in her seat with a forlorn sorrow on her face. She glanced up at the sound of him descending the stairs and froze when she saw Hammon, his arms looped around Elijah's neck. Her whole face flushed plaster white, like she was about to faint; even when he walked up, she could barely manage a whisper, "What did…?"

Elijah just grinned, "See, your son lives."

He gently laid Hammon in her trembling arms, her whole face a mask of stunned confusion. That lasted right until Hammon looked up at her, "Hi, mom, what's going on?"

Dema, burst into tears, clutching the boy so tightly he winced. "Sweetheart," she whispered, "you're back."

Elijah took a few steps back, even as Hammon shot him an utterly confused look. Clearly he didn't understand why his mom was so emotional. Elijah nearly laughed in relief. They could explain it to Hammon later, although he had a feeling the boy might not believe him.

Elijah knew, though. He knew what had happened, and, even still, he was having a tough time understanding it.

He had just prayed and someone had come back from the dead. In the history of the world, he wasn't sure that had ever happened. So of all the people in the world, why had God chosen to answer his prayer?

Across the room Dema finally gave up on trying to squeeze her son to death and carried him back upstairs to his room with a promise of breakfast.

When she returned Dema didn't speak. Instead she strode across the space between them in a few quick steps and caught him in a crushing hug, "Thank you." she whispered. "Thank you."

"I'm not sure I had much to do with it," he said with a chuckle.

Dema pulled back a half step, her eyes meeting his, suddenly serious. "You did, Elias," she nodded, "Now I know for sure that you are a man of God, and that the Lord truly speaks through you."

She caught him with another tight hug that seemed to last forever. Finally Dema pulled away. "Hammon's expecting food," she said with an almost giddy ring to her voice. "Would you like something?"

"Sure."

Dema nodded, her face aglow like a beacon in the night. She met his eyes one last time. "Thank you, Elias."

Chapter 17
The Call

The setting sun scattered a blaze of scarlet ripples over the Great Western Sea, and from his vantage point on the balcony, Elijah stared off to the south. On the horizon, the city of Tyre glittered like a ruby in the fading light. Sitting next to him Dema sipped at a cup of water, her legs curled beneath her, while a long skirt hung loose around the wicker chair.

Tearing his eyes away from the far off city, Elijah patted at his deep blue robe, grinning at the way his hand glided across the smooth fabric. "Are you sure it's...?"

"It's what?" Dema asked with an amused twinkle in her eye, "Nice?"

Elijah gulped, admiring the way the snow white sleeves stood out against the royal blue chest. "Well, you don't think it's *too* nice?"

"That's the point," Dema rolled her eyes, "I made it to be nice. Would you prefer if it came pre-torn?"

"No, just..." This wasn't the first time he'd worn the wonderful outfit Dema had sewn for him, but he still felt strange in it. "You're sure it's not too ostentatious?"

Dema shook her head with a laugh. "Trust me, if it was too ostentatious, you wouldn't have to ask. I could have sewn in little glass beads and drops of silver until you sparkled like a girl at her wedding."

Elijah sighed and tried to ignore the sensation he was wearing someone else's fine robes. "You're sure it's alright?"

"It looks good, Elias."

He gave a reluctant nod and was about to sit back on his stool when the sharp, urgent clang of a bell tolled across the small town. Once, then again and again came a monotone chorus of booming chimes.

Dema tensed beside him, and, as if on cue, Hammon dashed into the street below at a full out sprint. "Mom! Elias!" he shouted, "Fire in the stables!"

Just the word was enough to sober up Elijah in an instant. It had been three and a half years since he'd prayed for a drought. It hadn't rained since, and even though a few trees had roots that tapped down into water underground, everything else was dead. Dema talked about how the hills to the east had once been lush green slopes, but now they were brown wastelands, perilously close to barren deserts. Even this close to the Great Sea, the parched grass snapped like glass shards when he stepped on it. The whole place was a tinderbox that gave 'bone dry' a new meaning entirely.

Dema's face paled, and Elijah turned for the door into the house. "I'll go help."

"Not in that outfit you won't."

Elijah glanced down at his brand new clothes, "Oh, right." He made for his room to change. "I'll help with the fire, you and Hammon get down to the ocean and help with buckets.

By the time he swapped into an old tunic and sprinted towards the gathering pillar of smoke on the north end of town, Elijah was already out of breath. Rounding the last corner, he found a hellish scene of twisting fire draped like a plague of locusts over the stables and spreading fast.

More people from the village were already there, trying to organize a fire brigade and a jumble of shouts went up, "Get more buckets!"

"Stop it spreading into the grass in the back!"

"Keep it away from the houses!"

The stables were gone, and Elijah suspected the few scrawny horses still kept there had kicked their stalls to splinters to escape. The fire was spreading quickly, the powder dry grass going up like kindling.

"Elias!" the head man waved him down. "Get around back and keep it from getting into the trees!"

That was easier said than done. Elijah ran wide around the searing flames, but by the time he reached the rear, the fire was already licking across the grass like a wave on the shore.

"Beat it back!" Several men were already there fighting to smother the fire with salvaged saddle blankets, heavy cloth pads to cushion a horse rider. Normally they were fantastically expensive, but now they were consigned to desperately swatting back the flames.

Elijah grabbed one, and, choking through the thick smoke, he threw it over a small patch of fire, leaving it for a second before pulling it back to find charred grass beneath. Coughing, he stumbled a few feet over and repeated the process on another bit of grass, trying to ignore the pinpricks of heat that stung his face.

Somewhere nearby, people were screaming for water, but it was a quarter mile down to the ocean. Even with the whole village turned out they weren't going to get water very quickly.

He took a deep breath and charged in to smother more flames, as panicked shouts echoed around him. It wasn't enough though. The flames were moving too fast, jumping across the grass and making for the orchard nearby, where all the smaller trees were dead husks except for a few ancient behemoths that still clung to life.

He was near the center of the flames, but on both flanks the fire raced forward, threatening to cut them off. "Get back!"

Everyone ran to get ahead of the fire, but Elijah hesitated a critical second. Before he could escape the pocket, the flames on one side jumped into the trees. They curled around the first like a giant snake, erupting into the branches in an explosion of embers then leaping like a chain to the next and the next.

Faster than he could think he was cut off. He stumbled back as the smoke stung at his eyes and a hail of fiery flakes rained down around. Somewhere across the grass an echo of his name floated to him. "Elias!" Dema's voice.

He stooped low trying to find a way out and avoid the choking haze. As he did, the flames in the grass seemed to burst into a veritable wall of scorching heat, leaping twenty feet into the air and growing thick, almost solid, like no grass fire he'd ever seen.

Back over at the stable the flames pulsated into a glaring beacon, radiating off heat like the sun itself, while behind him more fire danced impossibly high in the sky.

He knelt down to shield against the waves of heat, but suddenly the pounding force of the blaze vanished. He peeked up to see a wall of fire swirling around him, so he couldn't see anyone on the opposite side. It wasn't quite fire though. It didn't burn right. Instead, the flames swirled and danced around him in beautiful geometric patterns. Oddly the smoke wasn't choking him anymore, and, despite the blinding flames, he couldn't feel the heat pricking his skin, just a reassuring coolness like the shade in spring.

As he watched, the patterns kept up their ballet, twisting palettes of red and orange, painting strange pictures and rotating around him like the eye of a giant cyclone. Suddenly, it clicked in his head and Elijah realized exactly what was happening.

The Lord was here.

Elijah lowered his head as the fire pulsed like a heartbeat, and from the heartbeat came a voice, a voice like thunder calling his name, "Elijah!"

He kept his face to the ground. "Speak, your servant is listening."

"Go and present yourself to Ahab," the voice declared, "and I will send rain on the land!"

Then the voice was gone. Elijah kept his head down as the searing heat of the fire swept back over him like a shockwave… but not for long.

Looking up, he saw the fires around him dying back, even the ones in the trees were fading. It was as if the Lord had stolen away most of the flames when He departed, leaving just a few smoking skeletons of trees.

The fire was low now, receding back into little more than

patches of burning grass, and through the smoke he saw Dema urging several men towards him with buckets. Their splashes of water cut a path through the flame, leaving just a blackened swath, and Elijah sprinted towards them.

The smoke seemed thicker outside the blaze than inside, and Elijah found himself coughing and staggering away, gasping for fresh air.

"Elias, are you okay?" Dema's frantic voice cut in, and he felt her hand on his back.

"Yea, I just–" He held up a hand and leaned over, taking deep breaths to clear his throat.

"What *was* that?"

"You mean the fire? It was hot."

"No, the sound!"

Elijah froze. "Sound?"

"Did you not hear it? When the fire erupted there was a noise like... like a thunderclap, the sort that rumbles on and on, but so loud!" She paused, "Almost like a voice, except it didn't make any sense."

Elijah hesitated before answering. Behind them the buckets had finally arrived in force, dozens of people sprinting water up from the seashore. The farmer in him cringed a little at the prospect of dousing salt water all over an orchard, but it wasn't like they had many choices. The smaller trees had mostly burned themselves out by now, only cinders like giant black toothpicks remained, and the bigger trees were mobbed by villagers flinging buckets to douse the glowing embers.

Somehow in a matter of just a few minutes, the stable fire had died out, leaving just ash and the charred skeleton of the building with a few flames desperately licking at the last patches of wood. It was like the giant inferno of the Lord's Presence had soaked up so much fuel that the fire was struggling to find anything else to consume. That was good, though. It meant they might just get things under control.

Elijah's thoughts jumped back to the message he'd heard. 'Go back to Israel and King Ahab.'

To be honest, that didn't sound like the best idea. Ahab hadn't particularly liked him to begin with, and Elijah doubted that ruining his kingdom with three and a half years of drought would have improved the situation. He could handle that, though. What really worried him was having to leave Hammon and–

"Elias?" Dema snapped her fingers in front of his eyes. "Elias, are you okay?"

"I'm fine, Dema."

From her look, she didn't believe him. "You sure?" she frowned. "Did something happen in the fire?"

It had, but Elijah knew well enough that now was definitely *not* the time.

"We can talk about it later." He grabbed her empty water bucket off the ground where she'd left it. "Come on, let's get more water."

***

The Next Morning

"Elias, you can't be serious," Dema fought as he brought his travel bag down the stairs into the main room. "Just because you hear a noise in a fire doesn't mean you have to run off and–"

"It wasn't just a noise."

"Right," Dema fumed, frustration in her eyes. "It was a voice, telling you to go. Except that no one else heard it."

"It wasn't just *a voice* either," Elijah insisted. "It was the Lord."

Dema threw up her hands. "And how are you so sure?"

Well first, he was a prophet, so hearing from God was an integral part of the job. He got the sense Dema wouldn't like that answer though.

"Look," Elijah stopped his packing a moment, "I wouldn't be so sure myself, except that this sort of thing has happened before. The first time, the voice came from a whirlwind, the second time it was from an earthquake." He paused, "That was the message that sent me here."

Dema covered her mouth with a hand, clearly upset, but

131

trying to hide it. "Well, if God sent you here, then why do you have to leave like this?"

"Dema, I can't ignore… I don't want to leave either. If I could, I would stay here."

"Then stay," she pleaded. "Please, don't go. What about Hammon, what's he supposed–"

"Hammon will be okay." Elijah tried to ignore the tug of her words. "He's good at taking care of himself."

"And what about me?" Dema's eyes misted, frustration and hurt swirling in her dark pools. "What am I supposed do?"

"You'll…" Elijah wasn't quite sure, and her accusation stung. He'd tried not to feel like he was abandoning them, but in a very real sense he was, and he didn't really have a good answer. He swallowed back his feelings and forced a weak grin, "You're pretty good at taking care of yourself too."

Apparently that wasn't the right thing to say, she looked away and sniffled. "So that's it then," her voice soured, "you're just leaving."

"Dema, I'm sorry. But I can't just ignore God. You don't get to pick and choose which orders you want to follow."

The woman stared at the floor, her arms pulled close to her chest. "You can't even stay for a few more days?"

Elijah almost said yes, but stopped himself at the last second. "If I did, I don't know that I would ever leave." He exhaled, "And I don't think God would send me away like this if it wasn't important. What if I had been a few days late coming here?"

That finally took some of the fire out of Dema's voice. "I…" she sighed and shook her head, "I still don't like it."

Elijah nodded, "I don't either. But I have to go."

Dema sighed, resignation on her face. "You'll need food for the trip then?"

"I'm going to Israel, either Jezreel or Samaria, so probably three or four days' worth."

"What are you doing there?"

"I'm going to see the king," Elijah answered, a hint of excited nervousness finding its way into his voice.

"You what?" Dema glanced at him like she'd misheard.

"You mean… King Ahab?"

"That's the one." Elijah nodded with a wry half grin.

For a moment Dema stared at him, slack jawed. There was an odd, almost knowing glint in her eyes, "Who are you, Elias?" she suddenly asked.

"What do you mean?"

"Oh please, I'm not stupid. That first day when we met, I'd have had to be blind and deaf not to see you'd made up that name. So who are you, really?"

Elijah didn't deny it, but he wasn't sure he wanted to have the conversation. "You didn't ask then, does it really matter now?"

"I was desperate," Dema narrowed her eyes. "It didn't feel like the time to question help. But it's been two years. I've trusted you, I haven't made a stink about it, but yes, I'd like to know, before you vanish forever. You owe me that answer at least."

Elijah mulled it over before giving a slow nod, "Alright then; my real name is Elijah."

Dema stared at him, absolutely motionless. "*The* Elijah?" she finally asked. "The one the Israelites say shut up the skies?"

"Yes."

Dema's eyes went wide, and for a moment she seemed torn like she thought he was joking. He could see on her face though, as she worked through everything that had happened, all the pieces finally dropping into place. "*You*" she whispered, her expression growing bitter and her voice rising, "What is wrong with you?"

"Huh?"

"Why would you do that?" Dema demanded. "Why would you stop the rain?

"Because–"

"Because what? Do you even hear yourself? Do you have any idea how this hurt everyone, how–"

"Yes," Elijah cut her off, "I do know. I've been living here too."

"Then why would you…" Dema's voice trailed off in stunned disbelief.

"Because," Elijah sighed. He'd thought about this a lot himself. "A long time ago, God spoke to the father of my people, Abraham. God promised that all the peoples of the earth would be blessed through him, through Israel and Judah. Except that Israel hasn't paid attention to God lately, and because of that we've become more of a curse than a blessing. I didn't ask God to shut the skies on a whim. In the scrolls, God says it's one of the punishments for my people if we abandon him. I'm sorry you got caught in the middle of that, though."

Dema still didn't look very happy about it. "Your God couldn't have gotten their attention some other way?"

"You don't think people tried? You don't think *I* tried?" He shook his head. "No one cared so long as things were good. Your Princess Jezebel, she and her priests and guards murdered my friends, the people who taught me about God. They walked into town one night and slaughtered them because they said Israel shouldn't worship Ba'al. After that I spent months wandering Israel, telling people about God. A few people cared, most didn't. So eventually I prayed to God to enact His curse on my people, and He did."

"And now you're going back to…"

"To end it," Elijah said. "I'm going back, and this time they're going to listen, because they can't pretend any longer."

Dema fidgeted with a loose curl of hair. "And what about Princess Jezebel? You don't think she'll kill you, like everyone else?"

Elijah wasn't sure. He'd definitely considered the possibility. An image stuck in his mind, for the last few years he'd envisioned himself as a tiny figure, running and hiding from the king, trying to stay alive.

This time though, he saw something different. Ahab and Jezebel were still there, still strong, tall, proud, and Elijah still felt just as small. But this time he wasn't alone.

Someone huge, like a mountain, stood behind him, Someone bigger than the king and queen, and all of Israel. In an instant Elijah saw the world in reverse. He'd always thought he was hiding from Ahab but it wasn't like that at all. Ahab was forted up in his cities hiding from God, and this was God's quiet, patient way of sieging him out.

Suddenly Elijah wasn't afraid.

"I'll be alright," he said. "God didn't bring me this far to drop me now. But I do have to go."

Dema gave a slow, unhappy nod. "Alright then, if you're sure, I won't stop you. While I'm making bread though, you do need to say goodbye to Hammon."

She headed to the kitchen to start on dough, but hesitated halfway and looked back. "Why didn't you tell me?" she asked. "Your name, when we first met?"

Elijah shrugged, "Would you have taken me in if you'd known?"

Dema considered it for a second. "I'm not really sure." She cracked a hopeful smile, "I'm glad I did though."

Elijah found Hammon out gathering wood, fallen branches in the orchard that had survived the fire the prior evening. For a moment, he watched the boy scuttling around the black scar on the land, snatching up the charred sticks and snapping them to see if they'd burned all the way through. Finally he walked over, bearing his bad news.

He didn't tell Hammon who he really was. He wouldn't have understood. He trusted Dema would tell the boy, but when he was ready. That didn't make saying goodbye any easier though, and he found himself locked in a long hug with a kid he'd come to think of as almost a son.

"Will you ever be back?" Hammon asked as the two wandered back towards the house.

Elijah didn't know the answer, but even so he forced a smile, "I'd like that. Someday, when things are better."

Hammon nodded, "Why do you have to leave?"

Elijah didn't try to lie, "Because God told me I have to go, and it's important to pay attention to Him."

He'd told Hammon about God during his stay, and the explanation appeared to make some sense to the twelve year old. Making sense didn't erase the sadness from his face though, "I wish you didn't have to leave, Elias."

Elijah swallowed, "Me, too."

Dema didn't just make bread for a few days; she prepared a veritable feast for the three of them. Elijah briefly wondered if her plan was to feed him so much he'd have to stay the evening. It was an excellent meal though, one of the best he'd had in a very long time. Almost like home.

Eventually the hours drifted away, and, as the sun passed midday, Elijah knew it was time.

When he said he needed to pack, Dema didn't fight. Instead she did her best to wrap up his food in a cloth travel pouch and found a spot for it in his bag. They lingered a few moments, just talking, a sort of stillness before the goodbye.

At last Elijah felt that sinking in his chest, the kind slowly pulling him towards the door. "I should get moving."

Dema took a long, shuddering breath but nodded then made a fuss over checking his stuff one last time. Finally, he stepped out the front door and looked back at Dema's house for what might be the last time. He wasn't alone though. Dema and Hammon both followed after him, like no one was quite ready to say their final goodbye.

The sun was still high as they headed for the edge of town. No one really wanted to stop and so they kept on walking, Dema quiet as she kept her slow pace with him, and Hammon bounding with distracted energy and darting off ahead to explore.

For a while, neither said much of anything. Finally Dema glanced over. "I don't suppose God told you what to say when you meet King Ahab?"

Elijah shook his head. "I was hoping to come up with something on the road." He shrugged, "I'm sure it will make more sense when I get there."

Another long pause. "Dema," he finally asked, "when I'm gone, would you promise me something? Don't forget about all this, about everything God has done. All the miracles, the impossible things, even if you never see me again, don't forget."

Dema's eyes were misty, but she smiled anyway. "You think I could forget about all this? About everything thing you...

everything God has done?”

“You’d be surprised. Israel has, and they’ve seen stranger things than you. Time has a way of erasing memories, chipping away until everything clear is just a haze.” He glanced back at Zarapheth. They were up in the foothills now, but he could still pick out streets and alleys he’d come to know well. Every step put them further away, more indistinct. “Just promise.”

Dema seemed to understand, and her hand brushed at his, taking a tight hold. “I promise,” she said softly, “I won’t forget, and if I do I’ll remember the promise. Besides,” her gaze drifted ahead to her son, as he ran pell-mell down a shallow hill, “it’d be pretty hard to forget Hammon. I owe him to your God too.”

Her voice choked up, and Elijah turned to see her tears in her eyes. In an instant she hugged him painfully tight, and Elijah met the embrace, his eyes a bit watery too, “I’m going to miss you,” she whispered.

He didn’t really know what to say, and for a time the two stood there, Dema sobbing into his shoulder.

“Are you okay, mom?” Hammon’s voice interrupted.

Dema gave a little laugh through her tears, and she broke apart wiping at her eyes, and trying to be optimistic. “Yes, I’m fine. Just… sad that Elias has to leave.” She took a deep breath, “I suppose we’re getting close to Israel aren’t we?”

They’d been walking for some time, and they’d moved from plains into the foothills that formed the northwestern border of Israel.

Elijah stopped on the dirt path and bit his lip. “I suppose so.” He took Dema’s hand. “This is for you.” He pushed a little pouch of silver bits into her palm, the money he’d saved from scribing, “Before I forget. To take care of yourself.”

Dema stared at the money pouch, “Elias you don’t owe me for…”

“I know,” he nodded. “It’s a gift, for you and Hammon. To help.”

“But what about you?”

“I’m sure God will come up with something.”

He could see Dema was hesitant about the offering, but she finally nodded. “Thank you.”

Elijah smiled, "There's one last blessing I can give." He took her and Hammon's hands, and the three all bowed as he recited the words he'd long ago committed to memory,

> *May the Lord bless and keep you;*
> *May He make his face to shine upon you,*
> *And be gracious to you;*
> *May the countenance of the Lord fall upon you,*
> *And may He grant you peace.*

He looked up and shared one last round of hugs then stepped back. "Goodbye."

"Goodbye, Elias," Dema said.

He walked and didn't look back until the top of the next hill. When he did, the two were still standing in the little valley at the base. They waved and Dema's voice echoed up to him. "Don't forget to wear your good clothes when you meet the king!"

Elijah laughed, waved one final goodbye, then headed over the hilltop. Dema and Hammon disappeared from view as he finally headed back to Israel and to his appointment with the king.

Chapter 18

The Steward

B a'al the powerful we beseech thee! Come hear our plea, send rain upon our land once more and take this sacrifice as proof of our loyalty!"

King Ahab stood in the paved courtyard surrounding the raised altar of Ba'al, along with dozens of others. He watched as his wife, draped in ornate robes of red and black, screamed to heaven to waken the god. The priests with her busily sliced a dead bull into pieces and spread them on the altar, an elevated stone table set on a dais and piled around with bundles of sticks to form a giant pyre.

Ahab tried to be patient as she went through the whole ritual of catching the blood in a basin then spilling it evenly across the altar, but really he was seething over the fact that she'd murdered his best bull. Apparently Ba'al wasn't answering them and sending rain because they weren't offering him their best animals. So now he was minus one more prize bull, and he had the sneaking suspicion Ba'al still wasn't paying attention. If all their sacrifices the last several years hadn't caught his eyes, Ahab wasn't sure why one gaunt animal more was supposed to matter.

He sighed and shuddered a little; at least this was better than the alternative. Originally Jezebel had tried to convince him they should have another child and sacrifice it to appease Ba'al.

He'd drawn the line there.

139

Frankly, he was worried about his wife. With every failed sacrifice she turned more desperate and frustrated. Anymore, he mostly tried to avoid her.

He knew he was supposed to stay and watch the whole burning of incense and lighting of the sacrificial pyre, but Ahab wasn't in the mood. Moving off to the side of the assembled crowd of priests, nobles, advisors and dignitaries, he slipped away and out of the colonnade surrounding the paved offertory courtyard.

Hopefully Jezebel wouldn't notice. She seemed pretty absorbed in her ritual, and he had a hundred other problems to deal with right now.

Wandering outside the secluded patio, he paused to glance across Samaria, trying to remember before all this. Before that cursed Elijah. A city perched on a hill amid a lush green valley, with the telltale rows of vineyards running up the sides, patches of orchards, and distant sheep dotting the upper ridge like speckles of cotton. Now it was brown, brown and dead. Ruined trees scattered like huge skeletons across the landscape, and the city was blanketed in a persistent fog of powder dust so thick it gritted in his teeth. The dirt hung like a choking cloud that never seemed to go away except when the wind kicked it into a thick, brown haze.

Further down, his steward Obadiah appeared out of a door. Ahab had never really thought about it, but he had an odd way of always being busy whenever Jezebel got in one of her frenzies. For once he was thankful, though. "Obadiah!" Ahab called, gesturing him over.

"Sir." Obadiah approached with a deferential nod.

"Where have you been?"

"The stables, checking up on things."

"And how are they?"

Obadiah hesitated to answer, and Ahab winced inwardly, his lips drawn tight. It grated at him to see his prize stallions as gaunt shadows of their former selves, living emblems of the impossible situation Israel found itself in thanks to that gods-cursed Elijah. There was no rain, no food, no hope. Just dirt to eat. He tried not to dwell on his kingdom being ruined, but these days the signs were hard not to notice.

"We're going to have to slaughter more of the horses, sir." Obadiah shuffled his feet as he spoke. "We just don't have the forage or the hay anymore for them. If we kill half of them, we may be able to add another season for the rest."

"Just one season?" Ahab cursed, his face darkening in pent up rage. "That's it?"

Obadiah paused, then continued, "If things don't improve, we'll have to slaughter more before then. The mules and cattle are in about the same way, worse maybe."

Ahab felt his frustration boiling over and ground his foot hard at the paving stone. "We have to do something." He rubbed at his brow. "How about this. Go through the land to all the springs of water and to all the valleys. Perhaps we may find grass and save the horses and mules alive, and not lose some of the animals."

That was vague as far as plans went, but Obadiah nodded. Anything was better than the raving fits of furious anger Ahab had been drowning in the last few months. At least this was actually doing something, "Is there anywhere more specific I should go?"

Ahab mulled it over for a moment. "I know a few places south towards the sea; I can go check them. You head up towards Jezreel and Megiddo, there may be something there. Go as far as you can and meet back here tomorrow."

Obadiah nodded, "Right away."

Obadiah traveled light, just a walking stick, a few pieces of bread and an ever so precious water skin. In a few quick moments he was ready to go and happy to be gone. Anything to get away from Jezebel and her twisted sacrifices to Ba'al. Just having all her priests strutting the halls was frustrating enough, especially since they hadn't been much besides a waste of perfectly good food the last few years.

He made for the main gate past a long, white stone building that served as sleeping quarters for many of the palace servants. As he passed, two young cleaning girls wandered by, their faces joyless and their steps quiet. The palace chef came not far behind. "Obadiah, sir," the cook caught him, "I hate to interrupt you, but we're getting painfully short on wine and oil. If we don't get some more the king may not even have bread to–"

"I know," Obadiah cut him off. "I've been told a shipment of oil is coming. If you can, try and stretch what you have at least a few more days."

The man continued, anxious, "But what about the wine, and the dried fruit… and really we need more fresh meat as well–"

The steward sighed, "I have to leave for a day. We can discuss it when I get back." He didn't mention that if his trip wasn't a success, they might have a sudden influx of fresh meat. Obadiah tried not to cringe at the prospect of that meat being horse.

He caught four guards lounging on their spear hafts at the hulking gatehouse. Watching out across the hillside over the city and chatting among themselves, they didn't see him until he was almost on top of them.

"Morning." Obadiah cracked a slight smile at the way they scrambled to attention, taking up places along both sides of the gateway. "The king's coming by a little later," he warned in passing, watching their backs straighten a tad at the news.

Staring out from the palace gate, the city proper was quiet, like a corpse. The drought had drained so much of the bustle he remembered from Samaria. Gone were the perfume and linen peddlers. Most of the smiths had closed up shop for lack of fuel, while the farmers and herders who drove so much of the business in the city didn't have money to buy anything anyway.

Instead, grim people plodded through the streets, the men with rags wrapped across their faces and the women veiled. A few chatted, but where before the rumble of the crowd would have been a dull thunder, now it seemed subdued, like they all knew a cloud of more than just dust hung over them.

The eerie stillness shattered when he stepped beyond the palace gates. Lounging in the shadow of the wall a dozen pitiable figures draped in filthy rags crowded towards him, women, children, even a few men.

Obadiah hadn't brought more than a few silver bits on the trip, but even so his hands fell protectively to his sides. A little boy no more than eight darted up, hands outstretched, desperation in his eyes. "Some food, sir?" he pleaded, before a middle aged woman pushed her way forward and elbowed him aside. "Please, I have children to feed, surely the king can spare a little grain?"

The people here recognized him well enough and crowded around. Anymore Obadiah didn't feel pity or sadness at seeing the beggars camped at the gate. It had been like this for so long that the only emotions he had left were sorrow and impotent frustration at the way the kingdom had been reduced to this, all by something so simple as rain.

Stepping out of the knot of hungry desperation, he held up his arms to quiet them down. "Everyone, there should be a distribution later today, not right now."

That didn't do much for most of the people. Obadiah figured if their places were switched he wouldn't have taken that answer very well, either. Still, he slipped off into the streets and though a few gaunt children tagged after him, they eventually fell away, not wanting to get too far from the palace.

He had to pass through the market on the way out of town and kept his eyes low towards the ground as he did, trying not to draw too much notice. It wasn't anything he'd done, but everyone still remembered when the prophet Elijah had come through years back, preaching about God's judgement. Most of them had mocked the man at the time, but now those same people were the loudest at cursing Ahab for not listening. Being associated with the king wasn't particularly good for one's health these days.

It was stupid really, Obadiah mused. They were just as much to blame. Maybe, if they'd actually listened to Elijah like *he* had, they could have stocked up on food that last harvest. Grain had been dirt cheap, and it wasn't like the prophet had been hard to understand. Instead, they shook their fists at the palace for hoarding all the food when they'd been the ones cheerfully selling it in the first place.

Even the palace was running out though, and Obadiah had no idea what they'd do then. When the famine had started, he'd sold them back their grain. When everyone had run out of money to buy it he'd started giving it away and buying what he could from Egypt, where they could grow food so long as the Nile flooded.

Anymore though, Israel was essentially bankrupt, and when they ran out of food…

He forced back the image of the restive Samaria bathed in blood as the granaries emptied, everyone turning on one another until there was nothing but a rotted husk of a city left.

Making for the city gates before anyone could recognize him, Obadiah headed north along the road, his eyes searching across the brown wasteland hunting for a hint of green. He plodded up the sloped valley that Samaria was set in, past dead vineyards and orchards. As the blazing sun soared towards its zenith, he crested the hill and the city vanished behind him, the only traces of green a few fortunate trees that had lived, but no grass.

Chapter 19

The Troubler of Israel

Elijah was sure it was supposed to be cooler up in the hills. Unfortunately, with the sun beating down on him, traipsing through Israel felt like he'd stepped into an oven. He was lonely, too. He'd been on the empty road for several days, and had taken to chatting with himself to relieve the tedium. "No, *you* Ahab!" he recited his imaginary speech, poking at the air and sweeping his arms wide, "You're the problem! You have ruined this kingdom!" He paused a half second. "Should it be *this kingdom* or *the Kingdom of Israel*?" Elijah stroked at his beard. "Maybe Israel sounds better but…"

He looked up and noticed a small figure descending the valley slope ahead, coming toward him. That was enough to put an end to his rambling rehearsal. Best not to freak out everyone straight away. He had plenty enough crazy saved for later.

For a moment he focused on the newcomer, just one man so probably not a bandit. As the man got closer, Elijah couldn't escape the sense that he'd seen him before. He couldn't place exactly where, though. The man was coming from the direction of Samaria, and about the only person Elijah could think of there was Ahab.

When they came close, the man raised a hand in a passing wave then froze, his mouth dropping open and his eyes fixated on the prophet.

"Greetings." Elijah offered.

The man didn't return the courtesy. Instead, he gulped down a panicked breath and bowed low to the ground. His tone turned almost reverent. "Is it really you, my lord Elijah?"

"It is." Elijah took a step closer to the fellow and offered him a hand, "Are you okay?"

The stranger rose and faced him again, excitement in his eyes. "I'm fine, I just… what are you doing here?"

Okay, what was going on? Elijah couldn't piece things together, "I'm sorry, but have we met?"

"Obadiah, your servant." The man offered another deferential bow at the waist.

It clicked.

"King Ahab's steward," Elijah exclaimed, the pieces falling into place.

Obadiah nodded.

A spike of nervous excitement stabbed at Elijah. This was perfect. "I've come to speak with Ahab. Go tell your lord, 'Elijah is here!'"

For a heartbeat Obadiah stared at him, eyes genuinely terrified. "Are… are you serious?"

"Typically," Elijah cocked his head a little to one side. He'd left for two years, and now Obadiah was staring at him like he'd lost his mind. "Why?"

Obadiah gulped audibly, like he was trying to gather an excuse. "Oh, sir, what harm have I done to you that you are sending me to my death at the hands of Ahab?" The man pleaded, "For I swear by the Lord your God that the king has searched every nation and kingdom on earth from end to end to find you. And each time he was told, 'Elijah isn't here,' King Ahab forced the king of that nation to swear to the truth of his claim. And now you say, 'Go and tell your master, "Elijah is here."' But as soon as I leave you, the Spirit of the Lord will carry you away to who knows where. When Ahab comes and cannot find you, he will kill me. Yet I have been a true servant of the Lord all my life. Has no one told you, my lord, about the time when Jezebel was trying to kill the Lord's prophets? I hid 100 of them in two caves and supplied them with food and water. And now you say, 'Go and tell your master, "Elijah is here.'" Sir, if I do that, Ahab will certainly kill me."

Oh. Elijah paused, glimpsing the panic in Obadiah's eyes, and not quite sure what to do. Apparently things had changed a lot since he'd been gone.

"Obadiah, I'm not trying to get you killed," Elijah explained. "I really am here to talk with Ahab."

"Where have you been the last three years?" Obadiah demanded, more than a little upset. "Do you realize the price Ahab promised to anyone who found you, and all of a sudden you just walk up like this? Have you seen what's happening in Israel?"

"I've been… busy," Elijah answered. "Learning. But now I'm here to finish all this."

At that he caught a flicker of hope on Obadiah's face. "You are, truly?"

"Yes," Elijah nodded. "Now go find the king. I swear by the Lord Almighty, in whose presence I stand, that I will present myself to Ahab this very day."

Obadiah hesitated, worried creases still on his face, but he managed a tepid bow. "As you say. It may be late in the day before I can catch him, but I'll go at once."

The steward turned and jogged off. Elijah watched for a few moments. Well this was it, the die was cast. Now he just needed to work out what to say to King Ahab. And more than just a speech, he needed to prove, prove without a shadow of a doubt, that God was real and Ba'al was just a statue. He wasn't exactly sure how, but his mind kept jumping back to Zarapheth, the impossible fire where God Himself had spoken.

Even the people there had realized there was something different about the flames. The way the fire had reared up, the way it had burned through hours' worth of wood in the space of a few heartbeats, it was unnatural. He was confident Ba'al couldn't do that, and he doubted his priests could replicate something similar either.

A few hundred paces ahead, a towering oak tree stood not far from the path, its leaves tinging a sickly yellow. It still clung to life though, and Elijah found a seat in its shade, his back to the thick trunk, still considering the possibility of a challenge.

He needed to get out, away from the temples. His experience in Tyre had taught him that much. The Temple of Ba'al-sur was imposing, even for him, and if he challenged the priests in a temple like that, it wasn't hard to imagine trickery. Somewhere open, where there could be no cheating, but also somewhere where they couldn't beg off the challenge. So outside, maybe an existing high place where people already worshipped Ba'al and Asherah.

As he mulled through the list of possibilities, his stomach gave an audible gurgle, and Elijah dipped a hand in his pouch, pulling out a hard crust to chew on. Food for thought.

The afternoon shadows were growing long when Elijah heard the beat of hoofs and the clatter of wheels on the rough road. Ahead, a chariot drawn by two roan horses crested the valley wall and charged down the slope at a full gallop, the horses gaunt and foaming at the mouth from exertion.

Two men stood in the back. The first had short cropped hair and a stubby beard that marked him as Obadiah. He flicked the reins while the other, a tall man with a spear in hand, a long pointed beard and a metal helmet scanned the horizon like an eagle.

Even from far away he recognized King Ahab, and Elijah tensed in anticipation as the king's eyes locked on him like razors. As the chariot rumbled close, he caught a narrowing in Ahab's eyes, a look that reminded him of his raven friends when they'd plunged on a rabbit for the kill.

Elijah stood to his feet as the chariot pulled up alongside the oak, and King Ahab stepped down, his knuckles white from clutching the spear haft. "Is that you, you destroyer of Israel?" the king spat and leveled his weapon.

"I have not destroyed Israel," Elijah met his burning glare, "but you and your father's house have, because you have abandoned the Lord's commands and followed the Ba'als. Now summon all Israel to meet me at Mount Carmel, along with the 450 prophets of Ba'al and the 400 prophets of Asherah who eat at Jezebel's table."

Ahab's lips curled in a grin, and he stepped forward. "Or I

could just kill you.”

Three years ago, the threat would have made Elijah’s hands tremble, but now they were rock solid, not even a flinch. Instead he held that image from before in his mind, him standing with God a bare pace behind, and a grin slipped onto his face. Apparently, Ahab still didn’t understand who he was messing with.

Ahab took another step closer. “I think I’ll do exactly that.” He smirked and gripped his spear for the blow.

“I suppose you could,” Elijah agreed, nonchalant. “I take it you like things this way, no rain and all?”

Ahab paused.

“Personally, I could do without the heat,” Elijah mused, “but if you’re happy with the way things are, then sure, kill me. Good luck finding someone to pray this whole mess away, though. From now on, it’s dust for breakfast, lunch, and dinner. I’d probably suggest moving your kingdom somewhere else.”

A breath of wind rippled through the valley, and for an instant it looked like Ahab’s rage might just get the better of him. At the last moment, he lowered his spear and jabbed the point hard into the dirt. “And if I do meet you at Mount Carmel?”

“Then we end this,” Elijah said, dead serious, “End this feud between Ba’al and God and determine who the real Lord is. Then we’ll ask whoever wins to bring the rain back. How’s that sound?”

For a moment Ahab said nothing, fingers rapping at the wooden spear haft. Finally he nodded, “Alright, then. Seven days from now, Mount Carmel.” He jerked his weapon out of the ground and marched straight back to his chariot, stepping up with a grim determination. “You had better be there, Elijah.”

Elijah couldn’t tell if Ahab intended a command or a warning, but he nodded, “At dawn, I’ll be waiting.”

Ahab didn’t deign to answer. Instead he gestured Obadiah to tug the reins and wheel the chariot around, back towards Samaria. “Let’s go.”

Elijah watched as the chariot crested the hill before vanishing from view, leaving him alone in the fading light of day.

With nowhere else to be, Elijah built himself a little fire from twigs at the foot of the tree and wrapped his traveling cloak tight. He'd head for Mount Carmel tomorrow, find a place to stay, and prepare for his battle with the priests of Ba'al.

Chapter 20

The Challenge

Elijah hiked through the city of tents and angled lean-to shelters that had popped up like wildflowers around the base of Mount Carmel. With the first traces of light peeking over the eastern hills, the coastal plain was bright enough to make out the vague outlines of the encampment. Even so, he still had to be careful where he stepped. He was wearing the bright blue and white tunic and robes Dema had made for him, and the possibility of falling and ruining his spotless outfit right before standing in front of all Israel kept circling in his head.

Fortunately, he knew well enough where he was going. Just a short walk south, Mount Carmel rose up like a dark behemoth out of the gloom. Reaching the base, Elijah started his early morning trudge up the shadowed mountainside. He'd spent the last couple of nights at a seaside hamlet down by the Kishon River, what was left of the river anyway, more like a trickle anymore. It reminded him of Zarapheth, all the way down to the shrine of Asherah stuck dead in the middle of town. These were his people, though, and today he intended to finally change their minds.

His foot slipped on a patch of loose gravel, and Elijah staggered a step before catching himself. That was a warning, and for a while he kept his mind strictly focused on not tumbling down the slope. He focused on one step after another and tried to ignore a churning in his stomach.

With tendrils of sunlight behind him, it slowly grew easier to see. Finally, the light broke over the horizon and danced out across the Great Sea in the distance. Pausing a moment to catch his breath, Elijah looked back and froze when he saw the multitude spread out along the plain towards the river. He'd come up here the day before and had seen plenty of people when he'd come down around midafternoon. Now, it was like waking one morning and walking outside to find a city tripled in size. The plain was thick with Israelites who'd come, and those were just the ones he could see from here. He was on the northern slope, but Mount Carmel fanned out much further, forming a maze of ups and downs dotted with peaks and ridges cut by sloping ravines. As he reached the top, he saw it wasn't just the people camped on the plain. Clusters were trickling in from every direction – men, women, and more than a few families hiking up through the shadowed mountain vales towards the summit.

Reaching the peak he'd scouted out the prior day, Elijah found two altars just as he had left them. On the left sat a shattered altar to the Lord, little more than a half torn down pile of worn stones, while not far off stood an ancient, withered oak with a small shrine to Asherah and an incense burner underneath.

"Sir?" A voice inquired behind.

Elijah turned to see a man a little younger than himself, clothed in a simple tunic down to his knees, a tan outer robe and a traveling cloak. Next to him stood a young woman in much the same fashion except with a longer, sun yellow robe and a bit more thought given to her smooth combed hair. At their feet bounced an excited young boy in a plain traveling outfit.

"Are you the one they call Elijah?" The man held out a hand in greeting.

"I am," Elijah nodded and shook. "And you are?"

"Abijon." He gestured to the woman who gave a polite nod, "My wife Naomi and our son, Ariah. We're from Succoth."

Elijah couldn't keep a flicker of surprise from his face. Succoth? That was… a long ways, almost the other side of the kingdom, and they'd made it all the way here.

The man didn't hesitate to cut to his real question, the thing on everyone's minds. "They say that you're the one to bring back the rain?"

"We'll see," Elijah gave the answer he'd been handing out to everyone. "It depends if King Ahab and his priests bother to show up."

"They're here," the man nodded eagerly, a touch of desperation in his eyes. "They arrived last night."

"Excellent," Elijah felt some of his nervousness vanish at the news. "In that case we'll begin when the king arrives."

He could see the man was hoping for more of an answer than that but nodded anyway. He guided his family back to a spot lower on the hill that offered some shade from the sun as it slowly crept above the horizon.

Elijah was ready to start right then and there, but with Ahab and his prophets nowhere to be seen, he settled down to wait. He'd been almost four years heading to this, so he could manage a little longer.

Before he could find a place to sit though, a girl's voice called out his name across the mountainside, "Uncle Elijah!"

He looked up in surprise as an older girl with flowing dark curls, a colorful shawl, and a beaming grin darted across the brown grass straight at him. For a half second he was sure his eyes were playing tricks on him. "Lila?"

She ran at him and half tackled him in a hug, her arms wrapping tight and nearly knocking the air from his chest. "Elijah, we missed you."

For a long moment he didn't know what to say, and he just held his niece close. Finally they broke apart, and Elijah looked down at little Lila, except… she wasn't so little anymore. The bouncing girl he remembered was gone, replaced with a blossoming young woman who'd sprouted taller like barley in spring. He realized with a start she was almost fifteen now, probably soon to be engaged. All the pent up excitement was still there, though, and her eyes were still the same.

"How have you been, Lila?"

A shadow crossed her face at the question. "Not great." She

fidgeted with a loose curl, "Not with the famine and all." She brightened a little, "But you're here now. Where have you been? You know the *king* actually came to town looking for you?"

"King Ahab?"

She gave an eager nod and lowered her voice conspiratorially. "He was in your house," she whispered.

"He was?" Elijah swallowed, the worst case possibility racing in his head. "What happened to my parents?"

"Oh, they're right down there." Lila turned and pointed down the slope, to a party of familiar faces trudging up the ravine towards the mountain top. "When we heard, dad didn't think it was you, but mom did. Grandma and grandpa came too, and Uncle Michael and – everyone." She paused, "They said you were going to talk to God?"

He smiled and nodded, "That's the idea."

"How?" she asked, a glimmer of amazement in her eyes.

"Well, if it works, you'll see, don't worry."

"Okay." She shuffled her feet a moment. "I… I did what you said," she added in a small voice. "When you left, I didn't worship Asherah."

The statement brought a wide, almost bursting grin to his face. At least one good thing had come of all this. "I'm proud of you, Lila."

He looked up to see the King's chariot, still a long way off but fighting its way up the mountain. He'd kept his retinue of spear guards close, men in leather vests studded with gleaming bronze scales and carrying circular painted shields. Behind them, strung out in a long column like a black and red snake, came the priests of Ba'al.

Lila followed his gaze and the joy dimmed on her features. "There sure are a lot of them." She hesitated, "Are you going to be okay?"

Elijah took a deep breath, "Alone… probably not." He caught her worried eyes, "I've got God on my side though. I'll be alright. Besides, Ahab needs me or he's going to be king of a desert."

He nudged his niece, "Go tell everyone to find a spot to sit, somewhere they can see, and we'll talk afterwards. We may be here a while too, so find someplace that's shaded, and make sure they have some water to drink. I think the sun's going to be blazing today."

Lila frowned, "But I thought everyone was here to bring back the rain?"

"Well," he nodded towards the priests of Ba'al, "with those guys trying, I don't expect too many clouds."

Lila giggled and gave him one last parting hug. "God be with you, Uncle."

"You too, little one."

Lila turned and jogged back towards his family, while Elijah turned his gaze to the king. He was a little surprised at not seeing the queen or any of the Daughters of Asherah here. Apparently, Ahab hadn't quite brought everyone the way he'd agreed. Still, his eyes wandered back to the long chain of approaching priests; this would work.

As Ahab ascended the slope, the crowd on every side kept swelling larger and larger. Soon the vale to the south was jammed full, and people carpeted the north slope like birds in spring. Other peaks that gave a good view were drawing crowds too as a sea of Israelites clustered around the mountain. Few came close though, and Elijah caught more than a few resentful glares. Apparently setting off a national famine hadn't made him the most popular person.

Soon enough the king's chariot broke through the thickening throngs of people, his guards having to shove open a path for him at the end. Ahab's chariot clattered onto the summit, his twin horses kicking up little swirls of dust, while the rest of his retinue of advisors and lordlings trailed close behind on foot.

Behind came the dull thumping of heavy hide drums as the Sons of Ba'al arrived, a long solemn procession. The noise of thousands of mingled voices had been rising to a dull, indistinct roar, but at the sight of the priests in all their finery, a wave of silence swept across the crowd.

The priests arrived on the plateau summit amid the rhythmic, rising beat of a dozen drums they'd brought along. Some waved smoldering incense burners, while others piped a harmony on flutes and trumpets as their striped scarlet and black banners caught the wind and spread like giant feathers on an enormous bird of prey.

As they halted, the throbbing drumbeats accelerated, the pulsing booms coming in pounding unison, faster and faster, finally hitting a crescendo as the trumpets blared a last defiant blast. Then, as all Israel watched they fell utterly silent, leaving the hollow whisper of the wind as the only sound.

Elijah decided that was his cue. "Morning," he put on an almost amused grin as he stood and paced over to the glowering Ahab in his chariot. "I see you made it well enough?"

Ahab narrowed his eyes, one hand clutching his spear tight, "Let's not waste time," he said curtly, "I'm here, the Sons of Ba'al are here. Say your piece and be done with it."

"Very well," Elijah's tone turned deadly serious. "Let's begin." He stepped forward, close to the waiting crowd and shouted so everyone could hear, "People of Israel!" His voice echoed in the ravines, "How long will you waver between two opinions? If the Lord is God, follow Him; but if Ba'al is God, follow him."

He waited a moment, but the only response he got was silence. He took that as a good sign.

"I am the only one of the Lord's prophets left, but Ba'al has four hundred and fifty prophets. Get two bulls for us. Let Ba'al's prophets choose one for themselves, and let them cut it into pieces and put it on the wood but not set fire to it. I will prepare the other bull and put it on the wood but not set fire to it. Then you call on the name of your god, and I will call on the name of the Lord. The god who answers by fire – he is God."

He left them a moment to consider the offer and quickly the jumble of arguing voices swelled like far off thunder, rising to a roar, thousands of people talking over one another. He glanced at Ahab, who suddenly seemed confused. Hadn't expected that now, had he?

Meanwhile, the vast crowd was rapidly coming to a consensus, and a chant of agreement rose from them, scattered at first but swelling to a roar.

Elijah raised a hand high, and the crowd went silent, as he

asked, "What say you?"

The shouts came back with the force of a wave off the sea. "What you say is good!"

He nodded his assent and turned to the priests of Ba'al. He couldn't help the victorious grin that tugged at his lips when he saw the evident worry on several faces.

Could their god not do that?

Too bad. He finally had them trapped for the whole world to see. They weren't about to sneak off now.

Not all of them looked scared though. From the crowd of priests a mature man in an elaborate embroidered robe stepped forward and walked out to meet him, supreme, almost arrogant confidence carved on his face. The High Priest of Ba'al. Elijah knew him by reputation only, Baltazar, the man who'd overseen the murder of his friends and the slaughter of the prophets of the Lord.

The High Priest strode out to meet him with a merciless gleam in his eyes, a look to slice iron and cut stone. Face to face, the powerfully built bull of a priest was intimidating to say the least. Enough so to force Elijah to remember back to the miracles he'd seen and gather his courage.

"So, little prophet," Baltazar demanded, "how shall we do this?"

Elijah forced himself to meet the man's granite gaze. "Choose one of the bulls and prepare it first, since there are so many of you. Call on the name of your god, but do not light the fire."

A wolfish grin spread across the High Priest's face, and he gave a condescending nod before turning back to his own and raising a fist. "Prepare the animal! Ba'al will feast!"

Elijah watched him go, sudden worries nipping at the back of his mind. For a man who worshipped inanimate statues, the High Priest sure seemed undaunted. The lone prophet whispered a quiet prayer, "Lord don't let this be for nothing."

He watched as two bulls were sent for, and the Sons of Ba'al went to their frenzied work.

Chapter 21
Prophet of the Lord

Outside his one nightmarish day in Tyre, Elijah had never watched an actual sacrifice to Ba'al. He had to admit, they were nothing if not efficient. By the time the bulls arrived, they'd swiftly fitted together stones to erect a wide, flat altar on which they added wicked looking bull horns that stabbed like curved spears towards the sky in the four corners.

The high priest wasted little time taking the halter to lead the lowing bull forward and drape a heavy silver chain around its neck. Standing before the king and his retinue, Baltazar raised his sacrificial knife as he dedicated the sacrifice. "An offering!" he shouted, "To Ba'al-Sur the king of the sun, invincible ruler of the sky, bringer of rain and great provider! So that he may once again return from his time in the underworld and bring with him rain and abundance upon the land!"

Baltazar stepped back, lowered his arm, and the peaceful tableau was shattered as a well-muscled man to the other side of the animal swung a thick hammer in a single violent stroke. The impact smashed at the bull's head and the stunned animal gave a distressed bellow as it swayed and cratered into the dirt. In an instant the high priest was there, slicing its throat in a sharp jerk and a crimson spatter.

He stepped back as the dazed animal bled out, making space for his acolytes to collect the blood in clay bowls.

Eventually, the bull stopped moving, stopped breathing,

stopped bleeding. Hauling the carcass aside, more priests quickly quartered it into manageable chunks, spreading out the meat on the altar while yet others piled around bundles of sticks for the fire. Soon, a delicately arranged offering was laid out across the altar stones, the meat fresh, and the tinder parched dry. It lacked only a spark.

***

Baltazar stood at the center of a swirling mob of priests, leading a low chant that told the story of Ba'al's battles and mighty victories. The eldest of the priests stalked in a wild circle around him and called back in unison after each of his lines. In the center of the circling mass, Elijah could see the priests coming forward one after another. Each sliced the sacrificial knife across his palm with a grimace of pain and clenched their fist tight to squeeze out a trickle of their own blood into a bowl. Nearby, the more junior priests were arrayed in a block doing much the same thing with numerous other bowls, their massed voices joining the dark hymn to raise a powerful chorus.

They'd been at it for nearly a half hour, and Elijah was more than a little surprised the chant had so many verses. They seemed near the end, though, and as he watched, Elijah saw the last priest accept the bowl from Baltazar. The high priest in turn drew the knife across his palm to mingle his blood with the rest.

Walking in a solemn procession, every priest with one fist clenched and many still dripping blood, they laid the clay bowls on the altar.

Then they stepped back.

Baltazar raised his arms toward heaven. "Oh, great Ba'al, see our offering, accept our blood and our sacrifice, and send down from the sun a spark of your eternal fire to light our offering!"

Behind him, the hundreds of priests intoned in unison, "O Ba'al, hear us!"

"Great king, show us your favor, return from the far land where you have departed!"

"O Ba'al, hear us!" The chorus rolled out across the people like a physical force, and Elijah saw many bow their heads in a mix of fear and reverence.

"We call you back from your slumber with the bounty of our offerings. See our devotion, see our blood! Return!"

"O Ba'al, hear us!"

Even Elijah couldn't help but be impressed as he watched. All else aside, the priests put on an excellent show. Watching, it made a bit more sense why no one had listened to him when he had spoken out against Ba'al. Massed together like this, the priests were an army, a terrifying force complete with strange weapons, daunting uniforms and the ear of a god himself. Compared to that, he was just... an itinerant madman raving about false gods and judgement.

The priests started chanting again, a slow, mournful melody. All around, the crowd shrunk back from them. For a long while they sang, trying to summon Ba'al. Distracted by the over-awing pageantry, it wasn't until several verses in that Elijah realized something else.

Nothing had happened.

The awareness hit Elijah like an angry goat to the backside, nothing *had* happened. The priests were still chanting in low, scary voices, but the altar didn't show any signs of fire, not even a smolder.

The sun was rising high in the sky now, and soon the priests had taken up another exotic chant, slicing themselves even more as they attempted to draw Ba'al's attention. Several of the chief priests had brought out incense to burn, but their attempts to light it instigated a loud scuffle. "They cheat!" one man shouted at seeing their tinderboxes. "They want to light the sacrifice themselves!"

Several more rose up in protest until finally the sullen priests put aside their incense and returned to their frenetic crying to the sky.

Their voices grew steadily louder as they shouted themselves hoarse, and they kept up their slow circling of the altar as the sun reached its zenith. In the heat of the day, the fresh meat was already beginning to bake dry. Now the priests took up a new cry, pleading with their god to send down a flicker of the midday heat to light their fire, grant them an ember of the sun.

No fragment of a star fell to the ground, though. As the moment passed, Elijah finally glimpsed worry on many faces, not just the initiates. Even Baltazar, the rock confident man he'd faced earlier, seemed confused... worried. But only for a moment. "We must awaken Ba'al!" he shouted to his assembled. "The Storm-lord demands blood! With the drops of the faithful he shall light the altar! Sacrifice and call to him so that he knows and hears our devotion!"

Elijah rolled his eyes. He couldn't for the life of him discern why a bit more shouting was supposed to work. They'd been trying that all morning.

"Shout louder!" he called over. "Surely he is a god! Perhaps he is deep in thought, or busy, or traveling. Maybe he is sleeping and must be awakened."

That earned him a flurry of vicious glares from the priests, but given their normal reaction was to murder dissenters, Elijah considered it a step up as far as civility went. "Maybe he had a big dinner and a little too much to drink!"

Somewhere near the front of the assembled people, he caught a snort of laughter. The priests paid it no mind, though, and kept up their screaming dance. High Priest Baltazar stood like a man possessed in the center, his face unshaken as he drew the knife down his own arms and even touched the blade to his face. The scarlet rivulets trickled down, tracing across his wrists and across his cheeks until it looked like he was weeping blood down his whole body. More priests joined him in slicing themselves. As the blood flowed, they took to dancing around the altar in a whirlwind frenzy. Their robes billowed around them as they swung their arms like wild men, speckling the sacrifice and each other in crimson.

"Try jumping, that might help!" Elijah added as he reached into his pack and pulled out the last of Dema's food, a week-old slice of hard bread, to nibble on. Sitting back against a large rock, he tried to ignore the beating sun as he watched. They had commendable endurance, he'd give them that.

As though his breaking out food was some sort of silent signal, he saw others in the huge crowd start pulling out snacks in a vast, undeclared lunch time. Even King Ahab, who'd been watching from a tent set close to the priests to show his support, finally gave in, with his servants bringing him and his assembled courtiers bread.

A palpable fear that had clung like an invisible mist to the hillside finally started to burn away as the sun passed noonday. The priests still raved over by the altar, but out in the crowd, people paid it less mind. By the time Elijah finished, the priests were more a sideshow as people chatted among themselves. Even Ahab had a disapproving frown tugging at his lips.

Elijah was tempted to keep toying with them, but with the sun past midday he got the sense it was his time now. Ignoring the screams from the other side of the hill, he stood and gestured everyone in close. "Come here to me."

Everyone had made plenty of space for the dancing priests, but slowly, almost timid at first, his countrymen pushed in close. Many of them still didn't look very happy with him, but they looked even less happy with Ba'al.

Fortunately, he didn't have to go scavenging for stones to repair the ruin of the altar. There were plenty all around. Elijah stooped down to lift a large block, hauling it over and setting it as a base. He spoke to the crowd as he worked. "You have all heard of our forefathers. First was Abraham, who was called out of a far land to come here, then his son Isaac and his son Jacob. When Jacob was young, he fled away to Haran and lived there for many years. When he returned, he met the Lord God across the Jordan, not Ba'al or Asherah, but the God of our forefathers."

His voice paused a moment as he strained to push another bulky stone over to pile on the altar.

"Jacob met the Lord in a place called Peniel, near Succoth. That night Jacob was alone and a man came close and they fought till morning, but Jacob clung to the man. It was there that the Lord gave him a new name, and said 'Your name shall be Israel. For you have struggled with God and with men, and have prevailed.' And so our father Jacob became Israel."

"Now Jacob had twelve sons from whom came the twelve tribes of Israel, the fathers to us all. For many years they were captives in Egypt, slaves. But the Lord raised up Moses and with mighty works of God set our people free, leading us to this land here. For a time we were one people, not Israel and Judah split in two, and all went down to Jerusalem to offer sacrifices to the true God. And just as there are twelve tribes and twelve sons of Jacob, there are twelve stones on the altar of the Lord."

As he finished, Elijah stepped back to observe the altar he had repaired, a simple affair, but it would work. "Bring me wood for the fire," he commanded the people nearby and the word passed back into the crowd. While he waited, Elijah set aside his robe, instead putting on an old rag of a tunic. He then dug a shallow trench around the altar and told them more. About the beginning of all things with Adam and Eve, about Joshua and how God had driven out the Canaanites to give them a homeland. About the sins of Israel long ago, and the judges God had raised up and appointed over them. About King David and Solomon, about a time almost forgotten before Ahab and his father Omri, before there were two kingdoms. Before Ba'al and Asherah had been the gods of Israel.

When the wood finally arrived, he spread the bundles on his simple altar, and gestured forward the servant who'd been holding the halter of the second sacrificial bull.

The stroke was quick, no blow to the head or crushing cut to the throat, just a simple, quick slice. The bull barely seemed to notice the severed artery, and instead stood there for several seconds before its eyes abruptly drifted shut and the animal passed out, crumpling to the ground. Elijah put a bowl beneath the neck to collect the blood, and looked back to the crowd, giving the animal several minutes to fully die.

"And the Lord spoke to our father Moses," he explained to the gathering crowd, "saying, 'the life of the flesh is in the blood, and I have given it to you upon the altar to make atonement for your souls; for it is the blood that makes atonement for the soul.' The God your fathers worshipped is not like Ba'al, he does not *need* our offerings. He does not feast on burnt meat and poured out wine; instead he has given sacrifices to us – a gift, a way to seek atonement and forgiveness for our transgressions. A way to be made right with Him."

Elijah turned back to the bull and got to the messy job of cutting up the deceased animal to prepare the sacrifice, talking as he worked. "The God of our fathers also spoke to Moses, telling what would happen if we were to forget Him. That He would turn the sky above us to bronze and the ground to iron. And so He has."

He paused and looked up from his work, his eyes meeting so many others staring back. "I know some of you – maybe most of you – look at me and see the person who stole your rain and your orchard and your vineyard. But this is all bigger than me, even than us. These were promises and vows made with God Himself back before our parent's parents were born. And we have forgotten."

His gaze swept the crowd, "You are all here because you want rain for the crops, water for the rivers, and you think that it's mine to give. But the rain belongs to God and He asks something more than just your presence here, He asks that you remember Him and the promises from long ago. Promises that if we kept his commandments, He would bless the land and bless us all. That's what the Lord wants, that we would be His people and He would be our God."

Elijah finished dressing the bull and laid the pieces on the wood of the altar. When he turned back to the crowd watching him, he saw curious looks on many faces, like they finally understood. Like for the first time, they saw clear as day who God was and what He wanted of them.

His mind wandered back to his time traveling the country, telling of the impending drought. It had been so rare to see faces like that and even rarer that they could go from scowling at him to nodding along with his words.

Suddenly it made perfect sense why. He'd come to them decreeing God's judgement, expecting that they understood and just didn't care. But he saw it differently now, *they hadn't known*, so how could they have cared? Suddenly, he wished it hadn't taken all this just for him to tell the truth and for them to hear it.

Perhaps things couldn't have gone any other way though, he mused. Maybe only *here* was he able to tell in a way everyone understood and only *here* were they ready to listen.

Regardless, Elijah felt a smile tugging at his lips, and not the vindictive smirk from watching the Priests of Ba'al exhaust themselves pleading to their god, but a genuinely beaming grin at what he saw in the crowd before him.

Elijah stepped back and regarded his altar with a satisfied nod. There was just one thing left, to prove that the Lord truly was God. A thought struck him and he turned to the crowd, his smile widening as he called out, "Fill four large jars with water, and pour the water over the offering and the wood."

Everyone looked at him like he was crazy.

It wasn't the first time that had happened, but to see the bewilderment etched on so many faces at once was priceless. "Do it." He gestured for them to fetch the water. "Bring water."

Some of the more exhausted priests of Ba'al had given up their dancing and were watching him now. They laughed when men came forward hauling pitchers of precious water, but Elijah didn't care. Instead, he made a grand show of stepping aside as the men upended their jugs and doused the offering and the woodpile, leaving his altar dripping wet. They finished and set the jugs aside, but Elijah gestured towards them with a sweeping wave, "Do it again."

He could have sworn people's eyes were about to pop out of their heads at the request. Even those who seemed like they agreed with him looked a little bit worried. They probably hadn't expected their champion to lose his mind. A ways back Elijah could see his own family watching, more than a little confused, and Lila nervously twisting at her hair

The men did it, though. They hurried back to where several large vats of water had been set up for the people to drink and dipped the jugs inside until they were brimming full. This time Elijah took the water and strutted over, enjoying the *glug glug* sound as he dumped it out, across the altar. When the four jugs were gone, he turned back to the crowd, who almost seemed to expect his next words, "Do it a third time."

By now literally everyone had their eyes fixed on him. King Ahab had pushed his way close to watch and crowd was pressing in. Even High Priest Baltazar was staring open-mouthed, his sacrifice to Ba'al forgotten as he and his acolytes watched the insanity unfold before them.

Elijah took the four final jugs and poured them over his sacrifice until the water flowed down all sides of the altar and filled the shallow trench he had dug. Only then did he nod that it was enough.

Stepping back, Elijah took it all in – an altar soaked with water and covered with wood, and a sacrifice with no flame to light it. He couldn't escape a slight nervous twinge that poked at his stomach, the possibility that somehow this might not work. He fought it back, though, remembering all the impossible things he'd already seen. A God that spoke out of a whirlwind, and a pounding flame. Ravens that brought him food. A flour jar that never ran out. And most of all, a little boy who'd come back to life because he'd prayed to the God of all creation and asked for something impossible. Against all that, one more impossible thing suddenly didn't seem quite so… impossible.

Elijah glanced up to see the sun slowly drifting lower as the afternoon ground towards evening, about the right time for the sacrifice.

He stepped a pace back, knelt before the altar, took a deep breath and prayed.

Chapter 22
More than a Conqueror

O Lord, God of Abraham, Isaac, and Jacob," Elijah said, "Prove today that you are God in Israel and that I am your servant. Prove that I have done all this at your command. O Lord, answer me! Answer me so these people will know that you, O Lord, are God, and that you have brought them back to yourself."

He bowed with his face to the ground, and overhead, a tremendous crack like thunder tore the air.

Elijah looked up to see the sun had vanished, hidden away behind a towering white cloud with a veiled brightness like the sun itself blazing from within. More peals of thunder shook the day, an earthquake in the sky, each punctuated by a dazzling flash from within the glowing cloud.

As he watched, the base of the cloud tore open. A silver white fire, like a lance of pure lightning, stabbed down on the altar in a blinding flash. Elijah lowered his head closer to the ground and pressed his eyes tightly shut as a hurricane of silvery flame whirled overhead, pulsing off waves of heat and tongues of wind that threatened to pull him from the ground.

The thunder overhead grew to a constant, deafening roar, so powerful it sent shudders through the ground. When Elijah dared to peek his eyes open he saw the dust around him being swept up into the cyclone, glowing like a shower of tiny embers as it was pulled into the vortex.

The fire blazed so hot Elijah was sure he himself was about to burst into flames, but finally the inferno lessened and Elijah dared to look towards heaven. The silver fire drew back into the cloud that now glowed painfully bright, spilling out flashes of pure golden lightning that lanced across the sky and vanished on the horizon. Slowly that dimmed, like he'd just witnessed a window into heaven itself and now it was closing. The majestic cloud began to spin itself to pieces, blasted apart by the last lingering traces of power.

Soon the sky had returned to its normal teal and the sun slid back into view, although now it seemed a pale imitation of what they'd just witnessed. All was almost the same as before, except for the altar – the altar was gone.

In its place sat a charred patch of ground scraped completely bare. The bull, the wood, the water in the trench, even the altar stones were completely gone, blasted into nothingness. For a second, Elijah stared at the spot in shocked disbelief; he'd been expecting a spark from the sky, not so much a silvery pillar of annihilation, but that worked too.

Standing to his shaky feet, Elijah looked back across the crowd to see every face, even King Ahab and the priests of Ba'al, pressed into the dirt in the face of the radiant supernova. Slowly a multitude of stunned, terrified eyes and ashen faces rose up towards him, and somehow Elijah knew exactly what to say. "The Lord!" he cried out, raising a fist, "He is God!"

The cry swept across the people of Israel, resounding a thousand-thousand times until it echoed back in a colossal, unified roar that every voice took up, "The Lord – He is God! The Lord – He is God!"

As the voices pounded around him, Elijah turned towards the king who was staring at him, his cheeks linen white and his mouth open, dumbfounded. Many of Ahab's courtiers quietly backed off, deserting him. Nearby, Elijah saw the Sons of Ba'al inching away, their arms streaked with dried blood, shock and fear inscribed on their faces.

Even the indomitable Baltazar looked shaken to his core. He didn't move, he just stared at the scorched space where the altar had stood, paralyzed.

Elijah wasn't about to let the Priests of Ba'al slink off to peddle their lies elsewhere. During his endless hours alone, he'd committed the entirety of his charred scroll of Deuteronomy to memory, and now the commandments sprang to his mind almost by instinct. The words of Moses were straightforward. If someone led Israel to worship gods other than the Lord, they were to be put to death. It was mentioned twice actually, which probably meant it was important. "Seize the prophets of Ba'al! Don't let anyone get away!"

The crowd surged in like a flood around them and despite a few panicked shouts and scuffles, the weight of people made it impossible for the exhausted priests to mount a resistance. In a few moments, two muscled farmers hauled a struggling Baltazar forward, holding the powerful priest by his arms. More men followed, dragging all the acolytes in their red and black robes, and a few who'd abandoned their garb in a desperate bid to escape. But marked out by the fresh cuts that marred their bodies there was no way to hide.

An older man with the bearing of a soldier stepped forward and offered a smart bow. "We have them, my lord prophet."

"Thank you," Elijah nodded and stepped forward to confront High Priest Baltazar, who'd recovered enough of his senses to finally speak. "Lies!" Baltazar shouted at Elijah, "Trickery, what did you do? How did you do it?"

"I didn't *do* anything," Elijah said, iron-eyed. "You saw as well as the rest."

"It was a trick!" Baltazar screamed and struggled to break free. "It was all a trick! I know it was!"

Elijah shook his head and turned to the man. "Take them down to the valley."

"Yes my lord." The man turned to the people and passed the word, "To the Kishon River!"

Together in a great wave they marched down the dusty slope to the half dried brook that flowed along the northern foot of Mount Carmel.

It was a short walk, maybe a mile, to the banks of the thin, withered stream. By the time they arrived, even Baltazar had grown quiet. Standing at the edge of the brook, Elijah's eyes flicked to the high priest and he caught the fury that traced the man's features. He really *did* think he'd been tricked, Elijah realized with a shake of his head. He'd seen it all and yet somehow missed everything.

Well, it didn't really matter now, he concluded as the priests were hauled to the riverside in a long line and roughly shoved to their knees. Elijah gripped his sacrificial dagger in one fist, raised the other for silence… then hesitated.

He'd never seen the Priests of Ba'al as anything more than enemies, the people who'd slaughtered his friends for believing in the wrong God and hunted him like a dog for daring to speak out. But kneeling before him, he saw something different, young priests, trapped and terrified, mixed with older men like Baltazar, too stubborn to admit they'd been wrong.

No one could disagree the priests were his enemies, and he had little doubt Baltazar would have cheerfully eviscerated him, given the chance. But looking at the army of defeated men, a stab of pity struck him like an arrow to the chest. He'd imagined this scene a dozen times, his moment of triumphant vengeance, his chance to settle the score for his friends, for Jesse. But holding the opportunity in his hand, it suddenly felt… hollow.

What if he did kill them? They'd murdered his friends for their god and now he was killing them for his. Did that really make him any different, or was it just a question of who held the knife on a given day?

Elijah's hand dropped as indecision shadowed his face. What was he supposed to do? The Lord's command wasn't ambiguous, and it wouldn't be the first time God had sentenced someone to death. But actually stabbing with the knife was harder than he'd imagined.

Did he let them go?

The thought echoed like a drumbeat in his head, *did he let them go*?

Elijah's mind flashed back to the image of his own friends kneeling, knives to their throats as everything they owned burned to ashes around them. Not so different from right now, just reversed, and if there was one thing Elijah would have asked for that night, it would have been mercy for his friends. He would have begged for them to be let go.

The image slipped away, replaced by another, the Priests of Ba'al set free, slowly plodding away in stunned silence as they returned to their mistress in Samaria because… where else were they supposed to go?

The thoughts quickened into a whirlwind of flashing images. He saw the hatred in Baltazar's eyes. Then he saw the priests of Ba'al as he'd watched them so many times before, a small troop marching along the road, raising little puffs of dust at each step as they made for another village. He saw them spreading like a strangler vine, teaching his people to offer sacrifices to Ba'al and purging anyone who disagreed. He saw them bleeding their poison into the entire kingdom, until no one was left untainted.

His last request to Dema rumbled like far off thunder, *don't forget*! Don't forget, because Israel had seen far greater things, and yet still they had. They had forgotten everything, and a part of him didn't doubt that they would forget again.

He saw the nation of Israel bowing down before the bronze god he'd beheld in the temple at Tyre. He saw his own people throwing countless screaming children into the enormous cupped hands to appease the thing that could never be happy, because it wasn't alive.

He saw more drought, famine, plague, war… death. His country razed to the dust, as God brought about more of the curses he'd promised if Israel abandoned their vows.

Finally, he saw the judgement that false prophets were to be put to death, the words carved into rock with letters deep as an arrow shaft.

Elijah sighed, shook his head, and raised an arm, silencing the confused murmurs sprouting up. "These men," he shouted, gesturing to the priests, "they have lied to you about the true God! You have seen it yourselves, they have deceived you, and opened the door to bring the judgement of the Lord upon the Kingdom of Israel. Moses warned of men who would speak lies and guide you to worship false Gods, that, as a consequence, they were to be put to death, to purge the evil from among yourselves."

Elijah gripped the knife, his fingers turning as white as many of the priests faces at the pronouncement. "They have tried to lead you to the pit!" he shouted. "To kill you in a way more permanent than death itself, and for that, the penalty is death!"

He swallowed hard and stepped forward, to where Baltazar knelt.

"I'm sorry it had to be like this." Elijah spoke quietly.

"Are you?" Baltazar demanded, with a last defiant sneer. "Really?"

"Yes," Elijah bit his lip, "but there are consequences."

"Ba'al will kill you for this!"

Elijah didn't answer, he raised his knife and hundreds more along the brook rose to follow it. "May God have mercy on you," he whispered.

Then his knife fell, and the Priests of Ba'al died.

Elijah walked back through the crowd and up the hillside, his knife discarded along the river bank. He didn't intend to use it again. The people parted before him in an almost reverent awe, and finally he made his way to the back of the throng, where he found King Ahab.

He wasn't particularly shocked that Ahab hadn't been leading the charge to punish the priests of Ba'al. His wife was more or less one already, and Elijah suspected the king preferred her with her head on.

He found Ahab ringed tight by a shield-wall of his guards, spears leveled outwards. The squadron seemed ready for a fight, and looking at them Elijah had a strange epiphany – Ahab expected he was next, didn't he? The look of grim determination on the king's face told Elijah the guess was spot on, and Elijah knew he could do it too.

It wouldn't be that hard, tell the people their king was just as bad as the prophets, and a few contingents of guards wouldn't stand a chance against the mob. He would only need a few words, and as Elijah walked up, he saw even the guards inch away, as though merely his presence carved an invisible path through their ranks.

The soldiers slid aside as he walked up to King Ahab, who clutched at his spear and met his gaze. "What do you want, Elijah?"

In truth, Elijah wanted Ahab dead. He didn't particularly like the man, and Ahab's family was behind many of the problems in Israel. Still though, Elijah sighed, Ahab had been deceived too, no different than everyone else, maybe worse. "Do you believe what you saw?"

There was a long pause, but finally Ahab assented, his voice quiet, "Yes, I do."

"Good." Elijah nodded and stepped back, noting the surprise on Ahab's face. "Go up, eat and drink, for there is the sound of a rainstorm."

Elijah turned and left.

After the fire from heaven and the chaos of taking the prophets of Ba'al down to the river, the massed crowd of people was in disarray. It was nearly time for dinner and wherever he walked, he saw packs of people scattered on the brown grass eating bits of food they'd brought along. Whatever organization they'd had was collapsing in the face of general hunger and confusion. The bulk of the people had stayed down by the river, getting water upstream from where the brook still tinged red with blood, and the crowd finally started to thin out as he tromped up the mountain slope.

"Elijah!" He spun at someone calling his name and through the haze of people, he caught a knot of familiar faces pushing towards him, his family. The kids broke through first, Lila and her not so little brother Tobin, along with Michael's youngest son Aaron, who was eight now, he realized with a start.

"Uncle Elijah!" Lila ran up and threw her arms around him while Tobin regarded him in wide eyed awe. Aaron blurted out what they all must have been thinking, "That was *amazing*!"

His parents caught up a few steps behind – his mom and dad, Hannah and her husband, along with Michael, Emma and their oldest daughter Mara.

His mom matched Lila for emotion, tears in her eyes as she clutched him so tight she might have been trying to crush him.

His father just offered him a smile and a handshake, "Well done, son."

"Thanks."

"Son, where have you been?" his mom demanded. "You know the king came looking for you, *to our house?*"

"Lila mentioned that," he nodded. "I've missed seeing you all."

Aaron grabbed at his arm, "Where did you learn to make fire from the sky?"

"Aaron," Michael cut his son off, "now isn't…"

"No, it's fine." Elijah knelt down next to the wide eyed boy with a messy mop of brown hair. "I didn't do much, I just asked God and He sent the fire."

From the look on the young boy's face he might as well have just explained how to go to the moon, but Aaron nodded anyway, and Elijah stood. "I guess we've got a lot to talk about."

He really ought to have gone to work on getting the rain back. But faced with people he hadn't seen since he'd walked out of Tishbi four years earlier, he figured the rain could wait a half hour more.

It was more like an hour later when Elijah finally hiked back up to the mountain with a beaming grin and Lila and Tobin both in tow. Aaron was a bit young to tag along, but the other two had insisted on going with him.

"So Uncle Elijah," Lila asked, "how exactly are you going to bring back the rain?"

"Well, it shouldn't be that hard," he explained, as they returned to the site of the altars, or, what was left of them. The altar to the Lord was gone and the one to Ba'al had already been torn down and stripped bare of meat and firewood. "I'll pray and God will send back rain."

He knelt down not far from the altar, his face between his knees, and prayed a quiet simple prayer. "Lord, your people have returned, we've followed your commandments this day. It's done, and now, so that they may know you are God, and I am your prophet, I ask you, open up the heavens and send rain on the land once again.”

He stood and glanced over at his niece and nephew. Lila had a half frown creasing her lips, but Tobin just seemed excited to be there, like he expected more silver sky-fire any minute. “Tobin,” he asked, “would you do me a favor?”

The young boy gave an eager nod.

“Go up and look toward the sea,” Elijah pointed to a little hill some distance away.

Tobin didn’t have to be told twice, and in a second he was off like a streak of lightning.

Elijah took a seat on the turf and patted a bit of grass beside him. “What is it, Lila?” he asked.

His niece toyed with her curly locks and mulled on whatever it was for a quiet minute before finally opening up. “I don’t get it,” Lila finally said, a bit discouraged. “I tried that before.”

“You mean praying to the Lord for rain?”

She gave a small nod, and looked at him, confusion in her eyes. “I thought you were going to do something special but… if it’s just that, then why…?” Her voice trailed off and the girl nibbled at her lower lip.

“You mean why didn’t it work for you?” Elijah said.

“Yes,” Lila agreed, “I don’t mean it bad, just… why does God listen to you and not to me?”

Elijah had to think on that one for a moment. As he did, Tobin dashed back up, barely breathing hard at all. “There’s nothing.”

“Go again,” Elijah said.

The boy nodded and jogged back off, leaving Lila’s question still hanging between them.

After a moment’s quiet, Elijah sighed. “I don’t have a good answer,” he finally admitted. “I do think it has a lot to do with things we don’t necessarily control though.”

“What do you mean?”

“Well,” Elijah said, “God has spoken to me very specifically three times, maybe four, depending on how you count it.”

“That’s a lot.”

“It is, I suppose, but every time, the way He’s spoken has been different, and I’m not really sure why. It makes me think there are factors that I don't quite understand involved." Elijah paused, "And I do think God listens, Lila, even if the answer isn't always yes." He shrugged, "I know that's not what you wanted to hear, but if you're looking for a ritual where you do something specific and God has to do something in return… that's what the Priests of Ba'al tried to do, and you saw how well it worked for them. If He *had* to do something you wanted, He wouldn't really be God."

Tobin returned, breathing a little hard, "Still nothing."

"Go again."

The boy rolled his eyes, but turned and took off.

"I guess you have a point," Lila said. "But what about the rain?" she asked. "If I had prayed, I don't think God would have sent back the rain."

Elijah watched Tobin running towards the hillock and starting to flag. "Technically, the rain isn't back just yet," he said with a wry side glance.

"You know what I mean," Lila arched her eyebrows just like his older sister Hannah had when he'd been younger. Just like his mom did too, he realized with an amused grin.

"About the rain, the way I understand it, the reason only I can pray for rain is because, as far as God's concerned, it's my," he struggled to find the right word, "responsibility."

From the way Lila tilted her head, that apparently didn't make much sense at all. "Huh?"

"Do you remember what I said earlier, about Moses, how he talked about all this hundreds of years ago?" She nodded. "I think God was… waiting, if that's the right word, waiting for someone to come along and ask for his promise to be fulfilled. I just happened to be that person. When I did though, I took on the responsibility and it became *my* thing, even if I didn't realize it at the time."

Tobin returned, panting, "Nothing."

"Go again."

The boy gave a loud huff, but ran off. For a while neither Elijah nor his niece said anything, they just watched Tobin dutifully keep up his jogging pace to the hill and back.

The boy came back with a frown, "Uncle, are you sure?

There's nothing there?"

"Go again." Elijah reiterated.

Tobin sighed but headed off anyway.

Elijah watched until his nephew got to the hill again and headed back before continuing, "I didn't mention the strangest stuff that happened," he finally said. "But some of it was pretty miraculous, and I really don't think God did it because I'm particularly special."

"Why then?" Lila propped her chin on her palm.

"I think… because I took on the responsibility, God prepared me for it. That involved a lot of miracles to bring me here, where I could kneel in front of that altar, and pray, and believe God truly would answer."

"Still nothing," Tobin ran back up, taking a deep breath. "Let me guess," he muttered sarcastically.

Elijah had a broad grin, "Go again."

Tobin left, and Lila sighed. "So what you're saying is, it could have been anyone who did what you did today?"

"Not *anyone* per se, but yes, something like that. I do believe most people would have needed to see some truly miraculous things before God sent them here."

His niece didn't raise an objection but she still stared at the dirt and gave a heavy sigh. "Lila," he put an arm around her shoulders and pulled her close, "don't think that whether or not God likes you depends on how many impossible things you get to see. If anything, it may be the other way around. I like to think you would have needed far fewer miracles than I did to believe."

That finally brought a hint of a smile to the girl's face, and she leaned up on his shoulder.

A moment later Tobin was back. "Okay," he panted, doubled over, elbows on his knees, "there is *nothing* there. Just sky. No rain."

Elijah shrugged, "Go again."

"Seriously?" He pointed at his older sister, "Why can't she go?"

"Because she's a girl," he said, deadpan. Next to him Lila smirked and stuck out her tongue in a profoundly unladylike fashion. Tobin fumed, but finally ran off after pausing to catch his breath.

"So" Elijah asked, "Anything exciting back home?"

Lila bit at her lip, her cheeks suddenly tinging red. "Well, I'm betrothed."

Elijah's eyes widened, "Really?"

Lila blushed, "To Samuel."

"Samuel? You mean little mister throws mud at people when they're not looking? I thought you hated him?"

Lila's whole face turned a furious scarlet and she shrunk down an inch, mortified. "He doesn't do that anymore," she affected an aloof voice. "And I kind of like him."

Elijah shook his head, "Well, I'm glad for you, little one."

"Thanks."

He turned his eyes back towards poor Tobin, still puffing on his seventh lap.

Lila cocked her head to one side, bemused. "Couldn't he have just – waited there, instead of running back and forth?"

Elijah gave a slow nod. "I was going to see how long until he figured that out."

Lila fought back a giggle fit, and eventually her little brother dashed back up, excited this time. "There's a cloud as small as a man's hand coming from the sea."

"Excellent." Elijah stood, and gave the boy a serious look, "One more trip?"

Tobin scowled, but assented. "Go and tell Ahab, 'Get your chariot ready and go down so the rain doesn't stop you.'"

Tobin's posture straightened up at the prospect of delivering a message to the king.

"When you're done, head down and find everyone else. I'm leaving for Jezreel so I may not see you."

Tobin nodded, "Goodbye, Uncle."

"The Lord keep you."

The boy was off like the wind and Elijah offered Lila a hand up. "We should probably head back."

As they wandered down the slope, Lila went back to fidgeting with her hair. "You're leaving again?" she finally asked.

"Hopefully not for long," he reassured her. "I think I'd like to come home. It's been a while."

"It has," she agreed and paused a second before adding a small blessing, "The Lord keep you, Uncle."

He grinned, "You too, little one."

Chapter 23
Small Blessings

Three Days Later
Samaria

He did *what!*"

"Jezebel, you weren't there." Ahab tried to placate his red-faced spouse. "You didn't see–"

"No," she snapped in a hot fury, "I wasn't there! Because if I had been, I would have his *head* as my *cup* right now!"

Ahab rolled his eyes with a sarcastic snort. "What was I supposed to do exactly? Try and fight my way through the crowd to save those–"

"You're still the king, aren't you?" Jezebel sneered. "Maybe try acting like one."

She turned away, hand clutching at her pottery cup so tightly her knuckles shaded white.

"Jezebel, he called down fire from the sky."

"You *actually* believe that?" She met his eyes with a strange darkness in hers. "Have you lost your mind? He tricked you, Ahab. He played you for a fool, and he... he..." Her voice faltered and Jezebel looked away, blinking back tears.

Ahab laid a comforting hand on her shoulder, but she jerked away like his hand was a viper. "Don't touch me," she snarled and stalked a few steps away.

Ahab had seen her upset before, but never like this. "Jezebel, please, just listen.”

“No!” She wheeled on him, death in her gaze, “I’ve done enough listening, *you* are going to get me that man’s head on a plate.”

Ahab stared at her like she’d lost her mind. “I will most definitely *not*,” he said bluntly. “I wouldn’t go after that man with an army at my back.”

Jezebel gave a disgusted head shake. “Fine,” she muttered darkly, and headed for the door, “I’ll do it myself.”

“Absolutely not,” Ahab caught her arm. “Jezebel you can’t–”

“I am *queen* of Israel,” she hissed right back. “I can do whatever I bloody well please.”

She tried to shake him off but Ahab’s grip tightened. “You don’t understand,” he lowered his voice, dead serious. “I am not having that man call down destruction on my palace just to satisfy your grudge.”

For a second their eyes met, a silent battle of wills. Finally, she looked away, “Coward.”

That shoved Ahab over the line, “What did you just say?” his face darkened.

“You heard me,” she taunted sweetly. “You’re *afraid* of a little man with a few strange tricks.”

“No, I’m afraid of a man who quite apparently has God Himself on his side.” Ahab’s voice turned mocking, “You should be too, dearest.”

She shook her head, the breath hissing between her teeth. “I told father it was a mistake to marry you.”

“Well, I didn’t get much of a say either,” Ahab retorted. “So that makes two of us.” He stalked a few paces closer, almost right in her face. “Of course,” his voice lowered, “you could always leave I suppose, but then you wouldn’t be queen.” He smirked, “As long as you are, though, you ought to remember that I am king *and* your husband, and as long as you want to keep it that way, I expect you to show a modicum of respect.”

Her eyes burned like twin infernos of furious rage and for an instant, Ahab tensed at the possibility she might just whip out her dagger and try to run him through on the spot. Instead though, Jezebel turned, hurled her cup at the wall so hard the baked clay shattered into useless shards, and stalked out of the room.

***

"Uncle Elijah," Tobin said in a furtive whisper, "Where are we going?"

Elijah didn't answer except to raise a finger to his lips for quiet as the two of them crept along the dark, deserted streets of Jezreel a little after midnight.

Peeking out of the side alley into the gloom of the main road, Elijah scanned the road for any more guards. Nothing moved and a moment later he gestured Tobin forward, "Come on."

The two crept out like shades, Elijah's heart pounding like a drum in his chest. In the stillness, he tensed as faint shouts drifted across the city. Guards, looking for him.

Crouched low, Elijah jogged across the street with only pale moonlight to guide his feet. Weaving his way through the alleys of the city, he kept glancing back every few steps to make sure Tobin was keeping up.

Darting into another bank of shadows, he paused a second to catch his bearings and his breath. When he did, the sinking feeling like a lump of bronze in his chest grew heavier. He found his eyes drifting back to little Tobin, the boy's hands fidgeting nervously. He'd offered to keep his nephew with him in Jezreel for a week before returning to Tishbi, but he was fairly sure creeping through back-alleys trying not to get killed wasn't quite what Hannah and Nathanial had been imagining. His older sister would have had his head if she could see them now.

He tried not to dwell on his situation, but reality had a sobering way of intruding back into his thoughts. It had been less than a week since his victory on Mount Carmel, and yet, here he was again, on the run, and this time with his scared nephew to look after. A single thought kept circling like a grim vulture in his head, 'this wasn't how things were supposed to have been.'

"You'll need to speak to Mistress Abigail," Naboth nudged at Elijah's arm.

"Huh?" Truth was, Elijah was barely listening. He had a hard enough time not getting lost in the mansion of a home, let alone keeping up with everyone's name at the flamboyant party.

"Mistress Abigail, this is her house. Wouldn't do to ignore her completely," his guide whispered. They navigated through the crowded upper room toward a richly dressed woman in a pearl white dress. She wore a bright yellow shawl draped across her shoulders and held an ornate cup filled with red wine in one hand. Naboth gave a polite bow. "Ma'am, I'd like to introduce you to Elijah, The Prophet of the Lord."

The lady's face lit up at his name, although more calculating than joyful. "Elijah," her tongue rolled over the word like she was savoring it, "delighted to meet you." She gave a slight bow, "I wish my husband could be here to share the pleasure but he's busy, business and all. I think he'd be the first to congratulate you on your work though, getting rid of all those priests of Ba'al."

"Thanks? I guess?" The last few days he'd gotten a lot of compliments on the fire from heaven thing, not so much on killing all the Sons of Ba'al though.

Before he could reply, Abigail's head swiveled to the side, noticing a commotion over by the window where the painted lights of sunset poured in, shimmering off a gorgeous young lady's dress. "Well, I simply *must* be off." She flashed him one last grin, "You have a good evening, dear. We're all very grateful to have you."

Elijah stared after her a moment, before glancing at Naboth with a frown. "What's her deal?"

"Her husband Jarius runs a silversmith," he explained. "She's just happy because people are coming in and getting their Ba'al idols melted down. Good for business. The way I hear, it's been tight the last few years."

The explanation gave Elijah pause; he'd never really considered people trying to profit from what he'd done. Naboth's casual explanation didn't help ease his conscience either. He'd come to respect the merchant over the last few days. After Mount Carmel, Naboth had invited him in while everyone else was still trying to sort out if he intended to incinerate them also. Elijah was starting to like the man, but he was suddenly a bit less sure about the rest of Jezreel.

Elijah watched Abigail strut off and Naboth nudged at his arm. "Come on, there's someone else I want you to meet."

"Is he happy about all the priests being dead too?" Elijah asked with a dry cynicism.

"He's in the grain trade, so I'd wager he's a bit more conflicted than our hostess," Naboth winked with half a grin.

Before Elijah could object, Naboth led across the room to where a short, older man with a thick beard traced with grey was sipping wine. "Caleb, I wanted to introduce you to…"

"The Prophet Elijah!" Caleb stepped forward to clasp his hand with a broad smile and a surprisingly firm grip. "Just the person I've been hoping to meet."

The man's almost aggressive friendliness took Elijah aback.

"What you did up on Mount Carmel, my boy," Caleb continued, "truly amazing! I've never been one for temples myself, Ba'al, Asherah, The Lord, it was always about the money in my scroll, but son, *you have proved me dead wrong*, and I've never been more happy to say so."

"Thanks," Elijah warmed to the man. "I'm glad I changed someone's mind."

"That you have," Caleb affirmed, with a forceful step forward to clap Elijah on the shoulder. "I'm just sorry I couldn't see you earlier, but with the rain back I had to hurry up to Tyre and get seed grain before the price went through the roof. You know how it is, opportunity comes to those who wait, and waits for no man. Felt darn good to be buying seed instead of just more flour grain for once. Can't say I've lost out on the trade, you know," he mused. "People needing food has been excellent for business and all, but I'm rather glad we're past all that now.

I think–"

"Caleb," Naboth interrupted politely, and Elijah got the sense the wizened merchant might just talk all day if given the chance, "Elijah and his nephew have been staying in my house the last few days and he showed me a scroll he has, one of the Scrolls of the Law of Moses. It touches on some very interesting subjects. Unfortunately, it's also been damaged. I was hoping you might be as interested as I was in getting it repaired and possibly finding copies of the others. I'm not sure if–"

"Say no more," Caleb cut in, excitement in his voice. "As the Tyrians say, I am *on board*." He looked to Elijah, a gleam in his eyes like they'd be talking the rest of the night if he had his way. Before Caleb could say more though, a commotion broke out across the room, and a man with a small messenger's satchel looped around one arm, stepped forward. Elijah was quick to note the knife strapped at his waist and a tunic clasped with the emblem of an ivory and gold horn – the sign of the king.

A path cleared for the serious-faced newcomer as he strode into the middle of the room. The assembled guests grew quiet as he spoke the fateful words, "I have a message for Elijah the Prophet."

The room went still as a corpse, and Elijah slowly stepped forward, "From whom?"

"Queen Jezebel of Israel," the man intoned, a flicker of worry shadowing his face. "She has heard what you have done to her priests, and has decreed, 'May the gods deal with me, be it ever so severely, if by this time tomorrow I do not make your life like that of one of them.'"

The messenger paused a second, a look on his face as though he half expected Elijah to summon fire on him following the pronouncement. Elijah didn't though, he was still jumping from the heady possibility of finally getting his Scroll of the Law repaired to the grim possibility that the queen was out for his head… again.

As it sunk in, the words kindled a spark of anger. After everything he'd done, everything he'd proved, Jezebel still hated him. Apparently some things would never change.

Across the room, the man pulled out his long knife, and took a pace forward. "I was ordered to bring you with me," he said bluntly. "There's nowhere to go, we have the doors guarded.

Elijah almost snickered, and stood his ground, "No."

He wasn't about to be arrested that easily, especially not in a house surrounded by friends. He waited a moment for people to rally to his side the way they had at Mount Carmel, but… no one moved. Even Naboth seemed frozen to his spot and for some strange reason everyone else was just staring expectantly at him.

Then the realization hit him like a sling-stone: they wanted him to do something else miraculous, didn't they? Maybe a few people supported him but they weren't moving to help, and the rest were just watching, waiting for an encore performance. Across the room, their hostess Abigail didn't even seem bothered by the proceedings. She just watched, sipping at her wine, excited anticipation in her eyes, like… Elijah's heart sank… like she was watching a game.

The man took another step closer and Elijah wilted, even as several of the ladies gave exaggerated gasps. Was that all he was to these people, a game? Someone who put on a good show?

The queen's messenger closed in and Elijah's arms turned to lead. No one was going to help him, were they? After everything they'd seen, they still didn't believe.

Back at Mount Carmel he'd had what felt like an inexhaustible wellspring of bravery, but now his courage deserted him.

Elijah bolted for the window and jumped.

He tried to roll but hit the packed dirt hard, jarring his shoulder, so he had to bite his tongue to keep from shouting. Fortunately, he'd come out in a deserted alley no one had thought to cover. Up at the window overhead the messenger's head poked out, "Over here!"

Elijah scrambled to his feet and ran.

* * *

"Uncle, what's going on?" Tobin demanded in a worried whisper. "Why are we hiding?"

"Shhhh." Veiled in the shadow of the narrow alley, Elijah tensed when he heard the pounding of leather sandals on hard dirt. He held out an arm to press Tobin back against the wall, and they crouched behind an oversized pot as the faint starlight was replaced by flickers of dancing torchlight in the street ahead.

The sound of footsteps grew until a squadron of guards appeared in the street, their blazing torches casting long shadows in the alley. "He'll probably head for the Water Gate to escape south." the commander snapped, "Ruben already had his men down there, so fan out and try to cut him off when he runs back this way. Understood?"

The guards answered with a smattering of 'Yes, sir' and a few nods before advancing off southeast, through the narrow city streets.

That was the direction Elijah had been heading, except with Tobin tagging along he hadn't been making much speed. Now though, his main path out of the city was neatly cut off, and he had little doubt the West Gate was being watched too. They were trapped in Jezreel.

As the footsteps faded, he turned to his nephew only to find Tobin's face had gone a deathly pale. "They're after us, aren't they?"

"Yes," Elijah bit at his lip, trying to imagine a way this didn't end with him and his nephew being murdered for Jezebel's amusement. "We need to find another way out of the city before dawn."

Tobin mulled it over for a minute. "What about the wall?" he finally asked.

Elijah shot him a skeptical look, "What about it?"

"We could get out that way? Right?"

Elijah nearly shot him down, but the idea stuck in his head. They *might* be able to; the wall wasn't *that* high. "I suppose it's worth a try."

He crept out to scan the now deserted street and waved

Tobin forward, as the two darted off into the night.

***

From far away Jezreel's main wall didn't look terribly tall, more like a low curtain of stone that ringed the city. Standing at its base though, the structure looked absolutely enormous. Fortunately, no one shouted as they crept up the wooden steps to the ramparts. Off to the far left and right he could glimpse little embers of light massed around the city gates, but here it was empty.

Peering over the stone wall it wasn't hard to see why. Lit up in the silvery rays of the crescent moon, the far side presented a sheer drop twice as high as he was tall. At the base, dirt spotted with patches of dry grass and jagged stones greeted them. Next to him, even Tobin didn't seem very fond of the idea now that they were actually there.

Unfortunately, they were out of options. Setting his pack on the walkway, Elijah turned to his nephew. "I'll go first then you drop my things over and follow. Got it?"

Tobin nodded. Picking an okay looking patch of dirt Elijah clambered over the wall, hanging down as far as his arms would let him before taking a deep breath and letting go.

In the semi-gloom of night he couldn't see to roll when he landed, and instead he slammed into the dirt, the impact force jolting at his knees. A sharp pain stabbed in his right foot, but gritting his teeth Elijah shoved it aside and gestured for Tobin to lob their packs over.

A minute later his nephew was over the wall, landing with significantly more grace and poise. Elijah checked his foot to discover a puncture wound where a needle pointed rock had punched right through the leather sole of his sandal, leaving a bloody gash. Every step sent a jab of pain racing up his body, but if someone found them outside the city walls at morning they were dead for sure. Gritting his teeth, Elijah forced himself forward, away from the city and towards... he wasn't sure what.

188

Chapter 24
Hunted

S ure I got a room," the old innkeeper said, his gaze drifting across Tobin and honing in on Elijah. "A shekel and a half for the night. That gets you an extra mat."

Elijah blinked, sure he'd misheard, that or the man was a highway robber on the side. "How much?"

"You heard me," the man shrugged, "times are tough. I'm sure a big-to-do fellow like yourself can afford it."

Elijah's eyes widened, "You know who I am?"

"You're that prophet fellow, Elijah." The man snorted in laughter and shook his head, stroking at his greying beard. "Son, I don't know anyone who *doesn't* know who you are."

Something about the man's brashness grated at Elijah. "And you're still charging a shekel and a half?" he demanded, indignant.

"Well, I assume your silver still spends like all the rest," the innkeeper eyed the obvious cloth purse laced at his side.

"That's not..." Elijah frowned, "I could just go outside and call down fire on your inn, you know."

Somehow, not even that fazed the man, who just rapped his fingers impatiently on the counter. "Wouldn't have a place to stay then," he said, in an almost bored voice. "It's getting dark, and in case you didn't know, it's six miles to the next town." The man eyed his obvious limp. "With a foot like that, I'd wager you're not going anywhere in a hurry."

Elijah scowled at being raked over the coals like this, but finally dug out a few bits and laid them on the greedy man's scales till the weight balanced. Back in Jezreel, Naboth had been hospitable enough to offer him some silver for his expenses around town. But at a shekel and a half a night, that wouldn't last long. As much as it irked him, he desperately needed a place to stay. If the man's inn had one thing going for it, it looked ramshackle enough that hopefully no one would bother looking for him here.

"I need some linen bandages."

"That's another gerah."

Of course it was. He mentally cursed the innkeeper and weighed out another twentieth of a shekel in exchange for a few strips of dusty cloth. Then he headed upstairs with Tobin to their cramped room and slumped down on the straw bed-mat.

For a few minutes he didn't move. He just pressed his eyes shut and tried to ignore the throbbing in his right foot from two days of walking on a painful cut.

"Do you need help, Uncle?" Tobin asked.

Elijah opened his eyes to see his nephew watching him with worried eyes. This wasn't the first time Tobin had asked over the last two days of constant flight from Jezebel's killers. "I could use a water basin," Elijah realized with a sigh. Hopefully, that wouldn't run up a bill also.

Tobin nodded and vanished downstairs, leaving Elijah alone for the first time since he'd left Jezreel. With the threat of imminent death gradually receding into the background, Elijah felt frustrated despair replacing it. Things weren't supposed to be like this.

The rumbling thought was enough to stir a spark of furious anger in his chest. What had he done wrong? He'd done exactly what God had told him, and yet here he was, on the run. *Again.*

He still hadn't changed anyone's mind… at least not enough to matter. The image of the party back in Jezreel flashed through his head – everyone watching him like a trained dog, eager to see his next trick. No one had tried to help, they'd just gawked. Now here he was, *The Prophet of the Lord,* and he couldn't even get a place to sleep for the night without being soaked for his silver.

Elijah shook his head. It was as if no one cared, as if they hated him, as if… he stared at the floorboards considering the grim possibility… as if it had all been for nothing.

The door creaked open and Tobin hurried back in, trying not to slosh a wide basin full of water. "Here you go, Uncle."

The water was lukewarm and the pounding pain faded some when he dipped his foot in. Tobin was quick enough at washing his feet, although a little indelicate. When they finished, the water was a clouded brown, but the caked blood around the cut was finally cleaned away enough to see a still nasty gash on the ball of his right foot.

Thankfully, Tobin was decent enough at bandaging up the wound, dabbing on some sort of mustard seed paste from a little pot Dema had slipped into his bag when he'd left. He'd seen her use it on Hammon's cuts. He wasn't sure how it worked, but the cooling medicine did soothe the pain.

"So, are we going home, Uncle?" Tobin spoke as he worked.

Elijah winced as Tobin cinched the linen strips tight. "I'm not sure we can," he said, "not with people looking to kill us. Tishbi would be the first place they'd look."

Tobin tried to hide it but Elijah saw his nephew's face falter at the news, and he felt a pang of sympathy for the youth. When Hannah had left for home, he'd been nearly bursting with excitement at getting to stay in the big city for a few more days. Clearly though, the adventure wasn't working out remotely like he'd anticipated.

Elijah sighed. That made two of them.

The next day, his foot feeling better, they left the little town called Ataroth where they'd stayed and tromped off south. Towards Judah. They skirted past Shiloh, staying safely east of the city and making for Jerusalem. That evening they camped outside, trying to conserve the scarce silver they still had. For the last three years, camping outside hadn't been much of a problem with the scorching, cloudless days, but the return of the rain presented a new dilemma.

Not long before dark, a light but persistent drizzle took up. Not enough to soak him and Tobin, but enough to be an annoyance. Eventually the two shifted from their impromptu campsite off the road to a thicket of low bushes. With everything damp, they couldn't even get a proper fire started. Finally, the two gave up and nestled down beneath the brush, using Elijah's cloak as a poor excuse for a blanket. After the long day, Tobin was exhausted enough to pass out straight away. But with his foot still aching and a rock poking uncomfortably at his shoulder-blade, Elijah lay there for a long while, the thoughts drifting through his head, trying to think what to do next. He'd go to Jerusalem and... his plan dead-ended right there.

Elijah was still struggling to summon up an answer, when he heard the distinctive *thunk thunk* of horse hooves on dirt, and not just one. Peering out from his spot in the brush, he saw several torches slowly bouncing closer in the night. He wasn't sure who would be traveling on a horse at night, particularly in a drizzle. Seemed like a good way to lame a horse.

In the still of the night, he caught drifting voices with heavy Tyrian accents. "Why can't we just stop?"

"Why can't you shove your belly-aching already?" the reply snapped back. "We're already behind. If we're going to beat that cursed prophet fellow to Jerusalem and earn the reward, we have to get at least a few more miles tonight."

"He's not *that* fast," the first voice gave a sullen mutter. "It's not like he can fly."

"I don't know," another voice chipped in. "The locals all say he summoned some sort of magic fire and still beat the king's chariot back to Jezreel on foot."

"Bah... superstitious fools," the first voice sneered, followed by the distinctive hack of the man spitting. "Bunch of country dopes."

The torches drew near along the road, maybe twenty paces away. "You don't believe he's a real man of the gods then?"

In the flickering light Elijah caught a glimpse of them, three dangerous looking men with torches and sword blades strapped at their sides. The one in front gave an almost pitying head-shake, "I believe in one thing, gold. If he is a man of the gods then maybe they'll be polite enough to pay for his sorry life, if not…”

“You shouldn’t say that. Not about the gods,” the other man admonished as the three horsemen drew close, without so much as a side glance towards Elijah’s hiding spot. “Ba’al is always watching, and he doesn’t take kindly to being mocked.”

They passed by and started to *clomp* away on their tired steeds, slow moving puddles of light in the gloom. The first man gave an angry mutter, something about paying Ba’al whatever he demanded when they were done.

As the riders faded into the night until they were little more than sparks in the distance, Elijah struggled with a grim reality of his own. With mercenaries looking for him in Jerusalem, he couldn’t go there, and as well-known as he was, he wasn’t sure anywhere in Judah would truly be safe either.

Three days later, he and Tobin wandered into Beer-sheba, a dust-blown town on the southern edge of Judah. The last stop at the edge of the end of the world.

Chapter 25
Lands Uncharted

As the hot morning sun rose in the east, Elijah didn't have a plan. He didn't have much money, either. Staring out at an endless expanse of wasteland pockmarked by rolling hills, he was out of places to run.

"What do you mean, go home?" Tobin asked, his expression more than a little upset.

"I mean just that," Elijah said firmly. "Go back to Tishbi." He unclipped the money pouch from his belt and handed it to the boy. Tobin was young, but in a year or so he'd be old enough to marry; he could manage the trip.

"It's a few days, but you'll be fine."

Still Tobin hesitated, "Are you sure you'll be alright, Uncle?"

"I'll…" Elijah didn't want to lie, but his nephew was already bearing up under the pressing weight of a lot of awful news. Besides, none of this was Tobin's fault. "I'll be fine, just tell my parents I'm sorry things didn't work out better."

That was a colossal understatement, but Tobin nodded anyway. From the look on his face, he might have guessed there was more going on, but after so many days on the run, Elijah could see he was tired, beat down, and ready for the not so fun adventure to be over.

"If more people come and ask where you are, what should I say?"

"Tell them," Elijah bit at his lip and gazed out across the endless bronze of the Negev Desert, "tell them they can find me out there."

His nephew gave a solemn nod, "Goodbye, Uncle."

Elijah shook the youth's hand one last time. "The Lord go with you Tobin, and I… I'm sorry."

They embraced, then Elijah watched as the boy turned and left, heading back on the long journey to Tishbi. He waited until the teenager was just a far spot on the horizon, then cinched up the strap on his water jug and struck off into the rocky desert. Heading nowhere.

For a little while the sounds of the town were still audible behind him, the noises carrying for long distances in the emptiness, far off shouts and clangs. Finally though, they faded, like the memory of a dream in the morning. As the sun passed its zenith, he couldn't hear anything except the soft rumble of the wind over the barren hills. It was a strange thing, solitude. Over the last several years he'd gotten used to being alone with his thoughts, but for the last week he'd had precious little time to do exactly that. He'd either been a celebrity, or he'd been on the run with Tobin. He'd thought a lot, but still there was something different about being truly alone.

Elijah almost didn't notice the passing of time as the thoughts swirled through his head, pulling into ever tighter circles. How did he go from calling down fire on the summit of Mount Carmel to… here? How could all that happen and everyone just abandon him? And maybe the biggest question of all: what was the point of everything, if it was going to end like this? If all his work was going to end in ashes, why had God gone to all the bother?

He didn't know what else he could have done differently. He'd followed the Lord's instructions. He'd gone to the canyon, to Zarapheth. He'd waited, and when God had told him, he'd been brave enough to speak to Ahab. He kept sorting through his memories, trying to think what he could have done differently, but it felt like every strand of possibility ended here, hiding alone in the desert from Jezebel's mercenaries. The last of the men of God.

In mounting frustration, he looked up at the sky. "Is this it?" he whispered, desperate for an answer to make sense of it all.

No reply.

His voice rose to a shout, "Is this it!"

He'd never been angry with God, not truly angry. He'd been upset, confused, lost... hurt... but seeing four years of his life's work crumble to dust in barely a week... Elijah was angry.

"Why!" he screamed, his shout lost in the vastness of the desert. In a sudden boil of rage he picked up the nearest rock, a palm sized, sharp-edged stone and hurled it with all his strength. It flew an unsatisfyingly short distance, before landing in the dirt with a muffled *thwump*.

Why? Why would no one listen? Why couldn't they just... no one believed, no one even seemed to bother. He'd warned them and they'd laughed. He'd performed a miracle like no one in the history of the earth, and they'd applauded like he was a trick pony, and then asked for another.

It seemed like no matter what he did, it would never be good enough. Moses had tried, Joshua had tried, Gideon, Samuel, David... they'd all failed, and now he got to add his name to the pile. A cold sadness gripped at his chest, his friends were dead and he... he'd missed his life for this. He had missed Lila and Tobin and Aaron all growing up because he was... he was living in a canyon with ravens for friends. All the while he'd thought he was fighting for something bigger than himself. He'd truly believed he could change things... and yet he'd failed. All his work swept away by one word from the vindictive queen.

He plodded on until another thought frothed to the surface. "Is this the end Lord?" he said. "Did you run me out here to die?"

Still no answer.

He raised his water jug for a drink but found only a few mouthfuls of water left. The possibility of running out of water was enough to jolt him out of his stupor. He turned around, wondering if maybe he should go back. The sun was descending in the sky now, the heat of the day nearly at its worst, but when he looked behind him, he couldn't see any tracks in the hard packed earth. The realization left him with a sudden panic like sinking in quicksand. He was lost.

More than that, was there anything left for him back there? A kingdom that hated him, a bunch of people looking to chop off his head…

He had been wandering all day and didn't know how to get back to Beer-sheba. The thing was – he didn't really want to. At least out here, he wasn't running anymore; he was just lost.

For a while longer Elijah walked. Finally, he found a solitary tree standing amid the rocky waste, a squat thing with thin, spiky needles, and close layers of wispy, pale green branches that spread out only a few feet above the ground. It was more of an oversized bush than a tree, but it cast a shadow. In the heat of the sun Elijah crawled under the shade, the fatigue of his long walk creeping up on him like a fox.

Sitting there with just the reality of his failure for company, Elijah felt as if he was being crushed, and after a long time considering it, he still didn't see a way out of his mess. Finally he shook his head. "I have had enough, Lord," he said. "Take my life; I am no better than my ancestors."

Still nothing happened.

Exhaustion closing in on him like a thief, Elijah lay down and drifted off to sleep.

"Hello…? Hello?" Elijah woke in the gloom of night to something poking at his back and an irritatingly buoyant voice somewhere nearby. "Are you okay?"

He rolled over beneath the tree to find a tall man in a long, oddly cut tunic, crouched beneath the bush, prodding at him. It was night, but close by a crackling fire cast an orange glow across the rocky desert.

"Oh good, you're alive," the man moved back a pace.

Elijah stared for a moment, completely lost. "Who are you?"

"I'm the person who found you under a broom tree," the man answered with a half grin. "I'm also the fellow who cooked dinner." He stood up, "Come on, get up and eat. I think you'll enjoy it."

Elijah rolled over and couldn't hide his open-mouthed shock

when he discovered a round of fresh bread sitting on a pile of neatly laid out hot stones, and a clay jug of water. "What is…?"

"I told you, enjoy," the man gestured to the meal with a wide grin.

Elijah caught a sniff of the bread and the scent was enough to kick off a gurgle in his stomach. "You didn't want any?"

"I'm good. Thank you, though." The man dropped down cross-legged by the fire a few feet away, cheerfully warming his hands close to the blaze.

Elijah watched for just a bit before the wafting aroma and his hunger finally got the better of him. He took a deep draught of water followed by a cautious nibble at the bread. He wasn't sure if it was his hunger, but it tasted fantastic, even better than it smelled. The inside of the loaf was still warm and moist, cooked through but not burned. It was light and delicate, with another flavor mixed in, a taste sweet like honey but with the flavor of pomegranate.

Despite his hunger he chewed slowly, enjoying the swirl of flavors in his mouth and glanced over at the man, shock written on his face for the second time, "This is delicious."

"I'm glad you like it," the man said, clearly pleased. "Sometimes I wonder if it's not a lost art, cooking. People these days are so good at making do with what they have, they don't realize what they can do with the right ingredients."

Elijah tore off another piece and took a big bite. He moved closer to the warmth of the fire as a cool breeze cut like a knife across the desert. "How did you find me?" he asked.

The man shrugged. "How does anyone find anything in the desert? I was here, and you were camped there under the bush. Since your water was empty, it didn't take a genius to guess you weren't doing great."

Elijah bit his lip for a moment and nodded. "Well, thank you."

"Of course, it's the least I could do."

They sat in silence for a while as Elijah took more wolfish bites. The loaf was big enough that he finally slowed down, his empty hunger sated. The bread was still too good to waste though, and he kept on nibbling at it.

"If you don't mind my asking," the man probed a little, "where were you going that dumped you all the way out here?"

"I'm not really sure," Elijah sighed. "I was trying to get away. This seemed like a good place."

The man gave a slow nod, but before he could press any deeper, Elijah chimed in with a question of his own. "What about you? What are you doing out here?"

"Oh, that's my job. I go all over the place."

"So, you're a trader or something?"

"Or something," the man agreed. "I enjoy the traveling; I get to see some incredible things."

"Like what?"

"Tall grass that reaches to the horizon, a forest of living sticks, a desert in a valley of trees, islands capped with fire, a land where the sun runs in a ring around the sky, walking mountains of sand, a sea of red dust." He paused with a smile, "If you ever get the chance you should go to Tarshish, the Hellenes call it Tartessos. Not the best city, but it has *magnificent* architecture."

In the face of the man's surprising travel pedigree, Elijah couldn't evade a hint of intimidation. "The furthest I've ever been is Tyre."

"Hmmm," the man nodded but his expression betrayed distaste, "Also beautiful but... dark. Like a dream gone wrong."

Close to the warmth of the fire, Elijah fought back a yawn and finished off the last of his bread. "You've been there?"

"Of course, the island of many ships, it's remarkable. I remember when it was just a rock, back when Egypt was still young and Ur was the place to be. I'm not sure they've really improved it much since, but it sure looks impressive."

"I've been to Zarapheth too," the man said with a modest half grin. "A simpler place but better perhaps."

The comment sent up a warning flag as clear as day. The man knew; Elijah couldn't guess how, but he knew. "Who are you?"

"A friend," the man answered, casually tossing a few more twigs on the flames.

For a long moment a tense silence hung between them, the

man watching the fire and Elijah watching him.

Finally the strange man glanced over, "You should get some sleep, Elijah," he said. "I'll keep watch."

The man knew his name.

Elijah almost ran, but he was in the middle of nowhere, in the dead of night next to the man that had been everywhere; he wasn't going to escape. He watched a moment, wary. The fellow *had* cooked him the best meal he'd had in days, and the man had already found him unconscious once. He still wasn't sure about the whole thing, but he was exhausted, even after his nap. He figured he could sleep now in peace, or worry a while and sleep later.

He wrestled with the choice before eventually settling down beneath his cloak, his face to the fire and to his strange new friend.

Elijah rolled over, half-awake on the hard dirt when someone nudged at him. "Morning, Elijah."

"Wha...?" It took Elijah a moment to recall where he was, but when he did his eyes flashed open to see the stranger from the prior night, still there. He looked different in the morning light... tall, wearing a long linen robe that seemed to put off a strange glow at the fringes. The hem should have been brown with dust from walking but instead looked fresh, like he'd just put it on.

The man didn't seem to mind the strange radiance; instead, he wandered back over to the fire and spent a moment stirring a clay pot of something that smelled like porridge. After a moment he looked back Elijah's direction, and gestured him over. "Get up and eat some more, or the journey ahead will be too much for you."

Elijah stood but still eyed him, warily. "What journey?"

The man shrugged, "Well, you don't intend to stay *here* forever?" He pointed to where he'd laid out another loaf of warm bread, some water, and a clay bowl of dates. "Might as well eat while you can, it's a long trip."

After his dinner the prior night, Elijah didn't think he'd be hungry again, but looking at the food his appetite swiftly returned, and soon he found himself savoring the meal.

Despite the good food, he couldn't shake his confusion about the man who'd helped him. "How do you know my name?" he asked after a few bites.

"You're a very popular fellow, Elijah," the man answered. "Were you expecting to find someone who didn't?"

"I… it just seems like everyone else who does, either doesn't care or wants my head."

"Now that's not true," the man said firmly, "and if it's any consolation, I believe your head was attached to the rest of your body for a good reason."

It wasn't much consolation, but Elijah tried not to dwell on the topic. Instead he found himself staring at the man. Last night he'd thought maybe he was a traveling merchant, but in the light of day, he didn't see a caravan. There were no mules or camels, not even a horse or a cart. Somehow the man was just wandering the middle of nowhere, on foot, with a lumber-pile of firewood and a full kitchen strapped to his back, making breakfast for strangers.

The man looked up with a perceptive gleam in his eyes like he already knew what Elijah was thinking. "You can ask," he assented.

"Who are you?"

"A messenger. And a friend."

"And this journey?"

"Well it's your choice," the man said, "but if you're interested it's that way… generally speaking." He pointed off in an arc south and a bit east, deeper into the desert. "You'll find the place you need."

"And when I get there?"

The man shrugged, "Did not knowing ever stop you before?" He finished with the porridge pot and ladled out a bowlful, handing it to Elijah.

Like the bread it was strange, traced with an exotic sweetness and mixed chunks of a strange candied fruit he'd never seen before.

For a while after eating Elijah didn't speak. Instead he mulled the possibilities in his head. He could go back towards

Israel and a bunch of mercenaries, or forward, deeper into nowhere. He wasn't sure which option scared him more. Either return back home to… pretty much certain death, or wander out into the wasteland, with no food or water, also pretty much certain death. Finally he shook his head. There wasn't anything for him back in Israel, so that just left one way to go.

He sighed, and pushed himself to his feet. "So, into the desert?"

The man nodded, and a hint of a smile cracked his lips.

"Thank you for the food."

"Of course," the man's grin widened, "it's been a pleasure, Elijah."

The prophet took a deep breath and, one foot after another, walked off into the desert.

Chapter 26
The Mountain of God

Elijah wasn't sure how long he had been walking. Time seemed to fade in and out like one more mirage in the endless desert.

The sun rose, and set. At night he stopped, sitting in the open beneath the waxing moon, his cloak pulled tight against the cold as the wind whistled across the rocky plains. He didn't sleep so much as doze, still half aware of the utter solitude surrounding him.

Every morning he rose with the sun, never tired, and continued. He didn't eat or drink, and he barely thought about it as he traipsed across lakes of golden sand and towering copper mountains. The occasional struggling bush or shrub gave way to vast, utter emptiness: a barren, bronzed land striped by rivers of sand and islands of hardened dirt where he could look forever in every direction, and see nothing.

Even the beating sun mattered little; he felt the blazing heat as a soft warmth, like the brush of the first rays at dawn, while the midnight chill seemed little more than a crisp, refreshing breeze.

It was as if the world flowed by all around as he traveled, always there but only reaching out and touching him with the gentlest caress. He'd always feared the desert, but freed from the need for water and food, he felt like he was seeing it for the first time, a vast, majestic world where sand flowed like water and swirled in twisting cyclones that cut across the land. Even when the dust blew in a thick bronze fog, he simply sat down until it passed, and the sun once again cut through the haze.

While he still didn't know where he was going, the strange man had been right; somehow he knew the way. Like a bird flying south, he just had a sense he was getting closer.

Finally, the landscape changed yet again, the desert giving way to wind-blasted rocky buttes that towered like red, monolithic sentinels above him. The maze of heights twisted and turned, narrowing to steep sided ravines with floors of fine sand before fanning back out like a rocky courtyard made by giants. At last he came to a place where the stones underfoot transformed from sand and gravel to rocks the size of his sandal, sharp jagged pieces smashed loose from the red pillars that rose up before him. And behind all that stood a giant, a huge mountain capped with blackened stone that soared up like a low triangle in the distance.

For a time it came and went, vanishing behind steep cliff walls and peaks of jutting granite, as Elijah wandered through narrow, desolate valleys. He always knew where to find it again; the awareness hovered like a beacon in the back of his mind. Almost as if he could have pointed to the mountain blindfolded.

At last he came to a wide valley, the far end flanked by two peaks with the black mountain top poised in the background behind. Walking between them, he found a level vale dotted with ankle high tufts of brush and, amid it all, a mound of boulders, each twice his height.

Even from far away the scratches on one boulder caught his eye. Coming closer, Elijah made out carvings, little etchings of bulls scraped in the rock, the outer shell transformed from red to black as if it had been burnt and stained with soot.

For a few minutes he stared, trying to figure out why someone would have carved a dozen bulls on a rock in the middle of the desert. At last the mountain beckoned him on. Crossing the sandy vale he continued upwards, following a winding gully scattered with sharp-edged, waist-high boulders.

Several turns in he discovered something else, three

columns of carved, circular, white stones and three parallel stone walls, each about a pace apart. The walls were as tall as his head, all in varying states of tumbled disrepair. They ran maybe twenty paces before turning and continuing an equal distance to a raised platform like an altar at the end, from above it would have looked like a wide V.

They were chutes, he realized, lanes to push sacrificial animals up to the altar. But why were they out here in the middle of nowhere?

He thought back to the engravings of a bull he'd seen in the rock earlier and in a rush, words came unbidden to his mind, from the scroll of Exodus, 'Then Aaron took the gold, melted it down, and molded it into the shape of a calf.'

This was *it*, he realized with a start. This was where it all began. He had wandered past the ruined altar of the golden calf, and now, here he was, standing at the altar where Moses had offered sacrifices to the Lord. He was standing at the base of Mount Horeb, the place where God had come down to meet with his people generations before.

Elijah glanced around him, suddenly seeing more than just rocks. He counted the white, chalk-like stones stacked together into the three pillars, four for each column, twelve in total.

More words sprang to mind, 'Moses got up and built an altar at the foot of the mountain. He also set up twelve pillars, one for each of the twelve tribes of Israel.'

This was *it*.

He swallowed at the realization. He wasn't sure anyone from Israel had been back here in... hundreds of years. He might very well have been the first since his people had decamped, centuries before. For an instant he almost imagined he saw it all, Moses, aged but still tall, and powerfully built, standing before the altar as smoke twisted towards heaven in a long ribbon. Behind stood the people of Israel, a vast multitude watching the sacrifice, Moses read to them the Book of the Covenant and the people agreed, making a covenant with God Himself.

His eyes drifted back to the Altar of the Golden Calf, now far out of sight... and then they'd forgotten, and ignored God.

Not so different from now.

Elijah sighed and shook his head, his imagined scene evaporating like mist. Whatever the reason God had brought him here, he wouldn't find it on a forgotten altar. When God had met with Moses it had been up on the mountain, so up to the mountain he went.

Close to sunset he reached the blackened peak. Most of the mountain was the same reddish stone of the surrounding desert, but near the top a line cut the stone and it abruptly shifted from red to a shiny, almost obsidian black, like it had been scorched by an impossible fire.

As darkness descended, he found a cave near the summit, a gaping opening maybe three times his height that led ten paces back to a small spot where he sat down for the night. Looking out, he could see the whole plain spread out below, the place where Israel would have camped in an army of tents.

Facing east he couldn't see the sun set, but as the last tendrils of light faded, gusts of wind picked up, whistling at the entrance. He heard something else too, like a whisper on the wind that grew louder, a whisper calling his name, "Elijah?"

He tensed, but answered, "Yes Lord."

"What are you doing here, Elijah?" the voice of God asked.

Huh? Elijah felt a stab of confusion, did God not know what was going on? He was here because… "I have been very zealous for the Lord God Almighty," Elijah answered. "The Israelites have rejected your covenant, torn down your altars, and put your prophets to death with the sword. I am the only one left, and now they are trying to kill me too."

Elijah stared out into the starlit darkness, waiting for an answer. He didn't understand, though. God knew exactly why he was here. Jezebel was out to collect his head. If this was about him leaving Israel, well, that was a fairly normal thing to do when people were trying their best to murder you. Was he supposed to just… not be afraid? Right up until someone ran him through?

He shook his head. No, he didn't think God was angry with him. If God was, why send someone to bring him food for his trip?

Outside, the breeze faded for an instant and finally an answer came, just not the one he'd expected. "Go out and stand before Me on the mountain."

As soon as the voice faded the wind whipped up outside, rising to a howl at the cave mouth. The gusts lashed at the mountain, and outside he heard the crashing of rocks. Even in the dim night, he caught the pitch black shadows as boulders overhead tumbled down the mountain, falling past the cave entrance.

Nestled in the back of the cave, Elijah waited. He kept expecting something like he'd seen before, an island of tranquility amid the storm, to mark the presence of the Lord. But it never came. Outside the wild storm shrieked like a banshee for what seemed hours, each gust followed by another that tore at the mountain, wrenching loose stones and hurling them like an angry god down the slopes. There was no God in the wind though.

At last, after what seemed forever, the wind diminished, the noise fading from a terrible scream back to a soft whistle.

He was still waiting when the rock beneath him pulsed with a shockwave of force, a hammer blow that shook the mountain. Outside the roar of tumbling rocks grew, and a heartbeat later another strike hammered at the mountain, one to knock him to the side even where he sat. More strikes followed, blow upon blow, rippling through the rocks of the mountain as though it was being torn from the ground and crushed to dust. The cave he sat in was solid stone, but even so, a few pebbles on the floor jumped at each smash of the earthquake.

He'd heard of earthquakes that lasted a few moments but this felt more like an army of giants marching to war. It went on and on, each pulse smashing free more rocks until the landslide outside grew to a thunderous cacophony. But there was still no God in the earthquake.

Finally the shaking diminished and outside he heard a different thunder. Clouds stirred above in swirling circles, flashes of light flickering in their depths, sending bursts of light spilling across the plain. From the back of his shallow cave, Elijah saw when the strikes began, stabs of liquid fire lancing down across the rocks of the mountain, more and more until the air itself seemed ablaze and he could see clear as day from the constant rain of fire. Wherever the lightning struck, rocks burned, an unquenchable fire that spread across the mountainside as if a plague of blazing locusts had descended on the slopes.

The fire gave off no smoke. Instead, it draped like an orange blanket across the mountain, not consuming the rocks but giving off a terrible heat. It crept right to the entrance of his cave but refused to reach inside. For a time the fire swept away everything in its path, but never was there anything like the impossible patterns of flame he'd seen back in Zarapheth. No voice of the Lord issued from the fire.

At last the inferno died down and began to evaporate. As the last tendrils of flame dwindled into darkness, Elijah was left alone and confused, more so than ever. Had he missed something? Had God wanted him to walk out into the windstorm?

Around him the quiet grew until it smothered everything. After a while he noticed he could hear his own heartbeat amid the strange tranquility, and... something else.

A whisper, "Elijah."

Rising, he walked to the cave entrance and hid his face in his cloak as the whisper grew louder. He prayed for an answer that made sense of all this, then spoke, "Speak Lord, for your servant is listening."

Shaded behind his cloak, his eyes couldn't see anything, but amid the cold night, he felt a warmth like the dawn sun ahead. He could hear the Lord's reply, clear as day, "What are you doing here, Elijah?"

The same question again, and it made little more sense this time either.

Frustrated, Elijah offered the same reply as before. "I have zealously served the Lord God Almighty. But the people of Israel have broken their covenant with you, torn down your altars, and killed every one of your prophets. I am the only one left, and now they are trying to kill me, too."

That wasn't strictly true, he realized as the words left this lips. There were probably others, those prophets that Obadiah, the king's steward, had claimed he'd hidden. But still, Elijah hadn't seen any of them standing beside him on Mount Carmel. He sure felt alone, and it was clear everything he'd done hadn't amounted to much, as far as the people of Israel were concerned.

The warmth before him seemed to diminish some at his answer, and a moment later the voice of the Lord rumbled again. "Go back the same way you came, and travel to the wilderness of Damascus. When you arrive there, anoint Hazael to be king of Aram. Then anoint Jehu grandson of Nimshi to be king of Israel, and anoint Elisha son of Shaphat from the town of Abel-meholah to replace you as my prophet. Anyone who escapes from Hazael will be killed by Jehu, and those who escape Jehu will be killed by Elisha! Yet I will preserve 7,000 others in Israel who have never bowed down to Ba'al or kissed him!"

As the words ended, the warmth faded, and almost before he could take in everything God had said, Elijah was alone again. There were a thousand questions Elijah thought to ask, the first being the simplest. Why? Why would God ask him to do something like that? Wasn't what he'd already done enough? He'd been working for the last four years for God, and to get to the end, only to be told to run further still, it...

For a long while he stood there at the entrance to the cave, his cloak covering his eyes, trying to answer the hailstorm of questions about what The Lord had said. At last he turned back inside, waiting until the first streaks of light painted the eastern horizon before beginning his descent down the mountain, and back home.

Chapter 27
Elisha

Elijah sat on a tree stump, staring out across the fields near Abel-meholah and trying to make up his mind, the words of the Lord still echoing in his head days later. For once he *really* didn't know what to do. He'd had an entire trip across the desert to consider it, but the burden of his instructions still hung like an iron chain laid across his shoulders. Anoint Hazael, King of Aram-Damascus and Jehu, King of Israel. It should have been simple, find the two men, pour oil on their heads, and tell them what the Lord had ordained. Yet it wasn't. There was the second, more terrifying part. Those who escaped Hazael would be killed by Jehu, and those who escaped Jehu would be killed by Elisha. He didn't know exactly what that meant, but it didn't sound good. Taken with the bit about God preserving 7,000 who had never bowed to Ba'al, he could guess.

It wasn't hard to imagine the armies of Aram tearing across Israel, slaughtering as they went. He had read about things like that before, the time of Gideon when the Midianites had descended on the land in a horde like locusts. God's judgement on Israel.

Elijah didn't dispute that God was right. He'd seen how no one in Israel cared – how they ignored the Lord to worship trees and little statues. Looking out over the fields, he caught an imagining of it all. Ranks of Arameans sweeping across a land

210

just now beginning to green after the long drought, cities lit ablaze, people screaming in fear, struck down like sheep on the roads. Worst of all he saw his home, Tishbi. It wasn't that far from Aram-Damascus, and he didn't entertain any illusions; if the world of Israel was to end, Tishbi would be destroyed too. His home burned, the orchard where he and Michael had played as children cut down, the town razed. People he remembered, friends, hauled out of their homes and butchered. His parents might get away, maybe Michael and his family too, but that still left his sister Hannah. She had worshiped Ba'al, and what about Lila and Tobin? He couldn't stomach the image that flashed through his mind of his niece and nephew, both dead.

He glanced across the fields, wishing his eyes could pierce souls to see who were left in the remnant God had saved for Himself. He couldn't though, and somehow the not knowing made the prospect of God's judgement all the worse.

Closing up the skies and killing the priests of Ba'al had been one thing. He hadn't fully understood it all when he'd begun. But now that he'd wandered a country of gaunt, thin people desperate for a bite to eat, he wasn't sure he could bear to bring the Lord's judgement on Israel again.

So, what did he do?

He knew God wouldn't delay forever, but maybe he could buy time? The possibility drifted idly through his mind, but Elijah latched onto it. What he'd done on Mount Carmel, challenging the Priests of Ba'al, hadn't ended the idolatry in Israel. But there had been some hope. His mind flickered back to the people he'd met in Jezreel, Naboth and Caleb, who'd agreed with him. Maybe there were others? It wasn't a perfect plan, but perhaps he could save more, like Noah in his ark. Or maybe he could change things, make it so God didn't have to ruin Israel yet again.

Granted, there was still Queen Jezebel to worry about. He didn't know what to do about her and her murderers. After seeing the true power of God on Mount Horeb, though, he was less afraid. Besides, God had told him to train Elisha to succeed him and Elijah didn't think the Lord would let him be killed before he finished his task.

Still dwelling on the idea, Elijah stood and wandered back to the road. "Ma'am," he got the attention of a nearby woman walking by carrying a bucket of water back to town, "Excuse me, but I'm looking for Elisha Ben-Shaphat."

The woman didn't seem to recognize him, not that he looked like he had back on Mount Carmel. He'd dropped weight and his clothes were a dusty mess.

At the question she shot him a look like he was crazy. "Elisha? You're sure?" Elijah nodded and she pointed several fields down where a number of men each behind a yoke of oxen were plowing the dirt, still damp from last night's drizzle. "That's him down there, the boy, Shaphat's youngest."

Elijah watched, picking out the boy she'd said. He was a youth, maybe fifteen or sixteen, struggling with the plow and a yoke of two stubborn oxen.

He walked towards the field. There were twelve yoke of oxen in total, many of the men of the town and their sons plowing together. The boy he was after was at the tail end. Wandering along the edge of the field, Elijah's eyes followed him as he worked.

Finally he cut across, his feet sinking into the freshly turned dirt. Elisha was still busy struggling with his animals, but he looked up when Elijah drew close, recognition flickering in his eyes. By right, Elijah could have pulled him aside, anointed him, and told him he *had* to follow him. Instead, he unclipped his cloak and tossed it onto the boy who deftly caught it across his shoulder.

"You know who I am?" Elijah said.

Elisha gave an eager nod, his eyes wide in awe.

"Good." Elijah left it there and walked on. If Elisha wanted to come along on this whole crazy adventure, Elijah wouldn't stop him. He wouldn't force him either.

He barely got five paces before he heard a shout behind him, "My lord, wait!"

He turned to see Elisha jogging up behind him, cloak in one hand, his plow and oxen forgotten. The young man swallowed, "You want me to come with you?"

"Only if you choose."

Elisha nodded, "Let me kiss my father and mother goodbye, and then I will come with you."

He hesitated, a flash of worry in his eyes like he thought Elijah might say no, but Elijah nodded, shocked at the boy's eagerness more than anything else.

"Of course," he said. "Go on back, for what have I done to you? You're not a prophet just yet, soon maybe, but there's not such a hurry you can't say farewell."

His new apprentice gave a low bow. "Thank you."

Elijah watched him hasten across the soft dirt of the field to his father, and felt an optimistic smile tugging at his lips. With a few more people like that, maybe there *was* hope for Israel. Elisha would still need to be trained. A flurry of practical details rose up. He would need a school like where he'd studied under Jesse, copies of the scriptures, a place to live. He had a lot to do.

And then there was the other part of God's command hovering over him like a falcon – what to do about Jehu and Hazael. For a moment he grappled with the question. Finally, he made up his mind. He couldn't destroy Israel, not again… at least, not yet. And he didn't see how he could train Elisha if the nation lay in ruins either. Elijah took the commandment and pushed it away, at least for right now.

That evening he ate with Elisha and his family, which constituted his parents along with two older brothers and a sister. His apprentice had slaughtered both his oxen for the meal. While Elijah had almost forgotten the last time he'd eaten, the first taste of cooked meat brought what felt like weeks' worth of hunger surging back, all at once. That evening he was a bottomless pit, although he tried to be polite about his ravenous appetite.

He also learned what had been going on in Israel since he'd been gone. He'd lost count of the days alone in the wilderness, but piecing things back together, he realized he'd been gone nearly forty days since meeting the strange messenger of God outside Beer-sheba.

The other encouraging bit of news was that, apparently, Jezebel had relented on killing him, at least for now. From what he could gather, the story of what had happened at the party had spread, until Ahab himself had been forced to rescind the order. There was no longer an axe hovering over his neck.

That night he went to sleep, flush with a good meal and very good news. The next morning he awoke to find Elisha already packed and eager-eyed. "So what are we doing?"

For once Elijah had a good answer. He'd spent the night thinking about where to start his new school, obviously nowhere near Ahab and preferably somewhere close to Judah where they could flee if the situation turned dire. On his travels he'd been to a spot near the west bank of the Jordan River, not far north of the recently rebuilt Jericho. It was quiet, out of the way, had plenty of water, and would make a good spot to start over.

Before that though, he needed to stop back at home, mostly to make sure Tobin had returned safely. From there, as much as he felt a distinct uneasiness in his chest, the next place on his list was Jezreel. If he wanted to do a school, he needed the scrolls of the law. The only way he knew to get those was to talk with Caleb and Naboth. Hopefully, they hadn't forgotten him completely.

He looked at Elisha, allowing himself a spark of cautious hope as he led his protégé outside. What were they doing? "Come on Elisha, we're going to save Israel."

Chapter 28
Sons of the Prophets

Years Later

Elijah guided in the heavy wooden roof beam, "Bring it down lower!"

Below, at the base of the house, one of his students led the mule serving as a counterweight a pace forward, and slowly the beam dropped down until it slotted into place.

Elijah stepped back, observing the work for a second with a grin. The house was coming together nicely, and when they finished they'd finally be able to house the new initiates who'd joined them the prior month. There had been a lot of grumbling about sharing space. Looking around, he couldn't help but marvel at how quickly it had all grown. He still remembered the first month here with Elisha, when two young men had shown up asking the simple question –We heard you were teaching about the Lord–

As he stepped down to help rig up the next roof crossbeam, he heard a familiar voice. "Master, they're here!"

Elisha came tearing across the open lawn set in the center of their little community, waving an arm to flag him down. "They're here!"

Elijah's heart skipped a beat at the words. There wasn't any need to explain who Elisha meant. In only a few seconds he scrambled down from his spot on the roof, grabbed his cloak and hurried to meet his young apprentice.

"Over by the road," Elisha pointed. "I saw them coming just now."

Elisha always surprised Elijah with his energy, but he was still quick to follow. Soon the two stood on a nearby hilltop, watching as a group of well-dressed men followed by several carts trundled closer. Even from a distance, Elijah could make out the familiar faces – Caleb, Josen and Naboth from Jezreel, Joel, Iscah and several others from Shiloh, Jared the Samarian and more. The people who helped support his school. Caleb had connections all across Israel and he'd done a magnificent job bringing them to bear, to help take a deserted piece of land near the river and transform it into a school for literally dozens of students. He'd gotten used to them stopping in whenever they passed by, listening to a few lessons or readings. There was only one reason they would all be here together though, one that sent a shiver of anticipation down his spine.

Hurrying down to meet them, he found Caleb in the lead, older than ever but still with an off-putting forwardness, "Elijah, my boy!"

Elijah tried not to wince at his handshake, firm enough to crush iron. "How have you been, Caleb?"

"Excellent," the man slapped him on the back, "and about to be better." He led Elijah back to the cart, where a tarp covered a long rectangular object. Everyone else crowded around as Caleb pulled back the sheet with a wide smile. "I presume you know what to do with this?"

Elijah stared at what lay there, and for a second, his breath caught in his throat. In the cart lay a decorative cloth sheath, sewn in ornate red and stitched with thread of gold. Wooden handles protruded from either end, the two ends of a scroll, and, on the protective cover was a single word, 'Deuteronomy.'

For the last several years they'd been working to procure a collection of the enormously expensive scrolls, Caleb rounding up money to have copies made. This one was an original though, the scroll he'd salvaged from the wreckage of his last school. They'd sent it to a man in Jerusalem to have the fire damaged sections replaced, but that had been months ago, and he'd pushed the excited anticipation to the back of his mind.

Seeing it restored to its full glory and so much more than charred hide, Elijah stared, not sure what to say.

Then he wept. Probably not the fanfare they'd expected, he tried to wipe back his tears. He'd just never expected to see it fixed and–

"Are you alright, Elijah?" he felt a hand on his shoulder and took a long breath to compose himself.

"I'm fine. Better than fine." He turned back to them all, brushing aside the tears that streaked his face, and reverently picking up the scroll. "Thank you."

A crowd of grinning faces looked back at him. Finally he glanced down at the precious package in his hand. "I suppose – I should probably read it, shouldn't I?"

"Probably," Naboth agreed, and with a nod he led them down into their little village.

Word spread impossibly fast in the school, probably Elisha's doing he realized, noticing his apprentice had somehow slipped away and was now making his way through the crowd. Regardless, by the time they'd arrived, most of the students were arrayed up on the grassy lawn, shooing off two munching goats mid-snack.

It took a bit longer to get everyone sat down to listen, but finally they did. After thanks to the men who'd made the scroll possible and prayers of thanksgiving to the Lord, Elijah opened the scroll and began to read, "These are the words Moses spoke to all Israel in the wilderness east of the Jordan…"

They didn't get through it very fast. The visitors had arrived mid-morning, and by lunch they weren't even through the first quarter. Just reading it straight through, Elijah recalled, the scroll would take several hours, and with a crowd full of questions, he expected it might be all day. And that was telling his students *not* to ask any questions out of respect for their guests, otherwise he suspected they'd be there for weeks.

After a quick break, Elijah continued, swapping out with Elisha and several of his older pupils at several points to save his voice. He was always good for the questions, though. Even missing a quarter of the scroll, he'd spent four years and a monumental amount of free time with Deuteronomy as his only reading material. Needless to say, he was well versed with most of it.

It was fun really, being surrounded by people who genuinely wanted to know more, and he was in his element explaining what he could, especially when they came to the part about God withholding rain as a punishment for idolatry. Everyone was particularly keen when they came to that bit.

He finished a little before sunset, raising his voice so the last words came clear as the fading day, "Since then, no prophet has risen in Israel like Moses, whom the Lord knew face to face, who did all those signs and wonders the Lord sent him to do in Egypt – to Pharaoh and to all his officials and to his whole land. For no one has ever shown the mighty power or performed the awesome deeds that Moses did in the sight of all Israel."

He lowered the scroll, and for a long moment there was quiet. At last one person began to clap, then more, spreading like wildfire until the whole green echoed in loud applause as he rolled up the fifth scroll of Moses.

With night falling he obviously couldn't send away their guests. Instead, several of the students prepared a simple but sizable supper: soup and bread, not exactly inspired, but it tasted excellent. Getting a bowl and a slice for himself, Elijah found Caleb and Naboth both sitting off to themselves discussing in quiet voices.

"You have space for one more?"

Caleb glanced up with a wide grin. "Of course, my boy, sit down," he moved over a pace. "That was excellent reading today. You know, before all this, I never knew Moses was such an interesting fellow." He paused, regarding Elijah with a wry grin, "You know, you're not so different from him yourself."

The comment caught Elijah utterly off guard, "I – what?"

"Moses," Caleb insisted in a boisterous voice, "You two aren't so different at all, except I suppose he's dead, that's a big difference."

"What do you mean?"

"Well, son," Caleb shook his head, half amused, "in case you haven't noticed, you've done some incredible miracles in the sight of Israel." The older man shrugged, "Just a thought."

Elijah wasn't really sure how to answer, so he filed it away for later, and changed the topic. "What's happening back in Jezreel?"

"Business, mostly," Caleb continued in his usual, excited semi-stream-of-consciousness ramble. "I believe the term to describe it is, *booming*. I just got back from Damascus myself, and let me tell you, there are some *fantastic* deals to be made there."

Elijah frowned. Damascus was a bit of a sore point at the school. Two years before, when the Arameans had invaded Israel, one of his fellows had gone to Ahab with a message of victory from the Lord. In the battles that followed, Ahab had twice destroyed powerful Aramean armies, but instead of finishing Aram, he'd freed their king, Ben-Hadad, and made a treaty with him.

Elijah had heard all the arguments. The Assyrians were on the rise in the north, striking closer every year, and Israel needed the Aramean alliance to survive. That rather missed the point, he thought with a sour taste in his mouth. If God had twice handed over Aram to Ahab's muddle of an army, He could do the same with the Assyrians. Besides, after their losses he wasn't entirely sure Aram-Damascus was set to be that helpful anyway.

During a pause when Caleb finally stopped to breathe, he glanced at Naboth. "And you?"

The man started and looked up, clearly distracted. "It's been fine," he said quickly. "Should be a good harvest."

"It'll be better than good," Caleb chimed in cheerfully. "I expect we'll be selling oil by the cartload to the Syrians now that we've whipped them. And rumor has it, there are problems down in Egypt too, low floods this year. If they can't send off their grain, the Tyrians will be coming to us for a change."

The evening passed pleasantly, with more than a few questions about the rest of Israel. Elijah had been busy at his school, training a group that had taken on the moniker, 'The Sons of the Prophets', and so he hadn't had much time to travel Israel, certainly not like he once had. He certainly felt like he was making a difference, though, at least with his students, and already they were spreading across Israel, making more differences in their own small ways.

Later, before they bedded down that night, Naboth came and found him again. "Elijah," he said, "I've been meaning to ask you something, from the scroll of Leviticus, about the jubilee. Why is it so important not to sell the land of your inheritance?"

The question was unexpected. "Well," Elijah fought back a yawn and had to think about the answer a moment, "I suppose there are a lot of reasons. In part so that no one gains so much land they can lord over everyone else. It ensures everyone, even the poor, have something. But I think the most important reason why is that it's God's land, we're just taking care of it, and that was the rule He made."

He was already tired and Naboth seemed to accept the answer, so Elijah didn't press further.

The next morning, after a festive breakfast, their visitors departed back to their various homes and businesses. That left Elijah with a still half-finished house to complete, and more lessons to teach. Elisha was getting knowledgeable enough that Elijah left him to work with some of the newest pupils. Over the next two weeks they settled into a routine, completing the newest addition to their school, and starting a long series of discussions and debates as the older students began looking at their newly refurbished scroll.

One morning, though, just as Elijah was crawling out of bed in his small room, he heard something strange. For an instant he was certain it was nothing, like an indistinct whisper that seemed to come from everywhere at once. Amid it all, however, he discerned a small voice, one that he recognized *very* well, "Elijah."

The prophet froze, stiff as a statue, then looked around, trying to find where the whisper was coming from. When he couldn't, he bowed and dropped to his knees. "Yes, Lord."

The voice answered soft but clear as Egyptian glass, "Go down to meet King Ahab of Israel, who rules in Samaria. He will be at Naboth's vineyard in Jezreel, claiming it for himself. Give him this message: 'This is what the Lord says: Wasn't it enough that you killed Naboth? Must you rob him, too? Because you have done this, dogs will lick your blood at the very place where they licked the blood of Naboth.'"

"Wait, what?" Elijah asked, "How is–" But the voice of the Lord was gone, leaving behind a swirl of question, with the chief one standing out like a beacon in the night, 'Naboth was dead? How?'

Before Elijah could settle his mind enough to think properly, a loud knock rung at the door along with Elisha's voice, "Master, there's a message for you with Caleb's seal."

Elijah swallowed and forced himself toward the door, where Elisha was waiting. Still in a daze, he barely spoke and took the folded papyrus. The message was simple, just a few words, but they hit hard, right to the chest. "Come to Jezreel. Quickly."

Elijah swallowed hard, not needing to guess the rest of the meaning.

Across from him, Elisha's early morning cheer had evaporated, replaced by confusion. "Is something wrong?"

Elijah's grip tightened around the message, anger in his eyes. "Yes, it is." He turned back to his room, "Get your things Elisha, we're going to Jezreel."

Chapter 29
The Vineyard

Jezreel
2 Days Later

Elijah," Caleb greeted him with a dark, grim expression at his home in Jezreel, "it's good you're here, I don't know how else to say it but–"

"Naboth's dead," Elijah interrupted. "I know."

Caleb's eyes widened in surprise.

"What happened?" Elijah asked.

The old merchant sighed, "You can see yourself." Caleb led him and Elisha into his plush house. Inside, the main room was dominated by low cushioned seats surrounding a knee-high table. Caleb found them a place to sit then vanished a moment. He returned clutching a sheet of papyrus, the boiling anger visible in his hard-set jaw.

"This," he slammed the note down on the table. "This, is what happened."

Elijah skimmed the letter, the first part was a set of perfunctory salutations, but it was a part halfway through that caught his attention. "Call the citizens together for a time of fasting, and give Naboth a place of honor. And then seat two scoundrels across from him who will accuse him of cursing God and the king. Then take him out and stone him to death."

He stared at the letter for a moment, eyes coming to rest on

222

the king's seal at the bottom.

Stalking the room behind him, Caleb was almost spitting fire. "You would not *believe* the trouble I had to go through to get someone to hand that over," he snarled. "And you know the most interesting part, when they dragged Naboth outside the city and left his body without even a proper burial, you'll never guess who they reported back to."

Elijah could have guessed right on his first try, but Caleb didn't give him the chance. "Queen Jezebel herself. That *witch* orchestrated all this. Murdered him, all for a spit of land."

Behind him Elisha spoke up, "I don't understand, what does Naboth's vineyard have to do with all of this?"

Caleb shot Elisha a confused side-glance, "You two already spoke to someone about this?"

Elijah waved off the question and didn't get into details. He'd mentioned the Lord's message to his protégé on the trip there.

Caleb didn't wait for an answer. "The king came and spoke with Naboth several weeks back," he explained. "I talked to his widow, Annalei and the short of it is, Ahab wanted Naboth's vineyard near the palace as a vegetable garden. Apparently he offered a better one in exchange, but Naboth refused, and said it wasn't right before God for him to give away his ancestors land." Caleb shook his head, "I knew the king could be vindictive but not like this. We have to…"

He kept talking but Elijah wasn't listening. He felt like a brick had abruptly dropped in his stomach at the story. Suddenly Naboth's reserve a few weeks earlier and his questions about the jubilee made more sense. He'd been wondering if he'd done the right thing, telling the king no.

The prophet closed his eyes for a heartbeat before looking over to his apprentice. "Elisha, stay here with Caleb. I'm going to speak to Ahab."

The merchant frowned, "I'm not sure he'll let you into the palace, not after–"

Elijah raised a hand to cut him off. "I know where to find him." Then, without more words, he turned and vanished outside on the streets of Jezreel.

He knew the way to the vineyard in question, a small walled enclosure near the summit of the hill where Ahab's palace stood. He hadn't let it out at Caleb's, but every step closer he felt his anger boiling at the injustice of it all. A devout man being accused of cursing God, of all things. It would have been laughable if it wasn't so sickening. Even worse, he couldn't escape the sinking feeling that it said something truly nasty about Israel that everyone had followed those grim orders. It wasn't just Jezebel, they'd all known it was murder and gone along with it anyway. Jezebel, he almost expected this from, but not the rest of his people.

When he finally reached the vineyard, he heard a soft humming inside. Stepping around the corner, he saw Ahab with his back to the entrance, cheerfully eating the ripe grapes off a vine one by one.

The sight of the king so indifferent finally set off his pent up anger. "Ahab!" he stepped into the open and walked towards the king.

Ahab spun around, his good humor instantly evaporating. For a moment he stared, his face souring, "So you have found me, my enemy!"

Somehow, the gall of the king riled up Elijah even more. He ought to be begging for forgiveness, but instead he was standing there, smug and sullen.

"I have found you," Elijah answered, "because you have sold yourself to do evil in the eyes of the Lord. He says, 'I am going to bring disaster on you. I will wipe out your descendants and cut off from Ahab every last male in Israel–slave or free. I will make your house like that of Jeroboam son of Nebat and that of Baasha son of Ahijah, because you have aroused my anger and have caused Israel to sin.' And also concerning Jezebel the Lord says: 'Dogs will devour Jezebel by the wall of Jezreel.' Dogs will eat those belonging to Ahab who die in the city, and the birds will feed on those who die in the country."

Ahab opened his mouth to answer, but struggled to force out the words. "I didn't kill Naboth," he finally said.

"No," Elijah spat back, "your wife did, you're just the one benefiting. Just like when she decided to get rid of me, actually.”

“Now hold on,” Ahab fought back, “I stopped her.”

“A few weeks late,” Elijah shook his head. “And for someone who disagrees with his wife murdering people, you sure looked like you were enjoying yourself just now. Maybe if she’s so nasty you shouldn’t have married her and stuck her on the throne of Israel in the first place.”

“You think I had a choice?” Ahab snapped, angry. “Neither of us did, I was *told*, and that was the end of it!”

“That doesn’t excuse any of this.” Elijah’s eyes narrowed like his gaze could slice iron. “I hope the vineyard was worth it, Ahab.”

Elijah turned and stalked away.

For a long while, Ahab stood there in stunned silence. Eventually, he glanced back at the cluster of ripe little grapes, but this time just looking at them left a taste like bile in his mouth. Finally, with a chill in his chest, Ahab turned and headed back to the palace side entrance down the street.

“Dearest, what’s wrong?” He bumped into Jezebel in the ivory hall, a long corridor, the walls inlaid with intricate pearly white carvings.

“Nothing,” he muttered.

Jezebel gave a stubborn frown and folded her arms, “You’re pale as a sheet, it’s not *nothing*.”

Ahab sighed, “I just met Elijah… or he found me, down at the vineyard.”

At the name his wife’s face twisted like she’d just swallowed something particularly nasty. “That false prophet again, what did he–”

“He’s not a *false prophet*,” Ahab interrupted.

Jezebel tensed at his words; this would make nearly a dozen times they’d fought over that particular point in the last several years. As much as Jezebel claimed he’d been tricked, Ahab knew what he’d seen on Mount Carmel. That made Elijah’s doom-saying all the more terrifying.

“Well, what did he want this time?”

“He was upset, about Naboth,” Ahab paused a pregnant

instant, "Elijah said you killed him?"

An irate sneer darted across Jezebel's face. "You know the charges, dearest. Naboth cursed you and–"

"Don't!" Ahab's voice rose in anger to cut her off, pointing an accusatory finger, "Don't lie to me Jezebel."

His wife took a half step back at the outburst. "Yes, okay," she finally admitted, "I had him killed."

"Why?" Ahab's anger boiled over.

Undaunted, Jezebel walked closer, laying a gentle hand on his waist, fixing him with her dark brown eyes. "Dearest," she said quietly, "I did it for you."

The words sunk like a dagger in his chest. "What do you mean?"

Jezebel leaned her delicate frame up on his arm. "You were so upset after Naboth said no. So I fixed it." Confusion and hurt flickered in her eyes, "I thought that would make you happy. I assumed you knew."

He… he had known, in a way. That was how Jezebel dealt with everything, wasn't it, more blood. He met her eyes again and something else leapt out at him; she didn't see anything wrong. There wasn't remorse, just confusion, like she'd tried her best to love him and couldn't fathom why he was angry. That was probably how they did things back in Sidon. Murder was how her father had come to power, he knew that much.

"It doesn't make me happy," he said, "not at all."

"Why? Because Elijah said a few words and–"

"Yes, *actually*," Ahab said. "That's a big part of it."

"Well what would?" Jezebel demanded, anger in her voice and mist in her eyes. "What *would* make you happy, Ahab? I assure you I've tried to help just about every way I know."

"And it's consistently made things worse." Ahab threw right back. "Your insisting on worshiping Ba'al nearly bankrupted the kingdom, your deciding to let Elijah go when we had him, this killing Naboth–"

Jezebel's voice rose, "And you agreed!" She jabbed him in the chest with her finger, "You agreed, Ahab, with all of it."

The words stung enough to give him pause.

For a moment he said nothing, and when he did speak his

voice was subdued, "I didn't say no…" he sighed, "and I guess I should have… a long time ago."

Jezebel wiped at her eyes, brushing away a frustrated tear that threatened her makeup, "Ahab, I did what I thought was best for Israel, surely you see that."

"I know," he nodded, understanding, maybe for the first time. "Jezebel, I know in Tyre things are complicated, but I didn't marry you expecting you to fight my battles. I never wanted a spymaster. I just wanted you to be my wife." He shook his head. "I'm sorry I didn't make that clear before. But please stop, with the schemes… all of it. It's already caused enough problems."

For maybe the first time, Jezebel didn't have anything to say. Ahab shook his head and turned to go. "I think we're in trouble."

Chapter 30
The Reckoning

Elijah returned from Naboth's tomb, still angry. They hadn't done much. Caleb had already seen to preparing the body the prior day, so they'd simply said a few words before laying the wrapped body on a burial table inside the family cave and rolling a stone across the stooped entrance. They'd be back in a year to remove the bones and place them in an ossuary, but for the moment there was nothing left to do.

He'd spoken briefly to Naboth's distraught wife, Annalei, but hadn't really known what to say, besides that he was truly sorry her husband was gone. There wasn't much else he could do, and in the end he was left with a sickness in his stomach.

Walking alone, he was just at the door to Caleb's house when a voice rang out in the street, "Elijah, wait!"

He glanced over to see a familiar face weaving through the loose crowd towards him, "Obadiah?"

"I heard you were in town." The steward hurried up, and greeted him firmly. "I was afraid I'd miss you."

Elijah might not have respected Ahab, or Jezebel, but he knew Obadiah was a man who feared God, and had little to do with some of the nastier palace doings. "It's good to see you again. Why are you here?"

"Well, I'd prefer to say it's just to see the Prophet of the Lord," Obadiah smiled, but then turned more serious. "Unfortunately, it's not entirely that." He nodded at the door,

"Could we speak inside?"

The others had lingered longer at the burial and Elijah was the first back so he led Obadiah into Caleb's house and the two found an out of the way spot in the sitting room. "I wanted to say I'm sorry about Naboth." Obadiah paused a second before continuing, "That said, I'm actually here on the king's behalf."

"I didn't think he and I had much left to discuss," Elijah's jaw tightened. "I made myself pretty clear."

"Ahab didn't tell me what you said to him," Obadiah admitted. "Whatever it was, though, it certainly made an impact."

"What do you mean?"

"I know you haven't been up to the palace, but he's in mourning over what happened."

"He is?"

Obadiah nodded, "When I left him, he was in sackcloth and was fasting for the next two days. He actually came to me asking where he could find you. I suggested it might be better if I went on his behalf, but he wanted me to say he truly was sorry about what happened."

Elijah was still having a hard time believing that Ahab could be repentant after everything he'd done. "Is he serious?"

Obadiah shrugged, "I suppose only God knows the heart, but I think so, yes."

There was a clatter from the front of the house as the door opened and he heard his friends returning. Obadiah stood, "I should probably go." He sighed, "It's good to see you, Elijah, I'm sorry it had to be under these circumstances."

He left as everyone else filed in. "Who was that?" Elisha probed.

"Obadiah, the king's steward." Elijah said, still not sure what to make of the news about Ahab. "He's an old friend."

With Naboth buried, there was the brief, but customary meal to be had, just bread and some wine, and once they finished, Elijah retired to the guestroom for a moment alone.

He was still trying to decide what to make of Ahab's sudden change of heart. Frankly, he felt like Ahab was more desperate than remorseful, but still, even that was surprising.

He was busy thinking when a flash of light caught the corner of his eye. He looked over to where a polished, silver-plate mirror stood on a low chest. The piece looked fantastically expensive with decorative engravings and jewels studding the outer rim, but what drew Elijah's eyes was the center, it was… glowing?

The next morning he and Elisha left Jezreel, beginning the long hike back to their school. It took until midmorning following the road up a sloping valley before Elisha finally got up the courage to ask him what was wrong. At first Elijah didn't answer besides to keep walking, his face locked in a permanent scowl.

It wasn't until they reached the crest of the hill and found themselves looking down at yet another green carpeted vale that he finally answered, "The Lord spoke to me last night. In my room."

His assistant instantly perked up at the announcement. "Well, that's good news… isn't it?"

"Depends," Elijah sighed. Normally he would have shared the Lord's declaration with his assistant, part of training him to recognize the voice of God. This time though, he had to fight the urge to keep it to himself.

The two followed the narrow dirt path all the way down to the valley floor before Elijah continued, "He's not going to punish Ahab."

"Huh?" Elisha glanced up like he'd been mulling over something else.

"God," Elijah explained, "He's…" He couldn't think of a good way to put it and just ended up repeating what he'd been told, "Have you noticed how Ahab has humbled himself before me? Because he has humbled himself, I will not bring this disaster in his day, but I will bring it on his house in the days of his son."

"So Ahab won't be overthrown?" Elisha asked. "But his son will, the judgement is postponed?"

"Certainly seems that way," Elijah said bitterly.

Elisha shot him a wary side glance, "And that's bad?"

The question left Elijah on very shaky ground. Was God's judgement bad? "You saw what Ahab did to an innocent person," he finally answered, frustrated.

Elisha wisely didn't push the issue. That evening they found a small family to take them in near Tirzah, a kind young couple with a small house and a single baby daughter. Apparently they'd both seen him when they were teens on Mount Carmel, and were ecstatic to have the famous prophet under their roof. They were about the same age as Elisha and the three found a never-ending stream of young person things to discuss.

With his mood already foul, Elijah found the strain of politeness grating on him. After an excellent dinner with a main course of quail and vegetable stew and dates for dessert, he found an opening to excuse himself.

Set out in the country, the small home had an olive orchard around back, and Elijah found himself wandering the gnarled trees. He couldn't help but note little details he'd learned working in his family's orchard, dead branches that needed to be trimmed or a tree that should have been pruned a bit more in winter. Unlike the trees at his home that dated back to his grandfather though, these were old... very old. Near the back stood one, a twisted mass of thick woody bark, a foot and a half wide with branches that fanned out at head height. He'd never been the best at guessing a tree's age, but this one could easily have already been old when Joshua had come through.

Back then, God had gifted His people with orchards they hadn't planted and vineyards they hadn't pruned. And here it was, one of those original gifts from God, sitting in plain sight, even as Israel forgot. The same question that had plagued the prophet all day found a way to the front of his thoughts.

Why had God spared Ahab?

It made no sense. If anyone deserved justice, it was the king who had ruined Israel with his idols and stubbornness, and yet, at the very last, God had pulled back His hand.

Elijah stared up at the rising crescent moon and twinkling stars in the night sky, and asked a simple question, "Why, God?"

For an instant, he almost expected to hear a voice thundering back, an explanation, *something*. All he received was a deafening silence. Folding his arms, Elijah's eyes drifted back to the ancient olive tree. It didn't make sense, he'd said what he was supposed to, and yet the Lord had…

A sudden thought gave him pause, *had he* said what he'd been supposed to?

Elijah's mind drifted back to the Lord's original pronouncement days earlier, *This is what the Lord says: Have you murdered and also taken possession?' Then tell him, 'This is what the Lord says: In the place where the dogs licked Naboth's blood, the dogs will also lick your blood!*

The more he considered it the less that sounded at all like what he'd said. He had talked about Ahab's sons being killed and dogs eating Jezebel, things largely unrelated to the original point.

Then a second possibility stung him like a brick flung at his back. What if Ahab had repented… because of him? He tried to shove the thought away. But as much as he didn't want it to, the notion made a great deal of sense. The original pronouncement was grim, but probably wouldn't have been particularly surprising to the king. It might not have elicited much of a reaction at all to know God was still upset with him. Instead though, he'd laid into Ahab in graphic detail… and so the king had repented; the exact thing Elijah hadn't wanted.

That was bad enough, but then another reminder slammed like a bell. Two words – Jehu and Hazael. The men he'd been supposed to anoint as kings of Israel and Aram. Elijah hadn't thought of them in ages, but suddenly the names froze in his mind.

What if he had anointed them? Ahab had fought two battles with Aram, and won them both, but what if Ben-Hadad hadn't been king of Aram, would Ahab have triumphed then? And if he hadn't, would he still be king, or would Jehu have deposed him by now? If so, would Naboth still be alive?

Elijah had told himself he couldn't bear to ruin Israel

again by deposing Ahab, but had he really saved it at all? Certainly he had gathered some followers of the Lord, but no more than God had said there already were, and he'd just seen the people of Jezreel stone an innocent man because the queen demanded it. He hadn't really saved anything, and he wasn't enough of a fool to think God's justice wasn't still coming. All he'd done was possibly leave a good man and a friend to die, for trying to do the right thing.

The sudden weight of it all pressed down on him like a rockslide. Dizzy, he laid a hand on the ancient olive tree to steady himself. He'd been so furious with Ahab for leading Israel astray, for destroying the work he'd tried to do, for killing an innocent man, and with God for delaying well deserved justice. But suddenly Elijah couldn't escape the possibility that it was his fault too.

"Master!" Elisha's voice echoed in the night and he looked back to see his apprentice running towards him through the trees. "Master, are you okay?"

Elijah was struggling to catch his breath, but he waved off his protégé, "I'm alright, I just–" Whatever words he'd meant to say died halfway out of his mouth.

"Master, what's wrong?" Elisha demanded, "You've been different all day. What is it?"

Elijah steadied himself and slid down to sitting at the base of the fig tree. He liked to think he wasn't *that* old, but he wasn't that young anymore, either.

"Elisha, I think I've made a terrible mistake."

He caught confusion on his apprentice's face, "Master, what are you talking about?"

"Why does God raise up prophets. Elisha?"

His apprentice knew the answer well enough. They'd read it in the scroll of Deuteronomy only a few weeks before, "To speak the words of the Lord," he answered simply enough, "to speak the truth to the people of Israel."

"And if the prophet doesn't?"

Elisha frowned, "Master, what are you saying?"

Elijah stared at the ground, "What happens to words, Elisha?" he asked. "Those spoken by a prophet in the name of

God but not from Him? Does it make one no longer a prophet, or does God make the words true simply because a prophet spoke them?"

"I don't understand."

Elijah rephrased it to a simpler question, "Am I a prophet *because* I speak the words of the Lord, or am I prophet, and *therefore* I speak the words of the Lord even when I try not to?"

Elisha tapped at his fingers for a moment before finally answering, "I don't know, but I would not be following you if I did not believe you were a prophet, master. I do not think that mantle is so easily given or taken away."

For a long while neither spoke. The only sound was the far off hooting of an owl. Finally, Elijah continued, quietly telling his apprentice what he had spoken to Ahab in the vineyard. When he finished, he fixed Elisha with a long stare, "There's something else, two men who should be king, but aren't. Because of me."

It took some time, recounting the story of his journey to the mountain of God, the impossible storm that had swept by him in the cave, God's strange question for him and, the command to anoint the two men king. When Elijah finished, his apprentice bit at his lip but nodded, seeming to understand why he'd been so hesitant to follow the Lord's last command.

"I'm sorry," Elijah said, "I didn't intend to leave all this to you. I thought at some point I would deal with it, but instead the moment came and went. Now I have the sense that it's passed me by completely."

For a moment Elisha said nothing. "I think I understand," he finally said. Elisha stood, not so much angry as thoughtful, like he needed time to really grasp what Elijah was telling him, "Do you mind if I…?"

Elijah waved him off, "Go ahead, I'll be back inside when I'm ready."

Elisha took a few steps to leave, but paused and glanced back, "Master, if I may, there's one thing I don't understand. When you encountered the Lord at Mount Horeb, what did He mean when he asked what you were doing there?"

Elijah shrugged, "I never figured it out. I assume He was

asking why I'd left Israel," he sighed, "asking why I... ran away."

"But you said yourself the Lord sent an angel to find you in the desert, so you could make the journey. And when God spoke, he asked you twice, even though you told him why you'd left." Elisha tapped his fingers together a moment before seeming to let the issue drop, "I guess it just doesn't quite make sense, that's all."

Elisha turned and headed back to the house, leaving Elijah to struggle with his own questions. Eventually he went back inside to sleep, but the next morning when they rose to finish the trip back to the school, he was still puzzling over Elisha's last question. Of all the things God had spoken to him over the years, he would say he understood most, except for God's strange double question on Mount Horeb. So what did it mean?

While the young woman prepared a simple breakfast, Elijah found himself chatting with the man of the house, a fellow named Efran. They found common ground on a topic close to both of their hearts, olives. The man was eager to talk about his orchard, the various ways he knew to fertilize the ground, how he grazed sheep between the trees to keep the grass low, the light pruning method that he claimed helped his trees' vigor.

Soon the conversation drifted to other topics, news from other parts of Israel, and eventually it circled back to the miracle of calling down fire from heaven. Efran had been a youth at the time, and apparently it had made quite an impression.

"If it's not too bold to ask, sir," Efran said, "after the miracle from the Lord on Mount Carmel, I thought... I thought things were going to change. Instead, you vanished and after a few years the priests of Ba'al returned. I've seen a few other people proclaiming the Lord but... everyone remembers *you*, sir."

It wasn't really phrased as a question and Elijah didn't offer an answer. A moment later Elisha appeared downstairs in a famous good mood, having taken the opportunity to sleep in.

As the two departed and began the long day's hike back to their school, Elijah found himself with a great deal of time and little to do but think.

God's strange question from long ago circled round and round in his head, and Elijah tried to transport himself back to that moment on the Mount Horeb to understand. He tried to remember, he'd been angry, confused, despondent, cheated...

The last gave him pause. Why had he felt cheated?

He vividly remembered the feeling, but he also couldn't recall being promised anything particular. And yet he felt like he had. Even now, years later, he could define it in almost crystal clarity. He'd served God faithfully for years, he'd followed some truly strange orders, he'd trusted the Lord, he'd been brave when God asked... and he'd expected at the end of it all that he would have earned Israel back for the Lord. Except he hadn't; so for a while he'd been upset, then he'd tried something different with his school, but still Israel prostituted themselves with Ba'al. He worked, and nothing changed, and he felt very cheated.

What are you doing here, Elijah?

Suddenly the words snapped into focus. God wasn't asking him why he'd wandered out to a mountain in the middle of nowhere. The question was, simply, what was his purpose in the world, and if the answer was to serve God, why did he feel cheated, that he'd never received something God had never promised in the first place?

He'd been working for years to try and rescue Israel, and yet he already suspected that wasn't going to happen. Naboth's death had put that reality onto stark display.

So what did he do?

Quit? That didn't seem the best answer. He still believed he had a purpose, but as for how – he found himself struggling to piece together a plan. Eventually he glanced over at his apprentice, wandering along three steps ahead, oblivious.

"Elisha," he took a stab in the dark, "where should a prophet be?"

The young man seemed to think it was a quiz of sorts, "Well, a prophet is supposed to speak the words of the Lord to the people, so I'd say he should be near to the Lord but also near to the people."

Elijah couldn't suppress a grin, the kid was pretty sharp. "Good answer," he said. "When we get back, I'd like you to pack your things. I'll speak with some of the older prophets about continuing the student's discussions, and we'll leave either tomorrow or the next day and do what you said."

Elisha continued walking with a nodded "Uh-huh," then abruptly ground to a halt mid-step, "Wait, what?"

Chapter 31
The Angel of the Lord

Several Years Later

"Good morning, Elijah."

Camped on the grass beneath a young oak tree with only a fur cloak for a blanket, Elijah's eyes cracked open at the unfamiliar voice. Then he abruptly panicked when he found a man standing over him, tall but youthful, wearing a bronze breastplate that glowed like the stars and a golden-hilted sword strapped at his waist.

Elijah bolted upright in shock, with a speed that did him credit for his age. "What…?"

He glanced over to see his apprentice, recently balding and in his late twenties. Wrapped in his cloak, Elisha was sitting by their small fire a few paces away, watching the whole scene in nervous excitement and nibbling on a strange, palm sized red fruit that he kept dipping in a slow bubbling pot of goo that looked uncomfortably similar to boat tar.

"Elisha," his voice lowered in worry, "do we need to have a talk about what 'keeping watch' means?"

Elisha shrugged, eyeing the man's gleaming sword hilt. "He said he was an old friend. I didn't think to argue the point. And he brought breakfast, you should try it." He took another bite of the small red fruit, "I don't even know what these are, but they are *amazing*."

It took a second for Elijah to look past the newcomers' burnished breastplate and gleaming greaves. When he did, though, the man's face did seem familiar, kind of like–

"Cooking is a lost art," Elijah suddenly guessed. "Right?"

The man gave a polite nod, "It's been a long time, Elijah. It's good to see you again."

"You, too." Some of the prophet's hesitance faded, his eyes lingering on the man's armor, polished like glass, but inlaid with silver and fine cut gems. Each gem glowed softly, like it held a little star within. Elijah wasn't typically one given to calculating values, but he had the feeling that he could probably purchase the Kingdom of Israel with the breastplate alone. "So, is this what you normally wear? At least when you're not wandering the desert cooking for people napping under broom trees?"

"Not always." The fellow gestured to the food he'd laid out, "Breakfast?"

In the short time he'd been awake Elijah had already caught the exotic scents of the man's unique food. Years later he still vividly remembered the truly incredible meals the man had made for him out in the Negev Desert.

Near the fire sat a loaf of savory scented bread and a bowl of strange bright red berries about the size to fit in his palm, while over the coals stood a small pot of slow boiling brownish goop. It looked disgusting, but as he watched, Elisha grabbed one of the berries by the ring of green leaves sprouting like a crown around its top. Dipping it in like a malformed spoon, Elisha scooped out as much of the thick liquid as he could and promptly shoveled it into his mouth.

Elisha glanced eagerly across to the newcomer who'd moved over to sit with them, his armor strangely silent when he moved. "How did you make this?"

The man shook his head, "Unfortunately, I don't think you'll be able to find the right ingredients. The berries are from northern Gaul and the stuff in the pot is from a place far over the horizon."

Getting over his revulsion at eating something that should have been slathered on the side of a ship, Elijah gave the berries and brown liquid a tepid try. He didn't regret it; the stuff in the pot was like earthy honey in his mouth and the berry was crisp and tart. It instantly set his stomach to gurgling and it wasn't until a few minutes later that Elijah paused to glance up at the man, "This is incredible, but am I right assuming you didn't just show up as a wandering purveyor of exquisite foods?"

"You would be correct," the man nodded. "Are you familiar with what has happened to the king?"

'The king', in this case, was Ahab's eldest son Ahaziah. Ahab himself had been killed a year and a half before. As best as Elijah understood it, following Ahab's twin victories over Ben-Hadad of Aram, the kings had fallen into an uneasy alliance and jointly moved north to ward off a major Assyrian invasion. The two forces had clashed at a place called Qarqar where the alliance had emerged victorious. Soon afterwards, Ahab had turned on his erstwhile ally and attacked Ramoth-Gilead, backed by King Jehoshaphat of Judah. Ahab's luck had finally run out, though, and he'd been killed by a rogue arrow in the battle, leaving the forces of Israel scattered in defeat.

One reverse followed another. Moab had taken the opportunity of Israel's weakness to cease their tribute and raise the flag of revolt, leaving Ahaziah scrambling to hold together his father's collapsing kingdom.

That was all Elijah knew, "Did something happen to Ahaziah?"

"He fell," the man in gleaming armor explained. "Several days ago a latticed window at the palace gave way and Ahaziah suffered a nasty fall. Since then his condition has worsened. As we speak he's summoning messengers to send to Philistia to inquire if he will recover."

"No surprise there," Elisha muttered.

The attempted humor earned him a withering, be serious, glare from Elijah, and a moment later Elisha gave a muttered, "Sorry."

"So," Elijah focused back on the angel of the Lord, "what about all that brings you here to us?"

The man stood, his voice and expression becoming grave, "I come bearing a message from The Lord of Hosts, He speaks thus: Go and meet the messengers of the king of Samaria and ask them, 'Is it because there is no God in Israel that you are going to inquire of Ba'al-zebub, the god of Ekron?' Therefore, this is what the Lord says: 'You will not get up from your sickbed–you will certainly die.'"

The message itself was gloomy, but even so Elijah's heart did a little somersault in his chest at the words. Ever since Naboth's death, he hadn't heard from the Lord. He and Elisha had mostly been traveling Israel, telling of God, but in the back of his head there had always been a niggling doubt, wondering if God had disowned him after his mistakes. Suddenly though, here it was, a very important assignment from the Lord Himself, unmistakable proof that he was still a prophet.

Despite the grim judgement on Ahaziah, Elijah couldn't hold back a wide grin. God still trusted him, and this time he wouldn't let the Lord of Heaven down.

He met the angel's gaze and gave an earnest nod, "Understood." He even repeated it a few times to make sure he had the exact wording down.

They were camped on a hill overlooking the main road south from Samaria. At a normal walk they were about an hour outside the city, but if the king's messengers moved with haste and took horses then they wouldn't be very long getting here.

"Come on Elisha," Elijah tightened his belt and donned his heavy cloak. "Let's get down to the road."

A few minutes later, the two stood in the middle of the otherwise empty road, "You have some very strange friends, master," Elisha commented, his gaze drifting back to the angel still atop the hill. He'd drawn his sword, a powerful, two-handed weapon made of a honed metal like liquid fire, and stood casually holding it at his side.

Ahead came a pounding of hooves, and a moment later, three riders crested a low ridge and came into view, moving at a quick canter. As they came close, one called out, "Make way for the riders of the King!"

Elisha shot him a worried side glance but Elijah didn't budge. Instead, he waited until they trotted even closer before answering, "Halt! In the name of the Lord God of Israel!"

He half worried they might just gallop on by, but instead the riders pulled their mounts to a sharp halt, a surprising fear in their eyes.

The lead rider stared at something behind him for an instant, before walking his roan mount up to Elijah, "Who are you? What do you want?"

"I have a message for King Ahaziah. Thus says the Lord, 'Is it because there is no God in Israel that you are going to inquire of Ba'al-zebub, the god of Ekron?' Therefore, this is what the Lord says: 'You will not get up from your sickbed–you will certainly die.'"

The rider hesitated, like he wasn't sure what to make of such an abrupt end to his mission. Eventually though, he swallowed and gave a curt, "Very well."

They wheeled and galloped off, and it was only when Elijah turned that he saw the angel had moved down the hill to a spot about ten feet behind them, his terrifying sword held across his chest with tiny tongues of fire licking along the blade. His armor glowed brighter now, like a beacon at dawn. Suddenly, it wasn't so much of a mystery why the riders had stopped.

Meanwhile, Elisha was all smiles, "That was easy."

Elijah wasn't so sure it was. The angel was still here, and in his experience, God and His messengers didn't hang around for long after the message was delivered. As Elijah walked over to the angel, the radiant armor diminished back to a soft glow, "Thank you," Elijah said.

"Of course." The angel inclined his blade back to the hilltop, "We should retire for the moment. The king's men will return."

A few paces away young Elisha anxiously tapped his fingers, "Shouldn't we *not* be here when that happens?"

"Nonsense," the angel spoke cheerfully, "you still have to deliver the Lord's edict to the king."

The color drained from his apprentice's face at the announcement and even Elijah felt a twinge of worry. Talking to the king was the absolute *last* place in Israel he wanted to be. He would probably get a better reception from Ben-Hadad in Damascus. Not only was bad news never the best thing to deliver, but in even his short reign Ahaziah had made it abundantly clear which god he trusted.

Plus, there was still Jezebel. He doubted she would take the news her son was going to die very well. When he'd been alive Ahab had held her at bay, but Elijah was fairly certain the Queen Mother still despised him, and with Ahab gone…

The king's men returned sooner rather than later, a full company wearing the ivory armbands of Ahaziah's personal retinue. Cresting the ridge, they cut straight as the raven flew towards the hilltop, only halting at the base.

The angel, who had sheathed his gleaming blade, drew it, the metal making a ring like music. Down at the foot of the hill, the soldiers formed in a tight squadron, spears lowered, ready for a fight.

Sitting under the oak at the top of the hill, Elijah waited. A part of him wanted to get up and start pacing, but he forced himself to keep calm. A moment later, a man wearing the double striped armband of a captain stepped forward and hiked up near the summit. He stopped a few paces away, spear in hand, his whole body tensed, "Man of God, the king declares, 'Come down!'"

Elijah glanced at the angel, sword held at a low guard, who merely shook his head no.

"And if I refuse?" He could guess the answer. Nobody sent a whole platoon to politely invite a guest back home.

The man's eyes lingered on the angel a moment, sizing him up. Finally he turned back to Elijah, "That would be a mistake."

Elijah gave a slow, understanding nod, so it was going to be like that. "Very well, then." He spoke loud enough for them all to hear his warning, "If I am a man of God, may fire come down from heaven and consume you and your 50 men."

That pretty much ended the discussion. The captain briefly glanced toward heaven but seeing nothing, he hurried back down the hill and rejoined his company, snapping out commands. As the three watched, the guards advanced in close formation, shields high and spears poised.

Then a flash like a second sun echoed in the sky above. A

beam of silver fire lanced down from on high, striking at the center of their spear wall with a roar that shook the ground and a force like a falling star. He looked away from the blinding blaze as the fire swept outwards, a swirling inferno. When the storm of white flames faded, they left behind a perfectly circular ring of charred grass and no one still alive.

That wasn't the end, though. From the ridge Elijah saw observers disappear back towards the city, and, soon enough, another company appeared from Samaria. This captain paused his men at the base of the hill, and glanced over at the circle of destruction before stepping forward, "Man of God, this is what the king says: 'Come down immediately!'"

The angel shook his head again and Elijah gave the same warning as before, "If I am a man of God, may fire come down from heaven and consume you and your 50 men."

That didn't seem to daunt the captain though, who ordered his men forward, straight into a cyclone of pulsing fire.

Elijah would have thought after that Ahaziah would have given up but the king seemed particularly wasteful of his men's lives that day for soon a third group appeared. This time, though, the commander halted his men some distance from the base of the hill, left his weapon and came alone to the summit.

When he drew close he fell on his knees before them, "O man of God, please spare my life and the lives of these, your fifty servants. See how the fire from heaven came down and destroyed the first two groups. But now please spare my life!"

Finally the angel gave a small nod, "Go down with him, and don't be afraid of him."

The captain stood to his feet, wild relief sweeping across his face and he led Elijah and Elisha down the hill. Glancing back Elijah saw the angel had abruptly vanished, but given the respect with which the captain treated them, Elijah figured they were in good hands.

The trip back to Samaria was short, and in less than an hour the captain had escorted them to the king's chamber. Inside they found Ahaziah, pale and feverish in his bed, with a doctor helping him choke down a bowl of nasty looking medicine. In the corner another young man, who could only be his younger brother Joram, sat on a low couch, while Jezebel stalked the room near her son's bed.

Elijah hadn't seen her in years, but the queen mother had certainly aged from the almost intoxicating beauty he remembered. She'd lost none of her deft poise, though. Straight backed and fiery-eyed, she seemed even more regal now that Ahab had passed.

She glanced up with poison in her gaze when Elijah entered. Her hand danced beneath her robes and Elijah caught a jeweled dagger beneath lustrous silk.

Jezebel moved towards them, but the captain intercepted her, "My queen, no," he pleaded. "Don't."

Jezebel paused, half surprised anyone would dare contradict her, but she stepped back a pace when the captain's spear-point lowered just a hair.

Coughing, Ahaziah propped himself up in bed so he could see Elijah, "If you have something to say prophet, I'd like to hear it directly."

It was only then Elijah realized what the king had been playing at. Ahaziah had heard the prophecy from his messengers. He knew exactly what the Lord's judgement was, but he *desperately* wanted Elijah to take it back.

That was why the king had wasted men he could ill afford to lose with a rebellion happening, just to apprehend a single prophet and his apprentice. Ahaziah had thought if he could haul them in here with spearpoints tickling their necks, then maybe Elijah would say something different, something nicer. Instead though, he'd walked into the king's chambers with his own personal guard.

Elijah spoke the prophecy one last time, "Thus says the Lord, 'Is it because there is no God in Israel that you are going to inquire of Ba'al-zebub, the god of Ekron?' Therefore, this is what the Lord says: 'You will not get up from your sickbed–you will certainly die.'"

He caught the dark scowl on Ahaziah's face, but there was nothing the king could do now. The words were out and Elijah couldn't take them back. Right then, the king collapsed into a coughing fit and, before he could recover, Elijah nodded Elisha

towards the exit. With the captain and the king's guard
protecting them, they departed Samaria.

Chapter 32
Chariots of Fire

Elijah liked to imagine Jericho must have looked much like this when Joshua had first destroyed it. Tall, thick walls built of adobe brick towered twice as high as him and an imposing gatehouse barred the way inside. Fortunately, it was open, and a steady stream of people, carts, and animals pushed their way in and out under the watchful eye of the gate guards and the sweltering midday sun.

Normally they might have gone inside, but he had more important places to be today. "Elisha," he gestured his apprentice over, "Stay here, for the Lord has told me to go to the Jordan River."

The young man vehemently shook his head though, "As surely as the Lord lives and you yourself live, I will never leave you."

Elijah couldn't suppress a grin at the answer, apparently he'd trained Elisha well, well enough to know what was going on. "Very well, then. So be it."

Together the two set off across the plain of Jericho, a mostly dry place dotted with occasional trees, brush and a few struggling figs, watered by a bitter spring that coursed down from the mountains. The hills that rose up behind them were barren scrub land where sheep and goats grazed at the desert weeds. Up ahead though they could just glimpse the far off ribbon of green that marked the Jordan River.

"Tell me, Elisha," Elijah mused as they walked. "Do you ever wonder what would have happened if you'd stayed with your plough?"

"I suppose I would be married by now," Elisha answered. "Beyond that, I'm not sure. I don't think I would be happy though."

"You enjoy wandering the country and sleeping outside?" Elijah raised his eyebrows in amusement.

"Not that part so much," Elisha said. "But I am happy to have done it at your side."

"And if I wasn't here?"

Elisha's face fell, but only for a moment, "Then… then I would still do it, but I might change a few things. I would buy more figs and fewer pomegranates."

That brought a half smile to Elijah's face and the two walked along until they came to the Jordan River. For a moment Elijah stopped, remembering when he'd crossed it all those years ago and begun his journey to tell Israel about God. Back then he'd waded through, but now he had a different idea how to cross.

Glancing back the way they'd come, he saw maybe fifty men standing on a low hill some ways behind them. All of them he recognized, students and teachers from his school, taught the way of God and sent out amid Israel. The Sons of the Prophets.

They watched, but didn't come any closer, a silent goodbye. Apparently just about everyone knew his time was ending.

There was still the river problem though and while Elisha dipped a tentative foot in the water to check how cold it was, Elijah set to a more practical approach. Unhooking the travel cloak from his back, he rolled up his mantle and, stepping forward, he struck the water. After all the other miracles he'd seen in his time, it was a small thing, but he still smiled when the flowing river split like an arrowhead. The teal water upstream surged at the sudden restriction and lapped against an invisible wall that held it back, piling higher and higher.

"Come on, Elisha." He walked out into the suddenly dry riverbed, admiring the strange view into cutaway depths of the Jordan River. Even in the murk he could see fish upstream, swimming so close he could almost reach into the wall of water and grab them. As they reached the bottom of the river, the water piled up higher than his head, like he was wandering an impossible valley of rippling blue.

Elijah lingered a moment, appreciating the rare sight of the whole Jordan river being held back, before finally continuing up onto the east bank. They hiked a little ways up the bank before turning back, Elijah unrolled his cloak and, as if by command, the invisible barrier vanished. The water surged forwards in a sudden torrent that roared off downriver towards the vast Salt Sea.

"It's just us now," Elijah said, and set off again at a leisurely pace, still heading east.

"So, we've made it to the Jordan, where to now?" Elisha asked in a knowing voice.

"Oh, nowhere in particular," Elijah didn't bother trying to send his apprentice away again. "You know Moses would have been here," he commented, "Joshua would have crossed the Jordan somewhere around here and Moses would have stayed behind and passed away on this side."

"Seems like we crossed the Jordan in the wrong direction then," Elisha astutely pointed out.

Elijah shrugged, "Depends on why we're here."

He turned to his protégé, trying to remember the youth God had sent him to find, and how exactly he'd become the young man standing before him. The flood of memories brought a grin to his face. "Elisha, tell me what I can do for you before I am taken from you."

He caught a stab of pain on the young man's face at the admission of what was about to happen, but Elisha summoned up an answer, "Please, let me inherit two shares of your spirit."

Two shares, the traditional birthright of the firstborn. Elijah pondered it for a moment, and finally gave a slow nod. "You have asked for something difficult. If you see me being taken from you, you will have it. If not, you won't."

Elisha accepted the answer well enough. Normally he was the sort to always race ahead when they were traveling, but for once he kept a half pace behind.

"So, are we heading for the place where Moses died?" Elisha

asked.

"We can, I suppose it would be interesting," Elijah admitted. "But as far as why we're here, I don't think it really matters." He sighed, and fell silent a moment, "You know you may not be able to save them, Elisha."

Elisha frowned, "Save who?"

"Israel, I tried a long time and…" He bit at his lip and shook his head, "Do what you can, save who you can, win where you can, but it may already be too late. Israel may be lost."

"And if it is?"

"Then it is," Elijah said bluntly, "I spent a lifetime trying to get people to remember and if they won't, then they won't. No one but God can change that. You can't carry that burden, I tried and it doesn't work."

"And if Israel isn't lost?" Elisha asked more optimistically.

Elijah grinned and slapped him on the back, "Then you're the person to find out."

As they spoke a pounding, the thunder of horses, came from above. Looking up, Elijah saw a gleaming star descend and arc lower in the sky, straight towards them. As it closed, he could make out a chariot, driven by two horses of pure white. Their manes danced like flames in the wind and their sleek bodies were coated with a fur of living fire. The chassis they pulled behind them was the same sort of strange metal he remembered from the angel's impossible sword, flames leapt to life, racing along the metal, yet never consuming it.

The chariot plunged towards them, and a sudden whirlwind drug them apart. Elisha staggered backwards and the chariot swept to the ground, landing between them, and the driver pulled it to a quick stop. A hand so bright Elijah could barely bear to look reached out, and taking it Elijah was pulled up onto the back of the chariot, while Elisha watched from the far side.

Instantly the chariot lurched forward and behind Elijah heard his protégé shouting, "My father! My father! I see the chariots and charioteers of Israel!"

Good, Elisha had seen him depart then, he'd receive what he'd asked. The chariot rapidly picked up speed, the wind rushing at them like a storm off the Great Sea. Elijah's cloak billowed out behind him in the wind, and at the last, the knot slipped loose. His mantle was swept back behind them and drifted to the ground, while Elijah was taken up into the sky.

THE END

Afterword

I'd like to thank you for reading to the end of The Days of Elijah. If you find yourself wanting more biblical adventures, then I'd encourage you to explore out my <u>Days of Joseph</u> series which explores the adventures of Joseph from the Old Testament and is available on Amazon.

Additionally, if you want to share Elijah with your friends, I've written a free companion Bible Study that looks at his life and journey. <u>Bible Study Download</u>

Finally, if you enjoy young adult space adventures with mysteries, explosions and questionable teenage decision-making, I happen to write that also and I'd encourage you to check out <u>Medea</u>, the first book in the Persephone Adventures Series.

A little about the book:

I've often heard it said that no one writes a book alone. I'm not sure that's entirely true, many books are penned in solitude, but that said, you wouldn't be reading this today without the work, help, suggestions, and feedback of many others beside myself.

For the core idea I am indebted to David Sinclair and

Cameron Schmeits, who showed up to church on an evening when there was no reason for them to be there, except that David felt like they should be. The two of them were kind enough to listen to my problems for the next two hours, and at the end they floated the concept for this book and encouraged me to do something positive with my skills. Proof that small acts of kindness and empathy do matter.

Additionally, although he may not realize it, I'd also like to thank Steve Glazer and Larry Perry for teaching me that's it's okay to ask difficult questions and struggle with difficult answers. I also would have likely never got up the courage to even try writing this book if Steve hadn't caught me off guard one Sunday and pushed me to a write and teach a lesson of my own the next week.

I'd like to give a special shout out to Ms Mary Baldwin of the West Michigan Homeschool Theater, who blew me away when she offered to adapt the storyline of the novel into a feature length play. On top of that, she was generous enough to invite me to come be a part of the performance. One of the small and very wonderful perks of being an author.

I should also extend my thanks to, Brett Kirk who helped me take a run-on manuscript with commas placed more or less at random, and transform it into something that a normal person could actually read. And, of course, my thanks also go to the people at Damonza who provided a beautiful cover that I never could have imagined, let alone created, on my own.

I'd like to thank all the good people at Rockpointe Church, who helped me through some very difficult periods in my own life with a great deal of compassion, understanding, and patience, and without whom I never would have even started writing this book.

Last, but in no way least, I'd like to thank my parents. Firstly, for putting up with me while I did write, and secondly for

always being there to help in their own ways. Without my dad
as an example, I'm not sure I ever would have had the
persistence to finish my first manuscript many years ago, let
alone this one. And a special thanks to my mom, who for the
last 12 years has faithfully read pretty much everything
creative I've written, and kindly told me that it's good and I
should keep trying, even when it wasn't very good and the
prognosis on 'keep trying' was highly debatable. I'm not sure
I can really summarize how important my mom was to the
book, from conception, to feedback, editing, and
encouragement along the way. Perhaps it will suffice to say
that the dedication in the front is, in no way an exaggeration,
and that without my mom, you would not have this book in
front of you today.

That said, I sincerely hope you enjoyed the Days of Elijah, it
was certainly an adventure to write and I hope it was an even
better adventure to read. I know not everyone will agree with
everything in this book. I've tried to stick close to the source
material, but of course I've taken a more modern approach to
the language. I operated under the view that, while Elijah
didn't speak modern English, he also didn't speak Victorian or
Shakespearian English, or any Indo-European language at all
for that matter. If it's a translation either way, I figured I
might as well choose a vernacular that makes sense to modern
readers.

In the end I hope you'll remember that this book is a work of
fiction, not fact. I've taken a great deal of creative license, but
I want to make it very clear that it's simply that, creative
license, otherwise known as making things up and as such, I
may have made things up wrong.

As I wrap this up, it comes to mind that perhaps I've forgotten
one other name who, more than any other, deserves my thanks
in this list. At the risk of sounding campy, and regardless of
whether or not you liked the book itself, perhaps we can agree
that the Lord God, to whom we owe the original story in the

Book of 1 Kings and much more as well, gets all the real credit.

THE ACTUAL END

Just kidding. Citations this way >>>>

Citations

Although Ancient Hebrew doesn't have quotation marks I used exact dialogue from the Book of 1 Kings where translators provided it. I mixed and matched Bible versions to find the translation I felt flowed best within the rest of the narrative so they are not all from the same bible version. Below are the biblical references for the book. The Chapter in *this book* where the citation is used is listed first and the biblical chapter and verse numbers are listed second. The appropriate version citations are shown last. I'd certainly encourage you check them out if you're interested. Note: full verses are often cited but only the dialogue is actually quoted.

1. Chapter 5: 1 Kings 17:1 (ESV)
2. Chapter 6: 1 Kings 17:3-4 (NIV)
3. Chapter 8: 1 Kings 17:9 (CSV)
4. Chapter 9: 1 Kings 17:10 (NLT)
5. Chapter 9: 1 Kings 17:11 (NLT)
6. Chapter 9: 1 Kings 17:12 (NLT)
7. Chapter 9: 1 Kings 17:13-14 (NLT)
8. Chapter 16: 1 Kings 17:18 (NIV)
9. Chapter 16: 1 Kings 17:19 (NLT)
10. Chapter 16: 1 Kings 17:20 (NLT)
11. Chapter 16: 1 Kings 17:21 (NLT)
12. Chapter 16: 1 Kings 17:22 (ESV)
13. Chapter 16: 1 Kings 17:24 (NLT)
14. Chapter 17: 1 Kings 18:1 (NIV)
15. Chapter 18: 1 Kings 18:5 (ESV)
16. Chapter 19: 1 Kings 18:7 (NLT)
17. Chapter 19: 1 Kings 18:8 (CSB)
18. Chapter 19: 1 Kings 18:9-14 (NLT)
19. Chapter 19: 1 Kings 18:15 (NLT)
20. Chapter 19: 1 Kings 18:17-19 (HCSB)
21. Chapter 20: 1 Kings 18:21-24 (NIV)
22. Chapter 20: 1 Kings 18:24 (NIV)
23. Chapter 20: 1 Kings 18:25 (NIV)

24. Chapter 21: 1 Kings 18:26 (ASV)
25. Chapter 21: 1 Kings 18:27 (NIV)
26. Chapter 21: 1 Kings 18:30 (NIV)
27. Chapter 21: 1 Kings 18:33 (NLT)
28. Chapter 21: 1 Kings 18:34 (NIV)
29. Chapter 21: 1 Kings 18:34 (NIV)
30. Chapter 22: 1 Kings 18:36-37 (NLT)
31. Chapter 22: 1 Kings 18:39 (NIV)
32. Chapter 22: 1 Kings 18:40 (NIV)
33. Chapter 22: 1 Kings 18:41 (HCSB)
34. Chapter 22: 1 Kings 18:43 (CSB)
35. Chapter 22: 1 Kings 18:43 (CSB)
36. Chapter 22: 1 Kings 18:44 (CSB)
37. Chapter 22: 1 Kings 18:44 (CSB)
38. Chapter 23: 1 Kings 19:2 (NIV)
39. Chapter 25: 1 Kings 19:4 (NIV)
40. Chapter 25: 1 Kings 19:5 (NIV)
41. Chapter 25: 1 Kings 19:7 (NLT)
42. Chapter 26: Exodus 32:4 (NLT)
43. Chapter 26: Exodus 24:4 (NLT)
44. Chapter 26: 1 Kings 19:9-10 (NIV)
45. Chapter 26: 1 Kings 19:11 (NLT)
46. Chapter 26: 1 Kings 19:13-14 (NIV)
47. Chapter 26: 1 Kings 19:15-18 (NLT)
48. Chapter 27: 1 Kings 19:20 (NET Bible)
49. Chapter 27: 1 Kings 19:20 (HCSB)
50. Chapter 28: Deuteronomy 1:1 (NIV)
51. Chapter 28: Deuteronomy 34:10-12 (NIV)
52. Chapter 28: 1 Kings 21:18-19 (CSB)
53. Chapter 29: 1 Kings 21:9-10 (NLT)
54. Chapter 29: 1 Kings 21:20-24 (NIV)
55. Chapter 30: 1 Kings 21:29 (NIV)
56. Chapter 30: 1 Kings 21:19 (CSB)
57. Chapter 31: 2 Kings 1:3-4 (CSB)
58. Chapter 31: 2 Kings 1:6 (CSB)
59. Chapter 31: 2 Kings 1:9 (CSB)
60. Chapter 31: 2 Kings 1:10 (CSB)
61. Chapter 31: 2 Kings 1:11-12 (CSB)

62. Chapter 31: 2 Kings 1:13-15 (NLT)
63. Chapter 31: 2 Kings 1:16 (CSB)
64. Chapter 32: 2 Kings 2:6 (NLT)
65. Chapter 32: 2 Kings 2:9-10 (CSB)
66. Chapter 32: 2 Kings 2:12 (NLT)

THE ACTUAL ACTUAL END